"The Fairies of Feyllan is a wonderful plunge for readers into the beautiful and intricate world of fairies. Both young and more sophisticated readers will be swept up in the action and revel in the gorgeous details."

–Rebecca Glenn, The Book Frog,
www.thebookfrog.blogspot.com

"With wonderful world-building and compelling characters, *The Fairies of Feyllan* is a magical fantasy adventure."

–April White, author of *The Immortal Descendants* series,
www.aprilwhitebooks.com

"An imaginative world of fairies and dragons, love and war, and the battle for power in the fairy realm, *The Fairies of Feyllan* will delight audiences of all ages as readers follow Varia and Loben's path into the secret lives of fairies."

–Elayne G. James, author of *The Lightbridge Legacy* series,
www.LightBridgeLegacy.com

Other Books by Cat Spydell

The Time Traveler's Apprentice at Hollywood High

Other Books you may Enjoy

The Lightbridge Legacy
By Elayne James

Flight to Andolin: Journeys of a Reluctant Heroine
By Roe Jewell

The Rain Must Fall
By Evangeline Maynard

The Fairies of Feyllan

Cat Spydell

MISCHIEVOUS MUSE PRESS   WORLD NOUVEAU COMPANY

The Fairies of Feyllan
2013 Cat Spydell
Published in partnership with Mischievous Muse Press
A subsidiary of The World Nouveau Company
Los Angeles County, California

Bio photo by Cassidy Spydell
Cover design by Gineve Lynnara
Design elements by Bruce Rudolph

Library of Congress Cataloging-in-Publication Data
The Fairies of Feyllan
Mischievous Muse Press/World Nouveau Company
ISBN 9781938208133
Printed in the United States of America

10 9 8 7 6 5 4 3 2 1
BVG

Dedicated to the Trees

This book is dedicated to the souls of trees,

To their beauty and ancient wisdom,

The slow song they sing on this planet,

And the divine property of every branch and leaf . . .

Blessed are the living lungs of the earth.

Acknowledgements

There are many people I wish to thank who have helped me on my professional, spiritual, and life journey, far too many to name. They all contributed on some level to help me write *The Fairies of Feyllan*. From my grandfather James Pearl Leach, a gardener who taught me to appreciate flora, and my friend Christina Zimmerman who loaned me a book that taught me about the deva influence in all things; to the many yoga teachers who taught me breath, and the amazing women at Long Beach WomanSpirit who introduced me to a unique spirit-path involving the fae . . . all of my life lessons to the point when I began writing *The Fairies of Feyllan* were pinned in place by remarkable people.

The animals that live at my private rescue ranch were a huge inspiration for the animal characters in the book: Drinian the Big White Dog is both regal and silly like Smote the Dragon (and as a puppy seemed to endlessly grow larger and larger as Smote does). The hummingbirds at our sugar feeder, the ravens that come to roost in the trees at night, my sweet pigeon Penelope, and even my creepy catfish Loch all contributed to my imagination just by being themselves. My weekly writing group was instrumental in helping me with editing, and individuals such as Stacey O'Brien (author of *Wesley the Owl*) and my last minute editor Nelida Heredia Larrañaga were gracious with their time to help me keep my deadlines. A very special thank you to my business partner Gineve Rudolph, who co-created the cover and the fairy Varia with her brother Bruce Rudolph. It was a thrill to watch my main character come to life before my eyes. I feel blessed to have spent the past few years immersed in the world of the fae. I loved creating Varia, Loben, and the families of Feyllan, and hope readers enjoy the story as much as I enjoyed writing it.

—Cat Spydell

The Fairies of Feyllan

Chapter One

The world of the faery exists, alongside the world of humankind. It can best be seen in a dew droplet at the first rays of dawn, or at sunset as the green flash brightens the darkening sky . . . in a crystal viewed with eyes crossed, and in the shimmering drip of an icicle in winter light. It is the Kingdom of Feyllan, the faery realm, and very few who have glimpsed it have remained unchanged.

Long ago the fae, or faery-kind, and mankind knew each other, as humans were sometimes rewarded with visits from the fae folk in exchange for offerings of rosemary and honey (a faery favorite), or plantings of orange nasturtium and lavender flowers, or dabs of baubles and beads, and bits of cloth. But the machine of mankind roared, the great time of industry pushed the fae from their woodland homes, and the diminutive creatures became reclusive, displaced folk, angry at the loutish destruction of human beings.

None of that mattered on this bright crisp morning to Varia, however. She flew from branch to branch, looking for the perfect round pink berry from a peppertree. Seeing one she liked, her small hands grasped the crinkly orb. She closed her eyes and tapped into the Devic energy of the pepper. She could visualize the origins of the tree, and in her mind a wellspring of information flooded in: long ago the pepper's seed, a non-native dropped by a bird, felt comfortable and warm in the sun, and then summer rains came. Soon the tree matured, and its few offspring flourished. It stood here, unknown to the world, a rare tree from a different continent far from its native land, untouched by human recognition. Varia opened her eyes; she had always liked the tree's story. She mentally asked the sumac to spare her the berry and upon receiving its consent, she pulled hard, flying backwards a bit as the pink peppercorn came free.

"Watch it!" her brother Ezia called from behind her, his luminous green and blue wings slowing as he hovered aside to avoid a crash. Flying in a V pattern beneath them were his comrades, who disappeared into a neighboring grove of pines.

"Why don't you get the peppercorns, then?" Varia asked in a miffed tone.

Ezia smirked. "Because it's your job, not mine. Your Devas guided you to the foreign tree grove, and mine bring me to the honey-filled hives. I have other, more important things to do."

"Oh yes, I forgot, you are the bee master, I beg your pardon, your highness."

Ezia, one of Erendome's bee tamers, spent an inordinate amount of time consoling the bees as the faery folk collected their honey. Each faery in the kingdom had a job of sorts, a speciality that one performed best, and it was a great honor to be chosen by the Devic spirits to become a master.

"It is an important chore," said Ezia. "One bee sting can kill, you know."

"I know," Varia replied. *He is so vain about his skill with the bees, I'll never get him to stop talking about it if I don't change the subject,* she thought. "Did you hear that the Wilhvyre FlightSoldiers are rumoured to have found an EarthSeeker colony in Birkendore?" she asked. It was old news to her, she was sure he'd heard it by now, but it would stop him from boasting about bee taming for a while. Varia straddled a tree branch, resting her blue, green, and violet-colored wings by tucking them neatly behind her. Ezia sat beside her, his wings spread, on the alert.

"No!" he said, his eyes the color of the pepper tree leaves, now scanning the horizon for signs of trouble. "Is it true? There have been no EarthSeekers in these parts in our lifetimes, I believed them to be extinct!"

Varia was surprised he hadn't yet heard the whispered rumour of the EarthSeeker clan moving in nearby. "I believe they still exist, and have heard that they were seen near the eastern mushroom pits, living in one of their dank horrible tunnels at the base of an ancient oak there. It is said to be a large colony, several families, all of their royal line." She shuddered at the thought of living underground.

"How did this news escape me?" Ezia wanted to know. Varia squirmed, sensing her brother's ire. Though their father Dreya was the king of their realm, Ezia felt as prince he should be in charge of the safety of the Alawe, although of late royal titles were unnecessary. Since their move to Feyllan's Ashenthorne region many generations before, life had remained peaceful, and mostly human-free. There was little for a king or prince to do, other than make sure that their homes and the majestic palace Erendome, high in the whitebeam treetop, were well-stocked and comfortable, and that the faeries who lived under the kingship were all getting along. Wild beasts were the main concern, and faery scouts had occasionally spotted humans from the outlying villages, though the nearest human dwelling was half a morning's flight away, and abandoned now. Except for the rare wandering lost sheep with a fretful herder following along behind, there were few threats in Ashenthorne. Varia could see by Ezia's hot stare that she had better distract him from thinking of EarthSeekers.

"Perhaps your brain has been too addled by the buzzing of bees to worry about what is being said at Erendome," Varia teased, hoping that mentioning the castle would now veer Ezia's agitated mind from the EarthSeekers, but it had the opposite effect.

"What does Rumedah say of these EarthSeekers setting up their home just outside the boundary of Ashenthorne?" Ezia wanted to know.

"Rumedah?" Varia asked, thinking of the elderly sage who counseled their father. "He loves only peace and communion with trees. He is old and addled, and no longer bothers himself with the politics of the faery world."

"He should be more alert, if our safety is at stake," Ezia grumbled. "Those dirty earth dwellers could attack, if they are so close by! Makes my skin crawl."

"Wouldn't you want to meet an EarthSeeker?" Varia asked, knowing she would be unable to distract him from the conversation now.

"Of course not! They are vile folk, who have no right to call themselves faery. No self-respecting Alawe AirWalker would want to say they'd met an EarthSeeker, if such monsters even still exist!" Ezia was riled up, Varia could see. She looked into his darkening face as he hovered above her.

He was a tall faery, three stems to her two,* his height from the ancient line on her deceased mother's side. Father was only two and a half stems tall, and Ezia was proud to tower over the king. Ezia lifted his chin, his luminous blue-tinged skin glowing as he raged within.

"Ezia, we do not yet understand the ways of these EarthSeekers, if they are even there or not. Don't be so quick to react! They could be allies, wanting peace and community. We do not yet know what to expect."

Ezia plucked a leaf from the peppertree without even asking its Deva, or spirit guardian, for permission. Varia was rather shocked when he threw it. She watched the golden-green teardrop shape whirl to the ground.

"I know what I know, Sister. Do not be fooled by their beauty that I have heard about in song! They are worm-like abominations to the faery realm!" Ezia buzzed in a circle, unable to still his anger. "And I will alert Father and the kingdom and suggest we patrol our perimeters. We should eliminate them before they take over all of the Ashenthorne realm!"

Varia realized that she would prefer Ezia's boasting to his rage. She placed her long fingers on his wrist to calm him, sending him a thoughtwave of peace. Ezia wrenched his arm away.

"Do not try to tame me like some common butterfly, Sister! I am not some beast who needs to be managed." He glared at Varia as he took flight, and before she could protest, he was gone like a hummingbird on the horizon.

Varia panicked. *What to do?* Ezia had been trained as a Wilhvyre FlightSoldier for the royal house's militia; he and all the faeries in their second-hundredth seasons were ready for a battle that had never come. Had she just caused one by alerting her hot-headed brother of the rumoured newcomers to their kingdom? With a determination that she had rarely seen in her young life, Varia made a bold decision, for she was a princess of Erendome, and had a responsibility to the throne just as Ezia did. She would fly to the EarthSeeker

---

*Note: The measurement of inches does not exist in Feyllan but has been translated here for human understanding. In Feyllan, Ezia stands 3 stems tall, and each stem equals about 3 inches.

kingdom in Birkendore, and if they had moved in, she would spy on them and see what the faeries were like. If they were a peaceful race, she could come back home and let her brother and the rest of the Wilhvyre FlightSoldiers, and especially her father, King Dreya, know that all was well, and the two tribes could live side by side without war or strife. She dropped the peppercorn, apologizing to the tree for wasting it, and flew as fast as she could toward the mushroom pits where it was rumoured the EarthSeekers dwelled.

Tired from her long journey, Varia arrived at the outskirts of the Birkendore Flats and drank thirstily from a flower holding the last remnants of morning dew, and then she curled up on a long leaf for a rest. The flight had taken much from her energy stores. *I am nothing less than crazy, coming all this way alone,* she thought. Part of her wanted to rest and then fly away home and never speak of it to anyone, but determination gripped her. Surely her father King Dreya would be proud of her efforts to discover the whereabouts of the EarthSeeker colony! The thought consoled her as Varia pulled the leaf tightly around her and napped to regain her strength.

A noise awakened Varia in the late afternoon; she opened her eyes and remained still upon hearing voices.

The voices were unlike any she had ever heard, yet far too quiet to be human. She trembled. As nervous as she was, she remembered to slow her breathing and mentally pull her energy into the leaf that hid her so that any passing animal, human, or even faery would not be able to recognize her as fae, but would merely see her as a leaf. Called deliquescing, it was the way certain fae have always remained hidden from the outside world, and in fact, at any given moment, a quiet wooded glen abundant with flowers, green plants, birdsong, and peacefulness may have a faery in it, but not so one could see. The voices grew louder as Varia listened. She could hear a slight rustling outside of her leaf cocoon, but knew that no other could hear it: It was the silent noise of faeries walking in the nearby meadow, probably looking for mushrooms, she imagined. She'd heard the EarthSeekers craved them and based their homes near their growing areas.

". . . not so, Cousin," a gravelly voice said. "Birkendore is a fine new home for us. Yes, we have lost much in our quest to come here, but we will rebuild. We should recommend to the king that we stay and continue our efforts."

"I'm telling you, there is something amiss! It is something I can feel in the quality of the air, and I have also felt it in the water of the river. This is not our place. Not here. We still should travel further north, send scouts to find new lands. This land is inhabited by other faeries, perhaps the AirWalkers rumoured to live in the West. I know it," the second voice, a soothing male voice that Varia could imagine listening to endlessly, interjected.

"Loben, our kinfolk are tired. We need to stay in one place, at least for another season. If there are others of the fae, why have they not yet come to greet us? I say we stay put. The king is my father, not yours. I'm afraid my word will override your opinion, regardless of your concern for the best interest of our kind."

"Then why ask me, Doon, if you are not willing to listen to reason?"

The gravelly-voiced one, Doon, chuckled. "I will listen when I am king and you are my trusted advisor, Cousin. Until then, I have to recommend to the council what is best for us Durndeng and all of our kin. We have already begun the slow careful process of building our splendid new castle. We can't waste our efforts for a hunch."

The soft-voiced Loben sighed. "Then as your underling, I will have to listen, but heed my words. I recommend against staying here, and will tell the king so should he ask at council."

"You know that it is not my wish to be king, Loben," Doon continued. "I am training myself for my own destiny, as you should yours. You will be my underling, but not because I wish it to be so! It is just the fate of our births. I am sorry to have to trump you yet again."

Varia heard the sound of wings, heavier than the whir of the wings of her own kin, and waited a moment before returning her own breath to the air and stirring from the leaf's folds. She peered out and found herself to be alone. She wondered what the EarthSeekers looked like; were they like her? Fair and willowy, with skin and wings the colors of the sky? She tried to remember the strange name they called themselves: *Durndeng.* Curiosity stirred within her, and she flitted to the top of a tree after sipping nectar to revive her powers of flight. The EarthSeekers tended to live low to the ground, favoring foods found near the earth, while the Alawe stayed in treetops, eating foods grown high; fruits, blossoms, nuts, and leaves. Whatever other differences they may have, Varia wanted to find out. She zipped from tree to tree, certain she was unnoticed. *They are EarthSeekers, involved with life on the earth's floor. They would not think to look up*, she thought. She closed her eyes and tapped into the energy of the tree she landed in, clutching a thin long branch and focusing her energy on the slow song of the old oak. It had known wars, and floods, and fire in its lifetime, Varia noted. And then it told her the story of the new ones, of the faeries who had a home down near the riverbank under another oak, a relative of this one. *I was never here*, Varia told the oak mentally, feeling a bit sorry that she had to ask it to cover up her existence, since the grand tree had shared such an interesting story of its life and would probably enjoy revealing that a faery had once questioned it. She rarely had to ask trees and plants to help her hide, but she was, after all, near what Ezia would consider "enemy camp".

Varia directed her senses to the earth: She could feel the river churning nearby and she noiselessly flew tree-to-tree, "air walking" over the tops of the giant oaks that towered above a lush understory by pulling down on a limb and releasing it, then catching it as it flew by and allowing herself to be hurled forward, keeping her wings tucked to draw less attention to herself should a hungry bird of prey or worse, the EarthSeekers, see her. It was a way to move quickly through the treetops without using too much energy.

Soon Varia found the river and the oak grove she searched for. She asked three different trees which one of them housed the fae; they had not been told to lie or cover the truth, something that surprised her. Did the EarthSeekers not know how to commune in such a way with the flora around them?

"Here," said the third oak. "The Durndeng fae that you call EarthSeekers dwell deep in my root system." Varia gasped. She had found them, but now what? The sun itself was dipping into the western sky. She should head home right now, but she still hadn't seen a faery! She couldn't risk flying home alone in the dark, and if she stayed away during nightfall, Ezia would certainly have a party of warriors out by dawn looking for her. Given their last conversation, he might convince the Wilhvyre Flight- Soldiers to come to Birkendore to look for her. The war Varia feared could happen might occur due to her own recklessness. Varia looked to the west and made her choice. She flew, whirring as fast as she could toward the golden rays.

ᴀrriving at the footfall of night, Varia entered her father's palace, Erendome, high up in the familiar giant whitebeam tree. The structure took up every branch and limb, mostly built of materials found in the sacred valley of Ashenthorne, where Varia's kin had lived in peace for many generations. Her home had tall arched ceilings, many stems high, carefully crafted from the soft bending branches of a willing willow tree near the Craggyrock Lake to the south. The rooftop itself, made of leaves hardened with the waxy resin from the maple trees that lived in groves to the north, supported crystal-clear domes popping up all around the glimmering leaf tiles. At sunset Erendome shone like amber in the evening light. Not that Varia saw the gloaming time; she could barely see the special luminescent glow of her home as she flew into the whitebeam and landed at the palace entry. In fact, the sky boiled into dark and angry clouds overhead as she pushed back the heavy door, woven of bark and leaf fibers, and ventured inside.

"Ah, here she is, here she is!" said the strong voice of her father, King Dreya.

"Father! I'm sorry if I concerned you, I fell asleep and was delayed," Varia said as she noticed that at least a dozen

Wilhvyre, the palace FlightSoldiers, were dressed in their warmer clothing for nighttime flight, at the ready to fly out. Ezia was among them, of course. Rumedah, her father's elderly advisor, gave her a curious look. Varia felt he could see right through her.

"You were not in the foreign tree's grove where I left you, Sister, and the peppertree told a story that you left with urgent haste."

Varia nodded, realizing with a start that the tree, if it was paying attention, could have told Ezia the truth about where she had gone. She made a mental note to ask the tree at sunrise to not share any part of a conversation it may have heard by listening to her thoughts. One never knows with trees, whether they are paying attention or not.

All eyes burned on her, and Varia felt like ducking back out the door into the dangerous night. She could see her sister Alshea and her favorite cousin, Irea, staring at her with concern. No, the look in Alshea's eyes was suspicion. Varia flushed.

"I remembered I had to visit with the linden tree, but alas, I was chased, by a marsh harrier. I hid in a comfortable leaf bed, exhausted from the pursuit, and thus slept."

"Ah," said King Dreya. "There we have it, the faegirl has explained herself. All is well and forgiven." The tension in the main hall melted away, and the FlightSoldiers on call meandered out of the room, clearly disappointed that their services would not be needed. Except Talow. He stayed. Talow, Varia's childhood playmate until things grew awkward between them as they merged into their maturity suns,* stood at attention, staring at Varia in a way that made her feel uncomfortable. Alshea and Irea noticed him lingering. Irea giggled, but Alshea glared.

"I apologize, Father, for any problems my absence has caused," Varia said. "I will take my leave."

"Very well," said King Dreya. His trimmed blue beard outlined his chiseled features, and he thrust out his chin in his kingly fashion and turned toward the entertainment hall.

---

*In Feyllan, one year is called a sun, and represents the amount of time it takes the sun to return from the first day after the first Frost Moon

Several of his subjects followed, but Rumedah touched Varia on the wrist. She looked down at his wrinkled claw of a hand on her skin and realized with a start he was thisselling, or "reading" her. She pulled her hand away.

"I see what is in your soul," Rumedah said in a voice as crinkly as his old face, that reminded Varia of the covering on a pepperberry. "Your intentions may be honest, but you must beware. Do not interfere in the world of warriors, Princess Varia."

Varia smiled at the man who had been like a grandfather to her as she grew up in Erendome. "I will be cautious, Sage Rumedah. I thank you for your concern."

Varia saw Alshea and Irea waiting for her by the ceiling-high door of the great hall. She joined her sister and cousin and they flew up the wide portals together into their bedchamber off the main hall, in the upper story of the old whitebeam tree.

Alshea burst into laughter as they entered the top room of the palace. "I apologize for any problems my absence has caused," she mimicked. Even the more reserved Irea smiled. Varia sighed.

"Oh, hush! Do you really want to mock me now, when I have news?"

"Oh, I know your news!" Irea said. "When it was first discovered you were missing, Ezia brought us to the spot he'd last seen you. Lucky for you, Cousin, I reached the tree before him and told it what to say. The tree told me you went out looking for the EarthSeekers!"

Alshea looked shocked. "What? I didn't know that, why didn't you say so, Irea? Truly, I've been with you since dawn!"

"Tell you?" Irea fluttered up to the high ceiling of the faegirls' bedroom, and floated easily down onto her soft bed, made of stitched-together layers of imported Mediterranean lambsear's leaf. "Yes, tell you, and then what? Have you whisper all that you know to score your romance points with Talow? I've seen the way you flirt with him. I believe you'd sacrifice your own sister to get on his good side."

Alshea turned bright red and said nothing, unusual for her. Alshea was prone to having much to say. Varia squirmed in the room's silence.

"I appreciate your tact, Cousin," Varia said to Irea. "And yes, it's true. I did look for the EarthSeekers!" Varia smiled at the shocked looks on her sister's and cousin's faces.

"I assumed the tree was mistaken, or that you were playing a little game!" Irea exclaimed. "You mean, you really flew all the way to Birkendore? Down to the river basin where the EarthSeekers are said to be living?"

Alshea seemed too stunned to speak. Varia smiled. "I did! I went there, it was a terribly long journey to make there and back in one day, but . . ." she shrugged. "I didn't see any EarthSeekers. But they live, the rumours are true! I heard them talking." Varia remembered the distinctive voice of the one called Loben.

Alshea broke her own silence. "You heard them!" she huffed. "You didn't see them? It could have been anything that you heard then, couldn't it? Even a human! Or one of our own kind. How is it that you didn't see the EarthSeekers?"

"I'm curious about that too," Irea added.

"I was hiding, in a leaf roll. It's such a far distance to Birkendore, and I am unused to long flight and slept to recover. But I was awakened, and not by the loud screeching voice I have heard is the way of humans, but by a voice . . . the voice of the fae. And not the Alawe, not one of our kind. I know it was an EarthSeeker by what was said."

"Oh, do tell," said Alshea in a mocking way. "Let us know what those wretched little EarthSeekers were saying."

Varia stared at her sister, stopping herself from telling what she'd heard in the meadow near the river bottom oak grove. Irea subtly shook her head as she lounged on her bed next to Alshea's. Varia bit her bottom lip, hesitating, stalling to find an answer.

"Well," she said, "I suppose I couldn't really tell specifically what was said . . ." Varia looked at Irea, who nodded in a slight, encouraging way. "Ah well. Perhaps you are right, Sister. Perhaps I didn't hear them after all and was fooled, as you said. Perhaps it was a trick, or a dream."

"Ha!" Alshea flitted upward again, hovering near the ceiling where she kept her jewelry in tiny little boxes built into the decorative molding. She took off fair rings and the bright jewels she wore about her neck, and then flew down and placed on its special table the headpiece she wore that announced herself as High Princess and next in line to an ancient faery throne. "It sounds to me, Sister, as if you slept and dreamt of a faery folk that are known from faechildren's tales of yore, but that no longer exist. I am going to retire now, if you two stay up to chatter, please collect yourselves in our other chambers." Alshea dove onto her bed and pulled up a coverlet made of pressed flowers of all colors. She disappeared under it, only the top of her head showing, her pearly hair swirling around her pansy pillow. Soon she fell fast asleep, and Irea motioned for Varia to follow her.

They lightly flitted out of the room so as not to disturb Alshea and went into a neighboring parlor that they shared and used to entertain their friends; its roof had a clear covering, made of dried silver dollar plant pods, and it was the reason the castle was called Erendome; named for the silvery glittering domed roofs, as Eren is the faery word for moonlight. The moon broke through the translucent film and lit the room with a filtered white glow.

"We need to talk, but there are too many ears in the palace," Irea said quietly. Varia nodded and they flew to the top of the room, and lifted up the see-through roof structure together. A light rain had spilled but the clouds were clearing across a velvet sky. It was their secret, that they could exit through the roof; and only Alshea knew of it as well. The three princesses often came outside at night to enjoy the moonlight and chilly air. They sat on the curved rooftop and stared out at the wide valley beyond the whitebeam's leaf canopy before them; the shine of the lake in the distance caught the moon and reflected it back to them. The moon itself was an effervescent orb in the sky, hovering brightly like a lit candle. Strange sounds of night birds filled the air, and in the moonlight tree leaves lacked all color, hanging limply black around them.

"That was dangerous," Irea said in a whisper. "I know that she is your sister, Varia, but do not forget that she will be our queen someday. Alshea is not to be trusted with this sort of information."

"You believe that I heard the EarthSeekers talking, then?" Varia asked, shivering in the cold night.

"I do. But you must use care. Now that we know they are there, we are at risk of war. Ezia came back from his time with you upset that he wasn't told by the Wilhvyre about the EarthSeekers."

"How I wish I hadn't mentioned it! I thought he would have heard the rumour, but I suppose those bee tamers don't chatter about the militia's duties. And Ezia hasn't been a Wilhvyre warrior for many moons."

"No one told him because he is hot-tempered and he craves war the same way the EarthSeekers are said to crave mushrooms," Irea sighed. "The Wilhvyre know to keep him blind of knowledge such as this. What will you do now? Go on and pretend that you know nothing? There may be a tree or flower out there that knows your secrets, Cousin. A secret is hard to keep from the fae."

Varia shook her head. "I am going back, tomorrow. To see for myself what they look like. If they are fair, like us, perhaps we can make friendly contact, and not be enemies, but become allies."

Irea scoffed. "You, a low-level princess, will bind the two tribes together! That is something that I would love to see, but you aren't being realistic! Alshea and even Ezia won't allow you to go, you know that."

Varia knew Irea was right, but she had to go! The thought of Loben's smooth voice filled her mind again. Could such a voice come from an enemy? Varia felt determined that she could bring the Alawe and EarthSeekers together.

"I must go," Varia said. "Now! I will fly out now, sleep near Birkendore until dawn, and then fly back here tomorrow and be back in time for supper. I will say I awakened early and visited the strawberry tree groves looking for berries."

"Now?" Irea shook her head. "You know you can't, that you shouldn't, fly at night!"

"Of course I can!" Varia said. "I will make it to Birkendore, I just need to watch out for certain things; predators, the cold air, and the like." Irea shivered, more with fear than cold, Varia guessed. "Worry not!" she told Irea.

No!" Irea shook her head. "Your own mother was killed in night flight, taken by a bird of prey. How can you risk it? It isn't safe!"

Varia hovered in mid-air. "If we do not establish friendly contact, then the EarthSeekers will soon know of our existence, and it will not be safe to live in Ashenthorne any longer. I started this by telling Ezia, and I must stop it before anyone is harmed. I can outwit the prey birds. I must go, please don't try to stop me!" She flew above her cousin, and sped off into the night. Irea hesitated only a moment before following Varia.

What neither faery knew was that at the palace, a guard had been placed at the door. This was not a usual occurrence, but now there were rumours of enemies afoot. And this guard, named Talow, watched in disbelief as two faery princesses of the royal line flew off alone into the night.

Chapter Two

Flying into the night was a reckless act, not only because of the habits of night-hunting birds, but because faeries have no tolerance for cold. When a faery becomes too chilly, the wings slow so that flight is stopped, and the faery floats to the ground, unable to move, and goes into a deep sleep until warmed again. This is how some humans have been able to catch faeries, though none of those humans have lived to tell the tale, because once the faerie's kin are alerted, an extraction occurs. A dreadful process for the human, and not so pleasant for the faery either.

Varia, feeling the chill of the night, knew that she must fly as fast as she could to keep warm. Now that she started her journey, doubt crept in and she mentally scolded herself; *Irea was right, how very dangerous, flying off into the night with no provisions, no water, no nectar, no food, and without any Night Flight clothing.* Just then she heard Irea's fast-beating wings behind her, and Varia turned in mid-air.

"Irea! You mustn't follow me, it is folly!" Varia said as Irea caught up and soared besides her, panting.

"I cannot let you go to the mushrooms flats alone again! What if something happens to you?" Irea said. "And if you are calling my actions folly, look at what you are doing! Your own dear mother was taken in the night, how could you risk it? Come back to Erendome with me. We will start fresh in the morning."

"I know it seems like the wiser plan," Varia said as she fluttered over to a scraggly lone pine in the gorse and rested on the branches, after feeling the tree's bark to see if any animals were dwelling there. The tree woke and responded that some sparrows were in the topmost branches before settling back to sleep.

"I considered leaving at dawn," Varia admitted, as her resolution grew firm, "but Ezia's suspicions are rising! I believe that he may organize a search party to find and destroy the EarthSeekers. I would like to discover if they are friendly by tomorrow's high sun, so that I can report back to Father. I fear Ezia rashness will start a war. Time is of the essence!"

"Then I suppose we must continue," Irea agreed as she leaned against the trunk, wings splayed. In the darkness Varia, with her keen faery sight, could see her cousin's worried expression.

"You should go back to Erendome," Varia said. "I will continue alone."

"No, I shall go with you," Irea said. "It is safest if we stay together, and I have come this far already."

Varia hugged Irea. "Very well, if I cannot convince you to return home, then please, be careful! I am hoping that our flight to Birkendore is uneventful. Let's fly."

Holding hands, the two fae princesses took to the air and continued flying at a fast pace toward the mushroom flats. As she realized she had missed the palace supper by coming home late, Varia wondered if she had the strength to fly all the way to the oak grove. She remembered a field of sunflowers at the abandoned human residence between Birkendore and Erendome, and decided to aim for it instead. There were large leaves they could hide in, the sun would hit the sunflower meadow and warm them as soon as soon it rose in the east, and they could gather their wits and drink nectar for flight fuel before spying on EarthSeeker faeries after dawn. Feeling relieved that their journey would not be so far, Varia pointed ahead.

"We won't go the whole way tonight, Cousin!" she said to Irea, whose raven-colored hair flapped behind her, sometimes tangling in her wingtips. "We will stop soon and rest in a secluded spot for the night."

"That is a good thing," Irea said. "Because I am unused to the cold."

Varia could see Irea struggling.

"It won't be long," Varia said. Out of the corner of her eye she caught a careening white glint in the moonlight. Far in the distance behind them, an angular shape bore down hard on the two faeries.

"Owl!" Varia called, and grasped Irea's cold wrist in her hand and yanked her cousin down just as the huge feathered creature whished past them with compromising speed. Irea yelped, and the owl turned, still searching for its prey. Varia knew that it was nearly impossible to outfly an owl; they were magicians of the sky, able to catch a meal in midair. Looking around, she saw no cover, for they were soaring over shrubby rock-covered heath. The ground was their only salvation. The owl nearly caught Varia, its huge talons grasping at air just next to her head. Varia seized the moment and held a tight grip on Irea's arm as she dove top speed to the ground. Once down, the faeries landed with folded wings, and ducked under a large white stone.

"Dig a trench under the rock!" Varia whispered, knowing with a sinking feeling that she'd given them away by making noise. *Owls hunt by hearing*, she remembered the childhood lesson now, too late. The faewomen tried to push their hands into the hard and unforgiving dirt but couldn't, so they found themselves stuck in the shallow shadow of a boulder.

"There!" Irea called, pointing to a deeper hollow. They ran into the moonlit heath, but were unused to running, being winged as they were, and had to leap over root and leaf. Their sanctuary, a nearby pile of limestone, sheltered a dark and foul crevice. As they ducked into the slit, there was no way of knowing what else might have found the cavern to be a comfortable home, but the faeries rushed blindly in. A horrific skittering noise and dusty wind rose up around them as the owl landed where they'd been, just missing his meal. The predator bird poked with frantic spurs, searching, an occasional earth-shattering preybird scream frightening Varia and Irea. The two clutched one another, inching back into the black hole. Irea tightened as the tawny pounded its rampaging hunt.

"Something . . . touched me," Irea whispered, and the faeries held very still. A clicking noise filled the den. Varia tensed, too afraid to move, feeling her impending demise.

"Shall we allow some light?" Varia whispered.

"Yes," Irea said in a tight voice. Varia reached into a leaf-made pouch she always wore on her belt and pulled out a lump of hestus, a bit of sand that the fae invented, known in the common tongue as faery dust or pixiedust. Varia blew on it, and the powder lit up, showering the cave with a dancing light. And there in front of them, bearing down, was a large hideous black face and attached, a body with too many gyrating legs. The thing squirmed, rising up tall, a wretched monster about to attack in the tight space. Varia held up the bright light toward it and the centipede shied and exited out the hole. The owl, in its angry hunt, stomped it dead, but not before a terrible moan rode the creature's last breath.

Shivering under the cold shale, Irea and Varia looked away from the carnage and waited for the owl to give up. They clutched one another to keep warm, as well as for comfort. Other enemies of the fae were near, but Varia kept a pile of lit hestus all around them, so a spider and a pill bug hurried on past, their own deep home disturbed by the tawny's tu-whoo and stomp. The owl flew off, and the faegirls quietly, in a way only faeries can, climbed out into the moonlight once more.

"Are you harmed?" Varia asked. "I wish you had not followed! I am sorry."

"I'll be fine," Irea said stiffly. She brushed herself off. "Just get me away from this hideous hole!" They flew into the air to avoid the strewn centipede remains.

"How can they stand it, do you wonder? The EarthSeekers. Living underground. It's horrible!" Varia wondered.

"I don't know," said Irea, "And right now I don't care. Let's just get to the sunflower field."

The two flew higher and continued east until they hovered above the meadow that Varia had told Irea about.

"This is a human dwelling!" Irea said in a shaky voice. Varia could see the outline of stone walls enclosing the field, and the decaying human house in the center.

"It's abandoned, no one lives there but some cats," Varia said, remembering Talow telling her about discovering it in their happier times. "The sunflowers were a crop they once sowed I imagine, that come back now each sun. But since these humans left, it has grown wild again as nature has taken it back. We can land here."

"Varia," Irea said, "I . . ." her voice trailed off.

"Irea?"

"I'm cold," Irea told Varia. Her wings began to slow and she twirled down to the ground, much as the peppertree leaf had that morning, unable to keep herself aloft.

"Irea!" Varia called. She dropped down after her cousin. Varia rushed to Irea's side, but she was fast asleep on the cold ground. The sunflowers grew tall above Varia. She couldn't lift Irea up that high to create a leaf bed for her. She'd have to make a sleeping area for her there on the ground. Flitting to the nearest stalk, she pressed her hand against its prickly surface and asked the sunflower permission to take the leaf. To her amazement, the sunflower told her no.

But I am of the fae, Varia said in an attempt to persuade the plant. *We are one with the earthbound beings, the plants and the trees and animals. I am in great need of the gift that you offer, and wish to bring it to my fallen comrade.*

Unused to faeries since the plant's family had been sown by humans, the sunflower declined again and then shut down, refusing to respond to Varia any longer. She went plant to plant, asking for help, with no luck. She would have to find another way to keep Irea warm until dawn. She looked up at the human house in wonder. Though she too felt woozy, with new determination she covered Irea by bending blades of grass all around her to create a hidden tent. She felt around in her pouch and pulled out a small wrapped package; inside was a dried bouquet of stinkweed. While it did not smell bad to Varia, carnivorous animals loathed it. She laid it at the base of Irea's makeshift shelter. Though it hid her well, it did not warm Irea as she lay on the earthen floor. If she grew too cold, it would take long to awaken her and they would not be able to continue their journey on the morrow.

Varia tiptoed through the overgrown cottage's garden, pushing aside stalks and leaves as she stole toward the human house door. She could hear the rumbly breathing of cats as they patrolled the fields for rats, and she was careful to avoid them, and the rats as well. In the moonlight she found a meandering pebbled path where less weeds grew, and followed it, stumbling over the chunky rocks as she walked. She stayed to the side and rounded a thicket of grasses when, heart thumping, she ran smack into a tall stranger.

Gasping, Varia fell backward and tumbled into the rocks, cutting herself. The stranger was so good at hiding even though in plain sight; she could detect no life in him at all. He looked like the figure of a small human, with a red pointy cap and a white beard, and a blue jacket. Varia stayed still, wondering if she could pass without harm. Would he come alive and grab her? She crept up to the man, two stems taller than her. With all of her courage, she touched him.

She thisselled, reading him by tapping into his being, and saw his story; he was not alive at all but a dead thing, made from the wood of a tree murdered by the humans, specifically the man who had lived here once. The humans had killed the tree, as Varia knew from stories of them that they often did without thinking twice about it, and then they had taken a portion of the poor tree's body and made a log. Then, she saw as she read the object's story with horror, the log was stripped of its bark, and carefully poked and prodded with a knife until the figure was carved into the log's surface. As if that hadn't been enough damage to the tree, the woman of the household had painted the thing to make it look like a little bearded man. Varia couldn't understand what it all meant or why humans performed such brutal rituals against trees, the very lungs of the planet earth. Varia recoiled and hurried past the dead thing, and found herself at the doorway of the house.

Easing herself through the broken bottom slat of the door, Varia ventured inside, sure she would see worse things than the man-figure. She did; she saw another dead tree carved into a flat surface, probably built for eating off of since it looked rather like the sturdy limb and leaf tables at Ashenthorne. Through the caved-in roof moonlight filled the room; the entire house seemed made of dead things, and Varia wondered how the humans could stand to live there. Furniture, skin coverings, all forged from dead trees and animals. Shuddering, Varia looked around until she found what she was looking for. One of the windows had material on it, similar to the flower petal dressings her faepeople wore. She felt it, trying to understand its origins, and when she saw a sheep in her mind she decided she didn't want to know more, but at least, from her moment of thisselling the shredded soft cloth, she realized the sheep hadn't been killed, but stripped of its wool. She flew up to the window ledge and with all of her remaining strength, she gathered a fallen piece of the torn fabric. Varia tied it around her waist and flew out the ceiling hole, not wanting to risk the strange garden again.

Exhausted, Varia found Irea and wrapped her cousin's cold stiff body into the material and bundled her tightly, and hid her again in the tall grasses. Even if a cat discovered her, the stinkweed would ward it off. Varia returned to the neighboring sunflower; she didn't need its permission to sleep on its leaves. Shaking with cold, hunger, and physical exertion, she wrapped herself up in the leaf in the faery way and if the sunflower protested, she didn't hear it, for she was asleep before her head was settled into her makeshift bed.

Morning didn't blaze hot but warm enough. Varia felt grateful when the heating rays of the sun hit the sunflower field. She sipped dew from a neighboring leaf, stretching her wings in the morning light. Once revived, she flitted down to the place where she had left Irea. She cleared the grasses. Irea was gone.

"Oh no," Varia said aloud. At least there was no purple-tinged fae blood in the strange human cloth remnants. "Irea!" she called softly, but loud enough a nearby faery could hear. The stinkweed, still bundled, lay nearby, undisturbed.

"Irea!" Panic seized Varia. She tried to fly straight up into the sky to get a better view of the area, but she only made it a short distance before she fell back to the ground. She stood up and brushed herself off, and tried again. Once more she found herself in the tall springy grass. Disbelief grabbed her as she realized she had not eaten enough in the past two days to fly any longer. She had heard of such things happening to warriors and vagrants, but she, as princess of Ashenthorne, had never experienced such hunger before. She searched her leaf pouch for a nectar vial, but found it empty. Knowing her predicament, she walked, looking up at the tall sunflowers around her. The seeds were green turning to brown, but they would fortify her enough to fly. She flew as far up onto the nearest stalk as she could, and began climbing the thick trunk. The prickly fibers scratched her legs and hands as she crept upward. Her strength waned and twice she nearly fell; the more energy she exerted, the more lightheaded she felt. She knew if she fainted, she would be exposed on the ground, to become a victim of some foul creature or EarthSeeker. As she reached up to take a bright yellow bract, the plant swayed dangerously. She hovered for a moment before falling, right into the path of a passing cat.

Her landing startled the cat, which jumped but then turned its harsh golden gaze in her direction. It leapt toward her. Varia barely had time to roll out of the way, into the thick sunflower forest. The cat followed her, its huge striped face a mere stems away. Swerving, Varia could feel the hot stink of the cat's breath across her wings, its paw with sword-like claws just missing her. She leaned up against the nearest sunflower plant, and deliquesced into its rough surface, consciously slowing her breathing. The confused animal hunted for her, and she could feel him nearby, waiting, watching. Her strength was utterly gone; she knew if she did not eat something in the next few moments, she would not even be able to continue even the delicate mental chore of making herself invisible. She held as still as possible, trying not to flinch at the smell of the beast hiding nearby.

"Shoo!" she heard from above, and a rock landed hard. The flustered feline ran off. Irea! She chased the cat away by throwing something at it, Varia realized as she fell forward to the ground, surrendering to her fear and lack of food. Irea joined her, and handed her a round ripe berry. Varia bit into it, the dark juice dripping down her neck. After a few more bites, she was able to stand. She continued to eat quickly, devouring as much of the food Irea had brought her as she could.

"Slow down, Cousin! You will choke if you are not careful."

Varia bit into a crunchy sunflower seed, eating shell and all. "I have never been so famished," she said between bites. "I was nearly taken by a cat, for I had not the strength to fly."

"After last night, when I was too cold to fly, I knew I could not let such weakness happen to you, so I went to gather our breakfast. You will be fortified now, and we can continue on our way to the EarthSeeker realm."

Varia took more bites and tested her wings, flying up to the nearest sunflower's face. She stole (without asking) a few sunflower seeds and placed them in her leaf pouch, reminding herself to never go anywhere in the wilds without food stores again.

Feeling stronger, Varia flew up higher to gage the area, Irea joining her. In the far distance they could see the oak grove where the EarthSeekers lived.

"This place is so strange!" Irea said, popping a final bite of berry into her mouth. She handed Varia her nectar vial, and Varia drank the few drops she needed to continue. "We really should get going, we have to get back by nightfall. I just hope we aren't in trouble at the palace."

Varia hugged Irea, glad that she was safe now. Varia breathed in, no longer feeling the panic of impending starvation. She started to tell Irea that she thought she'd lost her but changed her mind. "Okay, let's not talk then anymore, from here on out. Just quietly follow me, we will air walk. I suspect those ground dweller faeries are oblivious to the treetops and won't notice us. I hope."

"Let's go," Irea said, a catch of reluctance in her voice. Varia pulled herself in a hovering way across the tops of the trees and Irea followed. It was a favorite faery tradition, air walking, at least for the Alawe tribe. An effortless way to travel, it was also fun, and a faery could silently, without wing song, fly from tree to tree twice as fast as flying and without any effort.

A light rain gathered in the clouds above, and the cousins sought leaf shelter from the morning storm until white noon streaks of light broke free, and the water-sprinkled forest glistened. The cousins continued to fly and air walk toward Birkendore, and soon found themselves directly over the grove where the EarthSeekers were rumoured to live, and both Irea and Varia found comfortable spots and deliquesced, disappearing into the oak tree that housed them. Varia's heart beat wildly as, within a few wingstrokes, a warrior faery emerged from the hole under the oak, dressed in elaborate silver and black fatigues made of materials Varia didn't recognize. The faery was taller than those of her kind, taller even than Ezia. His face was finely chiseled, and his eyes were rounder than those of the Alawe. He was sturdily built and his skin was a deep brownish-green, a skin color Varia had never before seen, as her faepeople tended to have skin the color of early dawn. These faeries were the color of the earth. There was something about the way he stood, and carried himself, that Varia found fascinating. She covered her mouth with her hands to prevent herself from gasping audibly. Within moments, a second, heavier, and even taller EarthSeeker joined the first. Both carried lightweight weapons, like Wilhvyre swords, but with a broader blade.

"Let's go, Doon," the first said. Varia could understand them clearly with her keen hearing; she recognized the voice of Loben.

"Loben, I promise there will not be an invasion today. Let's let our tribe out in the air and let us all proceed with our jobs of getting provisions. Midsummer has passed. Winter is closer than you may think," Doon said.

"Just because the king agrees with you does not mean I am wrong," Loben said. His wings were different from Varia's, thick and short like a grasshopper's, compared to hers, which were iridescent and thin like a dragonfly's.

"You worry too much," Doon told him.

"I sense outsiders in our realm today even more than before," Loben informed him. Suddenly Varia saw a flaw in her plan; Loben's kind were called EarthSeekers only because they lived underground, but they could still fly. Just like her. And they were faeries, did that mean that they had all the same skills as Varia and her faepeople? Could they sense her and Irea in their tree, their very home, even with their cover of becoming one with the bark and branch? Varia knew not to panic; she would be discovered. She had to remain calm and focused. Doon looked around, but Loben looked up. Right at the spot where she was hiding.

"I will patrol with you if you like," Doon said. "But I would prefer to get the kingdom dwellers outside first and start our day. The sun sets earlier now and the night cold comes sooner. We must be prepared to get through the dark time of year in these unknown climes."

Loben continued to stare up into the treetops. "I sometimes sense these trees have eyes," Loben said quietly. He shrugged. "Very well. Let's go back inside and tell them they are free to leave the castle," he said. Doon went first. Loben watched the spot where Irea and Varia hid, and then he disappeared back into the hole under the tree.

"We need to get out of here!" Irea said in the smallest whisper, pulling on Varia's arm. In their excitement of seeing the EarthSeekers, the two had forgotten their vow to be silent.

"Don't you want to see the rest of them? How many there are, what the faewomen wear? Maybe even the king himself?" Varia whispered.

Irea looked exasperated. "Varia, that thinner one saw us! Or knows we are here. Let's go quickly back so that we don't accidentally start a war. We need to find a reason to get Ezia's mind off of these faeries and forget we ever saw them!"

Varia hesitated. "What about . . ." she said. She had no time for other words. The larger of the two EarthSeeker faeries, Doon, grabbed Irea and wrestled her wings into a pinned position. Varia felt a hard hand clamp onto her wrist but she wrested free and propelled herself upward. She felt herself being chased, a heavy breathing and the fast beating of wings just behind her, and she never looked back, but flew, grateful she knew her way around from her excursion yesterday. She could hear Irea calling for help behind her but knew if she slowed and was caught, there would be no way to save her. Ahead she saw the river and she dove for it, pulling up at the very last moment, just skimming the surface. Her pursuer followed, but didn't pull up fast enough. With great satisfaction she heard and felt the splash behind her. She risked one quick look before fleeing back up to the trees; it was Loben. He was wet, and furious. His eyes were narrowed angry slits, and that's all she saw before she got away.

Shaking in the sunflower field, where she now felt she was safe since faeries don't tend to like human dwellings, Varia raced through her options. Go home, and get an army of uptight Alawe Wilhvyre, the FlightSoldiers, to come rescue Irea and risk war. Go back to Birkendore, and try and reason with the EarthSeekers and ask them to consider peace, and risk her own capture. Return to the oak grove, to spy on the EarthSeekers some more, and see if she could sneak in and rescue Irea herself. Varia popped some sunflower seeds in her mouth, not even asking the uncooperative flowers for permission through their Devic spirit guardians. In survival mode now, she needed to fuel herself; she needed to be prepared. Varia drank water from a shallow divot in a nearby stone and wrapped pieces of the cloth she'd used to warm Irea into small bundles that she tied onto her belt. She put five more seeds into her leaf pouch, even though these things weighed her down and would slow her flying speed. She carefully braided her white hair in a tight weave around her head so it wouldn't hinder her flight. She was ready. She returned to the EarthSeekers' lair.

Careful not to touch the oak lest it give her away, Varia hovered nearby and saw the EarthSeeker's main door was being guarded now by different male faeries in the same unusual warrior clothing Loben and Doon had worn. She saw the fae of the EarthSeeker tribe still going about their business, but with warrior escorts. There was no sign of Irea, Loben, or Doon. She would have to get inside the castle to find her cousin, she knew. Somehow.

There must be a back door, Varia realized. No faery, or even animal, created a home without an escape route. *It was by exiting one of Erendome's escape routes that got us into this trouble,* Varia thought with a sinking heart. She hurtled up to the treetops and flew to the end of the oak's root line, and then spread her wings and stilled them to lower herself back down into the forested area near the river bank. Unused to walking but not wanting to fly, she tucked in her wings and leapt from rock to rock, trying to discover a back way into the underground tunnel she knew lay beneath her feet. Every so often a peculiar chill would cover her body, and she realized she could feel the strangers nearby; at those moments she leaned up against the nearest rock and leaf and leaned into it, disappearing until the threat passed. She didn't want to risk asking the tree to show her the way in; it may have been the tree itself who had tipped off Loben the first time. She saw a great root and wondered what might be underneath it. She tiptoed toward it and peered beneath the curved fortress; there was a tall slender door made from the base of the living oak itself. Taking a deep breath, she reached for the door handle and pulled. The door opened.

Chapter Three

A guard on the other side flew out as she stood behind the door, and she slipped inside and quickly deliquesced against the earthen wall. The door opened again and the guard peered in.

"Skag! Did someone come your way?" the guard called, mere stems from where Varia tried to keep her connection with the tree root that made up part of the wall of the entrance. Another guard appeared from further down the hallway.

"No, Grenden, why do you ask?" the faery, apparently Skag, wanted to know.

"The door opened in a strange way, with no one there to account for it. Come, guard outside with me, your weapon drawn. I don't like this one bit." Skag followed Grenden outside, and when the door closed again, Varia, sure she was alone now, released herself from the root and looked around. While Varia's time spent underground had been limited in her lifetime, she expected to find a dark, dank, earth-smelling tunnel, or worse. Surprise and delight encompassed her as she stepped forward. Before her a wide and tall hallway led into the labyrinth, and the walls were covered with a hard but beautiful iridescent coating. Stamped directly into this wall covering were strange but fanciful golden designs, swirls and curlicues. The hall was lit by a strange light at the ceiling. Varia looked up; she couldn't make out how the light was fashioned, but she did notice that the ceiling was the roughhewn wood of the very oak above her. *The ceiling is the oak's roots!* She realized with great awe. She wished to touch the wall to understand better its construction, but didn't want to risk the faery home itself giving her away. She had already risked enough hiding in the earthen tunnel.

Looking ahead, Varia realized that if a guard were to turn the corner, she would be discovered. Tucking her wings behind her, she walked forward and found a soft flowing drapery made of oak leaf; it was heavy and thick, and beautifully constructed, with thin golden threads woven through it. Trembling, she moved the leaf aside, hoping a family wasn't behind it in their private quarters, or worse, that she wasn't about to stumble into a guards' den. Again she discovered another lighted hallway, still following the organic pattern of the oak's great root system, but this hallway did smell of dank earth. Varia tiptoed in behind the curtain and wandered down the passageway. It abruptly ended with a length of earthen tunnel, and then, a solid dirt wall. *They are working on this part of the tunnel,* she told herself. *They are just moving in and still constructing their home.* Now she could see the process; the walls were dug and smoothed following the tree root roofline. Then some sort of a plaster was created and the walls were solidified, then adorned with the ornate patterns she'd seen in the first hallway. *And this is just their back door, not even their great hall,* she mused. *They are true artisans.*

Seeing the exquisiteness of their construction gave her hope; surely a faepeople with these finely honed skills could not be the barbaric tribe Ezia had described? They did not live in the dirt, as the Alawe had always claimed; they lived in a carefully-made architectural wonder. Varia was about to re-enter the first hallway and continue her quest to find Irea when she heard footsteps and voices coming from deep in the EarthSeeker cavern. She pressed herself up against the wall behind the leaf drape and listened, hoping she wouldn't be discovered.

"There is no stranger being held captive by the Vorku, that is just a rumour!" said a female voice.

"Dunheen, don't you believe that we are moving in to the outer region of an existing AirWalker tribe's territory? Everyone says so, how can you not believe it?" another voice, also female, said.

"If it's true, Kurnoon, then where are they? Why have they not shown themselves before now?" The two faeries walked past the leaf drape. Varia heard the door she'd entered open, and then close. She could hear the two faewomen talking with the guards on duty outside. Listening with her whole body, she sensed she was alone now. Quietly she tiptoed into the hall.

Soon Varia found another leaf-draped passageway, and she carefully moved the curtain back to find yet another hallway, large and spacious like the others. She listened, and hearing nothing ahead, she entered. This part of the castle felt different; warmer, more used than the last. A main passageway, probably used by most of the EarthSeekers to get around the large colony. Varia closed her eyes and aligned herself with Irea and felt that her cousin would be found if she continued this way. Creeping along, she moved stealthily through the tunnel. Hearing more faeries coming up the hall around the bend, she ducked into an alcove with a light above it. There was no place to hide. She sank against the wall, willing herself to become one with it. Now the chance that the oak would give her away was high, but the fae family that passed did not see her. She could feel the dirt behind the tunnel wall; it was happy to be part of the fae castle there, and the oak was honored that his deep root system was chosen for the site of building a faery home. *Thundendell*, the wall whispered, and she discovered the name of the underground castle, for that is what the EarthSeekers who now were inhabiting Birkendore called it.

The family, a mother with two children, all with the dark gold and silvery wings that she'd seen on Loben, turned the corner ahead unaware that Varia was there, and she pulled herself free from the wall, which seemed concerned about her presence. She touched the gold swirled plaster gingerly and sent the mental message, *I mean no harm.* It was an ancient faery statement of goodwill, and the tunnel and even the oak seemed to relax when she said it. Varia was about to exit the alcove when she heard voices. Deep male voices. She hid as two warriors passed.

"I for one hope it is true that we have captured an AirWalker spy! I would like to be the one to pull off his wretched wings."

"Ah, Druag," said the other. "Shows what you know! It is a female spy we have caught!"

"Gurhook!" said Druag. "You have cheered me. If I knew where they kept her, I could have a word, or two. Time with Druag and she would wish she had never come to Thundendell." Both faemen laughed and Varia shuddered, waiting for their laughter to disappear as they continued down the hall. Her stomach tightened as she mustered up her courage to continue.

When she felt safe again, Varia pictured Irea in her mind and asked her Deva to connect them, and an inner wisdom told her to turn down the last passage.

The leaf drape was made from a deep red maple leaf and Varia listened with her whole being before pulling it aside. She felt as if she were entering an important part of the castle, for here the tunnel was far taller and wider, and complexly built into a diamond shape, with the walls angling out away from the flooring and back in at the root ceiling. This time the walls were a beautiful shining white, like opal, and the etchings were a brighter gold and even more ornate. The ceiling held several elaborate chandeliers, and whatever magick lit them, they shone brightly, as bright as the outside world. Varia stood a moment taking it in; it was grander than anything she'd ever seen, even in the far-off palaces of her distant relatives that she'd visited long in the past. Varia felt simple compared to such majesty, and inside felt weak for her assumptions about the EarthSeekers. They were obviously an advanced race, more than she would have ever suspected.

Sensing her cousin ahead, Varia did not linger, but rushed to a portal covered only by separate reeds hanging from the doorway, not even a leaf drape. An apparent large storage closet of some sort, she pulled back the reeds and peered in. There she saw her cousin Irea sitting on the floor surrounded by woven baskets, cloth bolts, and tools, her wings tied firmly behind her, her hands bound, a gag over her mouth. Irea's eyes grew wide as Varia slipped up to her and released her wrists first, then her wings. Irea shook out her wings as Varia removed the mouth covering.

Let's go, Varia said mentally. Irea nodded. Varia clutched Irea's wrist and sent her a mental picture of the castle, a map of where the back door was. She gave a universal faery sign for *fly* with her hands held up and outstretched and the two of them stepped beyond the reed curtain and bolted full speed toward the back door.

They were almost to the door when Varia heard it, the whirring sound of a hundred wings behind them. Faeries

31

need to pay full attention to flight when either being pursued or pursing, and she heard no shout, just the ominous bee-like hum of fierce warriors in pursuit. Irea pushed the door hard and was free, and its violent opening knocked over the two guards that stood there. Varia followed her cousin. But so did an army of EarthSeeker FlightSoldiers.

The cousins broke free and zoomed for the skies, Irea heading back toward their home. Varia decided to give her cousin, bound for so long and undoubtedly stiff from having her wings tied, a fair shot at escape. She zigged and headed into the forest. She turned to look behind her, and she could see only two FlightSoldiers following Irea; the rest were now following Varia.

She headed for the treetops, hoping that the EarthSeekers were unused to the bright sunlight. Shooting up through the understory, she flew high. As the FlightSoldiers broke free of leaves, they slowed, uncertain at first in the full noon light, giving Varia the moment she needed. She flew the fastest she'd ever flown in her life toward the cragged mountains to the north. Away from home, but away from the FlightSoldiers too. They sped after her, and did not give up even when she was too sore to go on, her body weakened from fatigue and fear, and still she flew. Ahead she saw a deep cave in the hillside. She hurtled herself forward and darted straight upward, hiding in the top entrance stones of the cavern. Feeling around she found a retired bird's nest. It smelled of dusty bird droppings and she wretched. She would not be found here, she knew as she deliquesced, melding into the nest. She heard the FlightSoldiers fly in after her. But they too knew they were defeated. They searched half-heartedly for her.

"She could be hiding in this stone for all we know!" said one, kicking at a rock on the ground after some time had passed. "For I have heard that those foul AirWalkers can hide themselves onto any surface."

"I feel it is more important we report back to Doon," said another, "than to waste our time finding the AirWalker. We got the information we needed from the captive one."

"Hush," said the other in a reprimanding way. "That nasty AirWalker is here, listening to us now. Say nothing more."

There was silence, and then one by one, the sound of wingsong as the faeries took flight, leaving Varia alone in the cave.

After she was certain the EarthSeekers had all left, Varia climbed from the moldering nest and brushed herself off. She felt dirty, and exhausted. She reached into her pouch and pulled out the sunflower seeds and ate them to give herself energy. She would need more food, nectar for flight, and water. Her thoughts returned to the human dwelling and with determination, she flew quickly from the cave and headed for the house in the sunflower patch.

Loben felt the walls of his home, the castle Thundendell. He was beginning to glean how the AirWalker faery had done it; entered through the back door, crept into the unfinished hallway, and then? How did she make it through the main halls without being spotted? He felt the walls, listening, until he came across the alcove she had hidden in. Resting his strong hand against the smooth surface, he closed his eyes and discovered what he could. He was surprised; she had a skill his faepeople did not, and could make herself invisible. He had heard it was so but was surprised to find it to be true. But why was she here? He learned with his palm on the wall that she was not a SpadeWielder, a warrior. She was . . . a princess of her faepeople. She was only there to rescue the captive, a relative of hers. A cousin. Loben breathed in, trying to get a deeper sense of her story. The walls were protecting her. *Why?* He asked the partitions to answer for it, and learned that she had stated that she meant no harm. Loben pushed his senses deeper. She had been appreciative even, of the EarthSeeker handiwork; of their stately home, and lush leaf-cloth, and their sense of design. Loben pulled his hand away as if stung. This was not the enemy he had expected.

Varia stretched out on the bumpy pad of the sunflower and let the sun revitalize her. Her mind was filled with worry about Irea, but she also needed to find water, some sort of plant sugars, and more seeds for energy. But first, she needed rest. Not even bothering to cover herself, she fell asleep, her bruised and exhausted body soaking in the sun's warmth.

When she awakened the rays were slipping down toward the western horizon and she knew she had to make it back to Ashenthorne before she would be missed. She began to worry but guessed that Irea, like her, was revitalizing herself in a secluded place to make the last leg of the journey home. She knew that Alshea's suspicion of them would be her final hurdle of the day if Irea made it safely home, but she focused on the task at hand. She drank water greedily from a shallow stone divot and ate several seeds, until she was filled. She searched for nectar to make the flight safely back to the valley of Ashenthorne, to her home in the whitebeam, Erendome. She tried her tired wings, and while she did not feel up for such a long and arduous flight, she knew she must go on. She wondered where the unfamiliar berries that Irea had found the day before were; those were delicious. But probably they were to the north-east where more brambles grew, and she needed to head west. She knew of some nectar-filled plants in a hummingbird haven a short flight away; she would stop there for more nourishment. Putting three more seeds into her leaf pouch, up she flew.

She was tackled. A heavy body landed on her, catching her from behind, pinning her wings in an expert way between her body and her captor's. Her first thought was that it was a human hand grabbing her; the second, an EarthSeeker FlightSoldier. She squirmed, trying to break free. Looking down she saw two strong brown arms around hers, and she felt her body being lifted into the sky.

"Please, no! I have to get home," she called out, and she felt the heavy wing stroke hesitate. "I am no threat! I mean no harm. Do not take me back to your prison. Please!"

While Varia did not expect to change the FlightSoldier's mind, she was stunned to find herself lowered to the ground. But her hopes were soon diminished when she found a delicate golden thread wrapped around her wings, and pinning her arms to her sides. Somehow in a magical way she didn't understand, the part of the rope binding her became stiff and hardened like stone, but the portion her captor held was still flaccid in his hands. She was able to turn to look at him and she gasped. It was Loben who held her captive now.

Loben looked into the female AirWalker's eyes with wonder. Her skin was fair, the blue of an early spring sky, and her hair the color of a summer cloud. Her wings were doubled and much wider than his, and full of shimmering color; blue, green, purple, compared to his pale gold and black wings. She was shorter than his kin, but leaner too, and she wore a colorful thin shift of some papery plant he did not recognize, but the cut and design were advanced. They stared at one another, in a standoff. Loben knew he should take the enemy to his faepeople but he also remembered what the walls and earth of Thundendell had told him; that she had been appreciative of their ways. *I mean no harm* echoed in his mind.

Varia stared at Loben, trembling in fear.

"Who are you?" Loben asked, his voice harsh.

"I am Princess Varia of Erendome, third heir to Ashenthorne," Varia said, giving her full title as was custom when meeting fae outside of the family.

"I am Prince Loben of . . . Thundendell, nephew to the throne of Birkendore," Loben replied. Varia didn't know it was the first time he had given his full name since his family's recent move to this place.

"I am sorry I had to break into your castle," Varia told Loben, trying to steel her shaky nerves. "I had to retrieve your captive, my cousin, Princess Irea, as we are not supposed to be here. We will be in trouble if we do not get home by sunfall. Our Wilhvyre will come looking for us, and we may bring grave danger to your faepeople inadvertently if I do not get back to Ashenthorne."

"Why did you come here, then?" Loben asked, his distinctive voice softer now, the same one she had thought of many times since yesterday.

"I . . . was curious. My brother . . . Ezia, second to the throne, told me that you were—" Varia stopped herself. She didn't want to say what Ezia had said about the EarthSeekers.

"Curious!" Loben scoffed. "Two curious fae princesses would bring on the destruction of two faery tribes, causing a war? Ludicrous."

Varia felt her face redden. "It is not only that, Loben. I wanted to see for myself what your clan are like. I wanted to become a liaison, to bring our tribes together. Our FlightSoldiers are . . ."

"FlightSoldiers?" asked Loben.

"Warriors. Like those who chased me. Like you."

"A SpadeWielder? That's what our faepeople call our militia, in the common tongue."

"Very well, then, SpadeWielder. But ours are . . . restless. They have heard of your encampment at the edge of our province, and are concerned. And they are—"

"—Ready to make war on a tribe they know nothing about?" Loben asked. Varia hung her head.

"Something like that, yes."

Loben paced, the rope around Varia's waist dangling. She tried reaching her hands up around the binding to pull it free but it was solid. She sighed, and sat down. Loben spun around at her movement.

"Do you try to escape me?" he asked her.

"No! I . . ." Varia shook her head. "I'm tired. I just want to go home."

"What of your cousin? What will she say?"

Varia paused, thinking a moment. Irea was usually reserved.

"She will say nothing, Loben. She is of the same mind as I am. We are trying to prevent a war, not start one."

Loben looked perplexed. He checked the sun's position in the sky.

"You must go, then, but I am trusting you. The wrath of the Vorku, our SpadeWielders, is not something to take lightly. I am releasing you because I fear what you say is true, that if you do not return home your clan will hunt for you. Such is the way of my faepeople also. So . . ." Loben laid his hand on the binding rope and the entire thing softened.

Varia was able to loosen the knot easily and slip the lash from of her body. "Take this," Loben said, handing her a small container that she recognized as one the Wilhvyre used to carry nectar. She opened it, and the strong scent of honeysuckle juice greeted her nose. She drank greedily.

"I was going to suggest we share it," said Loben with an amused look on his face. "In comradery. I feel that we may both want to keep our meeting silent, and keep each other informed of upcoming problems. Perhaps if you and I are working to maintain peace within our tribes, we can stop any future uprisings."

Varia handed the nearly empty flask to Loben and wiped her mouth with the back of her hand. "How can we do that? Send messages, I mean."

Loben drank the remaining nectar and made a strange noise in the back of his throat like a bird's whistle. "Here." A striking ruby-backed hummingbird with a copper-colored throat came to him and landed beside him. Loben rested his hand on its head and looked fondly at the animal. "This is Zedah, and she will bring you messages. She knows how to be discreet."

"May I?" Varia asked, more to the bird than Loben, but he assented with a nod. She touched the bird on its breastbone; she felt the strong Devic presence in the animal. This was Loben's most trusted friend, she realized. She smiled at the bird. "Zedah," she said in greeting. "Blessings." She hugged the small bird's neck.

Zedah preened. Loben nodded toward the sun. "Be gone," he told Varia. "Zedah will find you if there is a change in our militia's plans that involve your faepeople. If you need her, call her in the voice you heard me use."

Varia nodded; she'd already memorized the call, as it was the faery fashion to do so, to remember the way to connect with all things wild.

"Thank you, Loben. I promise, you will not be sorry you freed me." Varia reached out and touched Loben on the arm. A small shockwave went through her body and startled her, and she looked into his golden eyes. He stared back, and she knew he felt it too. Quickly she left him, heading fast toward the fading sun.

Chapter Four

Spent and flustered, Varia caught the last red gleam of the sunset as she saw in the distance the whitebeam tree, her home, Erendome palace. She knew she would have to answer to anyone who might see her, and for that reason she went to the moon dome and carefully popped the hatch. She hovered through the hole, and closed it behind her, and floated to the floor of her shared parlor. There she found Irea, looking surprisingly clean but there wearing a scratch on her face.

The cousins hugged. "Oh, you're safe!" Irea said. "I was frantic with worry."

"As was I," said Varia. "I'm so glad that you're here. You even had time to clean up."

"You'd best do the same, for you look horrible, like the jackals of the dark have struck upon you."

Varia looked down; her clothing was soiled, she still had the bundles of material she'd taken from the human house tied to her belt, and her entire body, wingtop to foot, was covered with a fine layer of grime. She shuddered as she thought of the filthy birds' nest. Realizing how disheveled she had looked during her conversation with Loben, she flushed.

"I will go clean up, cover for me, will you?" Varia said. She left the parlor and was caught in the hallway by Alshea.

"So!" Alshea said, looking her sister up and down. "Have you taken to living near the swamp marsh, where the stinking willows grow? For you smell like you've just come from there."

"I was pursued by a bird of prey again," Varia said, her voice shaky. "I am on my way to wash up."

Alshea inspected Varia carefully before nodding her assent. "You'd best hurry with that," she said. "But do be more careful, Sister. You seem to be having too many high incidents lately. We are, after all, a peaceful kingdom." Alshea looked Varia closely in the eye. Varia squirmed under her sister's penetrating aqua gaze and looked away.

"Hmmm," Alshea continued. "Perhaps you need guidance, someone to keep a close eye on you? I could ask Talow, he enjoys your company."

Varia balked, knowing that Alshea only wanted an excuse to talk to Talow herself. "I will be fine alone, Alshea. I take your leave." She left the room and headed out to the garden balcony off the top level of the palace. Below was a cool crystal pool. She flew down to it, and ducked behind the ornate screens built of curled willow frames dusted with sparkling pollen sheen and covered in fast growing vines. She stripped from her filthy clothes and dove into the water. The refreshing cold energized her, but the feeling of growing too cold to fly hit her, and she quickly took down her braid and swished her hair in the calm, and then climbed out. Before her stood Talow, carrying her dressing gown.

"Your sister said to bring this to you," Talow said, averting his eyes. The fae are not shy folk about nudity, but there are rules not to ogle. Varia took the gown. "Thank you," she said, slipping the long warm leaf-made robe over her tired but clean body, carefully placing each iridescent wing through the wingholes in the back. She could have collapsed at that point from her overwhelming day, but she tried to maintain her composure. "You don't need to help me, Talow," she said. "Alshea is not queen yet. She has no right to ask it of you."

"She is our next ruler, and I do her bidding," Talow said with a slight bow.

Varia shrugged. "Very well. I'm going to retire. Thank you for your help."

Talow kept his eyes averted as Varia dressed. "The reason I do not mind doing Princess Alshea's bidding is because it is you whom she asks me to protect," Talow said softly. As Varia pulled the robe tight around her wet body, she looked the handsome Talow in the eyes.

"It is you whom she desires," Varia said. "I cannot stand in the way of my sister's heart."

"Even if the object of her love, loves another?" Talow asked in a soft voice, his gaze full of desire for her. Varia flitted backwards, putting space between them, as she could feel his heat for her.

"This is folly, Talow. My sister will be queen someday. I cannot steal her love."

"Even if that love is offered freely to you?" Talow asked.

Varia looked at Talow's chiseled face, knowing all palace faery girls favored him. She had felt the same once, not so long ago, but when Alshea had shown interest, Varia had trained herself to force down her own sparking feelings for Talow. She shook her head.

"I fear it is not mutual," she said in a quiet voice, and she noticed the warmth in his eyes dim. It wasn't true, and she hoped he couldn't feel her real attraction to him. And now that she had met Loben . . . she pushed the thought of Loben away.

"I have been watching you, covering for you!" Talow glowered. "And that is worth nothing to you?"

Varia laid a hand on Talow's shoulder but he tugged away. "I do care for you, Talow, but . . ."

Talow grabbed Varia and kissed her hard on the mouth. Varia pushed him away and spat at him.

"I will overlook this transgression for the sake of Princess Alshea!" Varia said. "You must follow me no longer! My business is not yours."

Talow released his grip on Varia's arm and flew backward with a shudder of wingsong. Shaken, Varia tied the robe securely around her waist and flew past him to the balcony doors that led to the upper chambers. She preferred to use the back way to avoid further confrontation by risking a meeting with her father or Alshea in the main corridors. Only a handful of the palace faewomen lived on the top floor, and she made it safely to bed without further interruption. Irea was already in the neighboring bed, almost asleep.

"We will talk tomorrow," Irea mumbled. Varia groomed her long white hair, her thoughts turning from Irea, the EarthSeeker Loben, and Talow's advances. She laced new braids and snuffed out the resin candle before climbing into bed. As she rested her head on her pillow, uneasy thoughts whirled through her mind.

Outside, Talow watched Varia fly to the window balcony on the upper floor of Erendome. He fumed until the upper windows went dark. Ready to head back inside, he looked around, wondering why Varia hadn't brought a dressing gown with her to bathe. Behind the willow screen in the moonlight, he saw her pile of clothes. He picked them up, surprised to find a bundle tied to her belt. Curious, he unrolled the material and examined it. It was completely unfamiliar; it was not plant based, like the textiles of the fae. He pressed his hands to it, and felt its energy, and learned his story. When he was finished, he looked back up above him to the top floor of Ashenthorne. A frown marred his handsome features as he refolded the cloth and flitted up to the balcony, and left her clothes there for her to find in the morning.

After sunrise Irea and Varia remained silent as the faeries congregated in the great hall for their morning meal. The tables were elaborately set with the usual palace fare; honey and seeds, nuts and nectar, leaf and herb salads and berries and fruit, and the peppercorns that Varia made it her goal to retrieve, a favorite of the fae.

After eating, Irea and Varia flew separately to meet at the peppertree grove. There the bees were swarming, but the faeries ignored them and they buzzed harmlessly by as the two sat in the morning sun, recovering their strength from their adventure the day before.

She suspected Talow was trying to follow her. She was right; she had taken the long way to the grove, stopping in the marshes, and there she hid. Soon Talow emerged from the trees, searching for her. When he was distracted by a pesky dragonfly, she quickly flew off to the grove where Irea was already waiting. After being hunted the previous day by Birkendore SpadeWielders, evading Talow was nothing to her.

"When did you get back to the palace yesterday?" Varia asked when she was sure they were alone.

"I arrived here far before sunset, and had time to clean and change my clothing," Irea said. "I didn't want anyone to notice that I was wearing the same clothes as the night before."

Irea peered at Varia from beneath a wave of dark hair. "Your clothes were on the balcony this morning, Varia. Did you leave them there?"

Varia's heart sank. "I left them by the wading pool."

"Someone did you a favor, then. I put them in our room, though there may be no removing the soiled bits. What a wreck you were!"

Varia winced. "You know I fled for my life. Do tell, Cousin, what happened in Thundendell?" she whispered.

"What's that?" asked Irea, a blank look on her face.

Varia peered at her darker-haired cousin. "That's the name of the castle you were held prisoner in, didn't you know?"

"Cas . . . castle? Prisoner?" Irea asked.

"Where the EarthSeekers took you?" Varia said gently. Irea leapt up in the air and hovered above Varia.

"Don't play games! I'm angry enough that I got lost in an attempt to follow you to Birkendore. Don't try to make me think those EarthSeekers live there now! I'm furious that we wasted a whole day's flight going to the mushroom flats, and then we were almost attacked by that owl, and that wretched centipede, and then I grew too cold to fly! And then what, just to fly home with no news whatever of another faery kingdom! A waste, and we were nearly killed!"

Varia gaped, uncertain what was happening. "You truly found our trip to be . . . a waste of time?" Varia asked.

Irea nodded and turned away. "I'm still angry I went with you, Varia. You are far too reckless!" Varia flew up beside Irea. She held her wrist.

"What are you doing?" Irea asked, pulling her arm away.

"I'm thisselling you," Varia said. "I want to know what it is you believe." Varia closed her eyes and connected with Irea's Devic energy, her spirit guardian. Only on few occasions had she done so with another faery; it was an intimate act. Irea begrudgingly let her. Varia saw Irea's story unfold. The owl, the human house, the cold . . . and the flight back. There was no EarthSeeker castle of Thundendell, no being chased or held by the SpadeWielders, no memory of their escape. It had all been erased from her mind, an EarthSeeker clever mind trick, more than any AirWalker was capable of.

Varia sat on a pepper tree branch and put her face in her hands, small sobs wracking her body. She was completely alone now. Irea had no memory of their discovery, and Varia alone knew of the other faeries' existence. Irea came alongside of her and put her arm around her cousin's shoulder.

"It's not your fault, Varia," Irea said. "Don't be sad, we weren't harmed. We had an adventure, but let's not do that again, shall we?"

Varia looked up at her cousin and stared at her, a bit jealous that she had been able to block the knowledge of what they'd learned from her mind. "I see that you think I'm reckless, Irea. I will be more careful in the future, I do promise you."

Irea smiled and linked her slender fingers through Varia's. "I must say though, Varia, that I always have the most fun with you. Even though I am stiff and tired today as if I flew for my life ten times." Irea leaned on Varia's shoulder and giggled. Varia patted her addled head.

From a neighboring tree, Talow watched.

Several days passed, and Varia grew more despondent and separated herself from her kin. She spent most of her days in the pepper tree grove, its alien feel perfect for the outsider she felt herself to be. It was there that Zedah found her. When the small hummingbird flitted up to her, Varia felt she was seeing a dear friend. She hovered up to the bird, holding her close. Zedah allowed the hug.

"Dear Zedah!" she whispered to the bird. Varia released her and the bird buzzed up into the air, making a quick circle, so fast Varia could barely follow with her eyes. "What is the message Loben sends?"

Zedah alighted on a slim branch and Varia placed her hands onto the hummingbird's breast. She read the story Loben had placed within the bird; a story of a faery colony on guard, of arguing and talk of going to war, of angry male faeries ready to fight to save their territory of Birkendore and their castle at Thundendell. Her very presence had caused these problems, problems that the EarthSeekers did not have before she sought to discover their dwelling. The bird also showed a story of Loben waiting for her, Varia, at the human ruin.

"I'm to accompany you, then?" Varia asked Zedah, trembling with fear. "Now?" The bird took flight, heading to the northeast toward the house. Varia looked around to make sure no one was watching and flew after the hummingbird, uncertain if she was making the right decision.

When Varia arrived in the abandoned human garden, she didn't know where to meet Loben. She hovered low over the clover and ate a few petals and found some dew to sip. She saw something she hadn't seen before; a large stone bowl. It had been used by human workers as a wash basin, she learned as she thisselled the carved rock. There was a clear pool of water filling it now. She peered into the surface, and she saw a reflection above her. It was Loben, who had flown in on a silent wing.

"How do you do that? When you chased me, I could hear your wingbeat as if it were my own, and now you are as silent as the sky," Varia asked.

"We have many secret ways, Varia of Ashenthorne," Loben said in the formal way of greeting. Varia sat on the rocky edge of the basin and folded in her wings.

"I know that your warriors erased my cousin Irea's memory of her detainment, and she knows not now that you dwell in Birkendore," Varia said. "Are those the secret ways you mean?"

"You are still the enemy, and you and your relative were in our territory," Loben said. "All is fair when warring parties are concerned."

"Is that why you brought me here? To have my memory erased as well?" Varia asked. A sense of foreboding filled her, as she wondered if this meeting might be a trick.

Loben sat beside her. "No. We must decide what to do. I have heard that we have military parties planning to sneak into Erendome. They will discover your castle and spy on your faepeople, and bring back information on your weaknesses. Then they will send another party to conquer your clan." Loben looked at Varia, his eyes holding hers with his gaze. "We can't let that happen."

"How many are they sending?"

"For now, two lead scouts, Gurhook and Druag. They are patrollers. We have only two for the time being, but I would imagine . . . there soon will be more."

Varia remembered hearing the names Gurhook and Druag. They were the guards who walked past her in the hallway at Thundendell. She shuddered at the memory of their words, and couldn't imagine such louts hiding like insects and spying on her kin in her beloved Ashenthorne.

"What can we do to stop it?" she asked.

"I hoped you could tell me. I fear to allow them to be sent, yet I am a small voice in the castle. I am but far-kin to the throne, and most find me . . . cautious. Too cautious. But war is the thing I fear most." Loben's jaw tensed. Varia felt herself wanting to hold his hand, the pain in his eyes was so great, but she said nothing and remained still. As if sensing her desire, he reached over and held her hand in his. He lifted one hand to her cheek and held her face, staring intently into her eyes, as if reading her very soul. Varia felt a connection between them, but she averted her gaze, too intense was he.

"I must get back, but now I know too much, and not what to do. Shall I ask for extra patrol to be put on guard? Or less?" The burden of war filled Varia's thoughts as she unhooked her hand from Loben's hold.

She looked up to find Loben staring at her again. She tucked her hair around her fingers and pulled it behind the point of her ear. A commotion from the nearby sunflower patch distracted her as two large faeries in SpadeWielder vesture flew up toward Varia, swords at the ready. Varia screamed.

"Fly!" shouted Loben, who buzzed up and put himself between Varia and her captors. Varia whirred backwards and turned and flew fast toward the west, hoping to lose them in familiar territory. Two more SpadeWielders cut her off, and she was easily caught.

"You would betray me!" Varia yelled at Loben, teeth gnashing, but she soon realized she was wrong: Loben too was being held captive by the first two SpadeWielders. They both were prisoners.

Varia struggled but found the familiar gold lasso tighten around her, and felt it grow firm like metal, pinning her wings and arms. Loben was outfitted with one as well, and they were each flown back to the castle, being towed in the air strapped and bound.

Chapter Five

Varia sat bound on a fae chair, one in which the faery rests forward on their knees so their wings can be spread behind them. Incarcerated in a small room, Varia noted it was a different one than the one she had found Irea in. She wondered if her memory would be erased. She felt sorry to think that in mere moments she may not remember Loben, or Zedah, or the beautiful castle called Thundendell. Fear gripped her as she reminded herself that they hadn't released Irea, even after they had erased her memory, but seemed to mean to keep her prisoner. Varia's heart thumped as she realized none of her kind knew where she was.

With a swish of the thick green curtain, the two guards who captured her came into the room. One of them, the stockier of the two, leered at her. Varia looked away.

"Looky what we caught, Gurhook," the stocky one said.

"This one is for the king to decide about, Druag. Too bad for us. Look at her, she looks terrified," Gurhook said in an eely voice.

"She should be afraid, she's an AirWalker spy!" said Druag.

"Not according to Loben. He says she's an emissary of peace. We need to await the decision. Doon says to guard her, because she may have been the one to let the other one go."

"Are we supposed to . . . alter her . . . memory yet?" Druag asked in a small voice, as if Varia couldn't hear as well as she did.

"Not yet, and stop yacking, you shouldn't be letting the enemy know about that," said Gurhook, his large fist smacking Druag in the shoulder. Druag looked like he wanted to pounce on Gurhook but he held still.

Varia wondered if she could talk them into letting her go, but knew she could make things worse. She couldn't stop shaking; it must be dark by now. The palace at Erendome would be sending search parties out for her. The entire Wilhvyre army could descend on Birkendore like an ill rain at any moment. Varia rested her forehead on the pillow of the chair, waiting for something to happen.

Varia pretended to fall asleep and Druag grew bored. "I'm going to go and see what is taking so long, surely they must want her to talk!" he said, leaving through the curtain, flipping it with disdain, adding. "If it were my castle, I would have built the dungeon first!"

Varia kept her eyes closed, and Gurhook had trouble keeping his own eyes open, as soon raspy snores emitted from him as he leaned against the door frame, his stubby gold and black veined wings holding his balance. Varia sat up and stared at Gurhook, at his thick muscled dark arms, the way his black and gold veined wings went limp like a leaf blanket around him as he fell into a deeper sleep. She gleaned that the different faery races had different skills. The EarthSeekers obviously didn't know about hiding in plain sight, just as her faepeople knew nothing of memory erasing. She deliquesced into the fae chair and coughed. Gurhook stirred awake.

"What?" he asked himself as he recovered from his nap, looking around for Varia. Not seeing her, he jumped up to his feet. He moved along the wall, looking in every corner for her. "Druag!" he called, running through the leaf curtain, leaving the room. Varia willed herself back to visibility, and stood. Though her arms and wings were bound, her legs were not, and she pulled the curtain back with her foot, risked a look into the empty hall, and slipped out, trying to get her bearings. She headed for the back door again. This time she would have to walk out of here; she couldn't count on getting away by flying. She would have to use her wits and figure out how to release the wrist bindings later.

Hearing Gurhook and Druag yelling as they entered her now-empty room, she slipped up against a drapery and melded herself to it. To her amazement, a regal looking faery, the King of Thundendell himself, walked down the hall after Gurhook and Druag. She heard his voice roar when he discovered her missing. Several SpadeWielders ran down the wide hallways toward the very door she wanted to exit. She could see Loben running with them. He was free; he must have convinced the royal court that she was an emissary and that he was not guilty of treason. Fearing she had made a mistake by escaping, she wondered if she should reveal herself to him. Loben stayed a few lengths behind the SpadeWielders and was about to pass her. He slowed, and looked right at her, though he could not have seen her, as while deliquescing she resembled the folds in the leaf drape. Gathering her in his arms, he pushed her through the curtain and they both fell through to the other side, into an empty room, Loben heavy on top of her.

No one seemed to notice Loben's sudden disappearance, and they were alone. Loben covered Varia's mouth and did some trick to free the rope that bound her. He pulled her along behind him and flew into a deep pocket of the room where another small corridor led to an unfinished flat. Loben shoved her inside. There was no leaf covering on that door, but they couldn't be seen if anyone peeked into the hallway. Above them moonlight shone through a dome, not unlike the ones at Erendome. Varia hugged Loben, trembling.

"I am sorry!" she whispered. "I didn't mean to escape, I just . . ."

"I thought you might," Loben whispered back. He touched her face where her hair had fallen in her eyes and pushed it away. Their bodies touched, he was so close. She could feel his warmth against her. She leaned her head on his shoulder, glad to be free, and with him once again. Her attraction to him overpowered her senses. As if feeling it too, he held her and kissed her, and she forgot all; that their faepeople were on the brink of war, that the entire SpadeWielder army was searching for her, that she might never see her own home again. None of it mattered; Loben's sweet embrace was all she knew. As they separated, all she wanted was to be back in his arms again. She could tell he felt it too.

"This is dangerous," Loben said. "We need to get you out of here!"

"And then what?" Varia asked. "They know where I live in Ashenthorne, they know our meeting spot, and my own brother is the one who told me where to find your colony, so the only next step is war if we can't stop this madness now!"

Loben rubbed his hands up and down Varia's arms, hers pale blue compared to his brown ones, and pulled her to him. They rested their foreheads together, the universal sign of the fae for love.

"If I can get you out, then we will have time to negotiate. They don't know that I have you with me now, and won't suspect me. I was with them when it was discovered that you had escaped."

"Aren't they all swarming around here? How can I go free now?" Varia asked. Then she looked up. Could she pry the moon dome off just as she did at home? The construction and materials were different, but the concept was the same. She pointed.

"I can escape that way," she said. "I do it at home."

"There is something I didn't want you to know before, Varia," Loben said. "But your kind is faster than we are. If you can get free, you can outfly them." The idea of having to fly the entire way home alone in the hostile night frightened her. It was so risky, and she was already weakened, and hungry. And she knew if she flew away now, she may never see Loben again. She didn't want to leave him.

"Do you think I could stay here until morning?" she asked. Loben gave a small smile; he looked around at the unfinished room still being built by the Durndeng workers.

"I think this is the safest place you could stay tonight," he replied, pulling her toward him. She smiled and leaned into his firm chest. In the corner they found some unfinished leaves, raw materials that were piled for making the leaf door to the flat. They quickly put together a bed, and as the moonlight filtered softly down on them, after a time, they slept.

Their night together was surprisingly peaceful, as the Vorku SpadeWielders were stationed outside. No one had suspected that the enemy fae was still inside Thundendell, and as Loben explained to Varia, he was the only Durndeng who had learned the gift of "reading" the walls. Varia slept well, although she and Loben had awakened partway through the darktime and talked quietly about their lives, and kissed, and held each other, and more. Now she felt reluctant to leave him.

"Can you come with me?" she asked.

"I do not yet know," Loben said. "I should go to breakfast as if nothing has happened; I will eat and try to smuggle some food back for you. You will need nourishment for the trip home," Loben whispered as he left.

Varia was hungry and thirsty. She checked the belt on her tunic before putting it on; she had three seeds in her leaf pouch and she nibbled on one. It did nothing to dissuade her hunger, and in fact made her hungrier. Slowly she dressed, dreading her day after such a blissful night. She looked around the room and decided she'd better rest more until she could eat. She deliquesced under a leaf and slept until a hand nudged her awake. She woke with a start.

"My princess," Loben said, and he pulled a large vial of nectar from his belt pouch. He laid nuts, seeds, berries, and fruit before Varia, and she ate ravenously.

"I love watching you eat," he whispered. "I could do so endlessly."

Varia sipped down the nectar. "You keep catching me between meals," she told him. "Normally my table manners are impeccable."

Loben chuckled, and leaned back on the leaf and placed his hand on her thigh. It made Varia want to stay with him another day and night, but she knew it would be difficult enough to explain herself to her father. A missing princess, even one not next in line to the throne, was a serious matter.

Sated, Varia leaned against Loben, their entwined wings wrapping like a cocoon around them both. She did not want to go back to Ashenthorne for the first time in her life, but she also knew that to stay was folly.

"I'd best leave now," she said in a quiet voice.

"Yes," said Loben. "Be careful. Remember you can outfly them!"

51

"I will remember," Varia said. Neither stirred, still seeking comfort in the other's warmth.

Finally Varia untangled her wings from his and stood. She hovered to the dome but couldn't see through it well enough to see if any SpadeWielders were standing guard.

"Go, my love," said Loben. "I will send Zedah when we can meet again."

"Blessings, and go sweetly," said Varia, the usual fae farewell of lovers. She carefully popped the dome from its base, the same trick that worked at home, and peered out. Seeing no one, she opened the dome, climbed up, shut it behind her and flew off quickly toward the West.

For what she hoped was the very last time, Varia was escorted into Ashenthorne by the Erendome Flight- Soldiers who had been searching for her, and she told her father that once again she was trapped by a bird of prey and was unable to get home before dark, and that she slept while hiding in the woods. Talow then was on her trail at every turn, but his eyes were dark now, and he did not bother hiding the fact that he followed her on the orders of Princess Alshea. Varia did her best to ignore him.

Over the next few days, Varia's mind wandered often to her time with Loben. She knew that Irea could sense something was different about her. As they flew out gathering seed pods and nectar balls and pepper seeds, Irea often turned toward Varia to stare at her, as if trying to read her secrets.

"Is it that you're in love?" Irea asked as Varia rested on a leaf in the sun. Almost asleep, her mind jolted awake.

"What?"

"The reason you're so mopey and distracted. I can't place it. I've not seen you this way before, Cousin. I suspect it must be a moon spell, love, that's come upon you."

Varia blushed and Irea laughed, wings fluttering, as she tucked her dark hair behind her pointed ears. "I knew it! Will you tell me who it is?'

"I . . ." Varia had no idea what to say. Irea had always been able to figure out Varia's feelings, often before Varia herself knew. She closed her mouth.

"Shy?" Irea giggled. "That's so charming Cousin!" She flitted up and tugged on a leaf above her head, asking the Deva to release it. She dipped back down and covered Varia with it. "There now, you look so comfortable, and ready for a nap. Perhaps if you are drowsy you will speak in your sleep and accidentally share your secret with me!"

"Irea!" Varia sat up and pushed the large leaf off of her, and it dropped slowly to the ground far below. "Stop teasing me now. I'm not ready to tell anything, and with good reason. You'll have to wait to find out 'my secret', as you call it."

Irea pouted and turned her back on Varia. Varia sighed and flew to her, putting her hand on her shoulder.

"Cousin . . ." she said, but Irea turned her back again, not before Varia could spot the tears in her eyes. "Oh, please don't cry!"

"I am *not* crying," Irea said, though it was not true. "Let's just go home." Irea flapped off toward Erendome. Varia whizzed after her and blocked her from going farther.

"Come, let's sit and talk, don't be this way," she said, breathless from her quick flight.

Irea shrugged but allowed Varia to take her hand. They went to a nearby hazel tree and sat on its round leaf with the sharp edges, careful to keep their legs up as the points were scratchy, even more toothed than their whitebeam palace tree leaves. It wasn't the most comfortable place to talk, but neither was the conversation comfortable, for Varia knew she would have to lie to Irea to keep Loben's tribe safe.

"Why are you crying, Irea? I have not said that I am in love," Varia said in a soothing tone. She rested her hand gently on Irea's wrist, hoping her cousin wouldn't notice she was trying to calm her, just as Ezia did with angry bees.

Irea didn't notice, and she wiped her tears. "I don't know, I just don't like the feeling of . . . separation from you lately. I can't place it, but ever since our adventure, trying to find those mysterious EarthSeekers, you have often been absent, not just in body but in your heart and your soul."

Varia thought about what her cousin was saying, knowing she was right. It was as if she had been ripped in two, and half of her loyalty was with the Alawe, and half with Loben, whom she now knew she loved.

Varia nodded. "I think I feel restless and ill at ease, perhaps because we never finished our quest," she said carefully.

"Varia! You are not considering trying to go back and find the EarthSeekers! You must admit to yourself, they are not living in Birkendore as rumoured!"

Varia patted Irea's head and pulled her into an embrace. "I will be safe, whatever comes," she said. "Do not worry. I am sorry that I am distracted and have caused you inner pain."

Irea sniffed and smiled up at Varia. "I forgive you. You always were the adventurous one, but I never thought that you would be more like a warrior than a princess, off to find the enemy in a faraway land."

Varia thought of her content life until the day she left for Birkendore, when her world expanded, and her mind changed. She could never go back to being a somewhat pampered but happy princess. Now she knew too much.

"I will pay more attention to you, starting now. So don't worry about whether you think I'm in love, Cousin! I will tell you if one of our fair Alawe faemen catches my attention."

Irea smiled. "Talow undoubtedly has feelings for you," she said.

"I know," Varia whispered, looking around to make sure he wasn't in earshot. "He told me so just the other evening!"

"Ah! Did you kiss?" Irea wanted to know.

"He tried! I told him the feelings were not mutual, and that it was my sister the future queen who loved him, and that I could not stand between them lest we risk a family feud!"

Irea looked shocked. "You told him that? But he has loved you since you were both very young! His spirit must be crushed! He always thought you were the one for him."

Varia saw her cousin's glum look and held her hand. "I know. This was the nicest thing I could have done for him, for perhaps he will get over me more quickly this way and turn his affections toward Alshea."

"Alshea! Alshea!" Irea cried. "How tired I am of her always having her way! Ever since she was born, my life has been a conundrum of caution for what is said, and bowing down to the whims of the future queen!"

Instinctively Varia glanced around. "Hush, cousin! Such words are treasonous, even if she is not queen yet!" She opened out her green-blue wings to give them more privacy in case there were nearby ears or eyes, for she had begun to suspect Talow was not the only one keeping watch on her. "You at least had several seasons of peace before her birth," Varia said in a low voice. "I have been in her shadow since my first breath in this world, and I do understand your feelings! But you must hold your tongue, lest someone from the court hear you and report back. For know that I am being followed and watched."

Irea's eyes grew round and she looked around. "You are?"

"If I cannot see Talow, who follows me in the open on Alshea's orders, I can feel a presence with me always of late," Varia said with a shrug. "And sometimes, as I fly, I hear a second set of wings, that come to rest as I do, even when I see Talow before me. It is undoubtedly more of Alshea's spies, as Father does not mind my wanderings, nor fear for the safety of the palace as she does."

"Alshea is restless now too, I've noticed," Irea whispered. "There is something pressing on her mind."

"It must be her love for Talow!" Varia said.

The cousins grew quiet, listening. Far off in a neighboring tree they heard a faint rustling, but even their keen ears could not decipher the origins of the sound.

"It is probably the wind, or a bird," Varia said, but her doubtful look said otherwise.

Beneath them a cluster of Bee Tamers, including Ezia, emerged from the canopy. Ezia spotted the faeries and flitted up to them, the rest following.

"What have we here?" he asked. "Conspiring cousins?"

"We are just resting our wings in the warm sun, Ezia. How is the hunt for honey today?" Varia asked, reminding herself to stay aloof.

Ezia nodded to four faeries carrying a large woven basket full of liquid amber. "We are nearly done for the day," Ezia said. "There is rumour of ample nectar in the honeysuckle jungle so we are making a stop there on the way." He folded his arms over his chest. "You two, on the other hand, seem idle."

"Our baskets are filled, and wait in the pepper grove for the transportation litter to come collect them," Varia replied. "We too have finished our day early."

Ezia humphed. "Cousin," he told Irea, "you risk much by being seen with my sister, for Varia has the whole of our Wilhvyre armies on her trail!"

Varia flinched and Irea raised her chin in defiance and replied, "Then the armies must have little to do in Erendome, if they are so idle that they must follow a court princess as she gathers pepper berries for her tribe!"

Ezia gave a broad smile. "Perhaps you are right," he said. "Or perhaps they are right to follow her, since there are whispers of her searching for the enemy encampment!"

Varia flew up into the air. "Come, Irea, we don't need to sit here and listen to the spewing of a mad faeman!" She grabbed at Irea's wrist, but Ezia flew in and grabbed her hand and held her tight, glaring into her eyes.

"Do not call me the mad faeman, when you are the one leaving our kingdom for your own pursuits! For Sister, if I discover that the tales about you are true, then I will be the first to administer swift justice upon you!"

Varia wrenched her arm away and flew backwards. "So be it, Brother. But until I am caught in the act of doing something that you fear may bring the wrath of Father's militia down on me, then leave me alone, for I too have more important things to do to help my faepeople!" She flew fast toward the pepper grove, Irea close behind. When she landed in her favorite familiar tree, she sat on a limb and sobbed into her hands.

"Don't let Ezia get to you so, Varia," Irea said. "He is just hot-headed."

"He is a threat to me now!" Varia cried. "For he has no sense of the ruin a war would bring upon us!"

"A . . . war?" Irea scrunched up her face, marring her pretty features. "You speak as if those underground worms live in Birkendore!" She smiled to herself. "I told you that the EarthSeekers are probably extinct, now merely a faechild's story, told for amusement around the hestus flame on a chilly night. Don't argue with Ezia over the dirt dwellers! They are not worth a fight."

Varia sighed, feeling more alone than ever before. Far below on the woodland floor a group of faeries, carrying a large platform with handles, lifted the pepperberry buckets onto it and continued on their way, the litter crowded with baskets holding other delicacies from the neighboring trees and plants.

Irea laughed and flitted up to the treetop, and Varia followed. "Cousin! Since when are you a connoisseur of doom and gloom! We have done our work. Come along now, the day is fine! Let us be out in it." Irea flung herself by pulling down on a branch, "airwalking" to another tree. Varia grabbed hold as the branch flew upward, following her cousin. Her mind thickened with worry, Varia wondered how she would ever break free of her own clan to meet Loben should he request another meeting.

Chapter Six

Zedah arrived with the flit of a wing the following week, just as Varia was beginning to lose hope. The bird hovered in front of her as she gathered pepperberries, and flew quickly away upon sensing someone else nearby. Varia followed the hummingbird fast enough to temporarily lose her shadows, Talow and whomever else followed her. Panting, she hid with the bird under a large creek-side plant, its pendulous leaves the perfect foil. Varia deliquesced against the water lily's stem, while Zedah, used to making herself invisible, stayed perfectly still nearby. After risk of discovery and Talow had passed, Varia emerged and hugged the bird's neck. She breathed in her honey-scented feathers and placed her hand on her breast, listening for her message. Gleaning that she was to meet next sunset in a secluded area north of her home, Varia's felt her insides quicken.

"Will you come and show me the way tomorrow?" she asked the bird. Zedah bowed her head once, acknowledging that she understood. Varia nodded. "We must be swift and careful! This will be a very reckless attempt to meet. I must cover my absence this time!" Thinking of ways to do so, Varia parted from the bird, saying, "I will meet you here during the midday meal time, then. Fare thee well!"

Flitting off, Varia thought about how on earth she would escape the Wilhvyre army to meet Loben again. An idea formed in her mind. It was dodgy, but it just might work.

That night Varia barely slept, and she went up to her secret moon hatch and climbed up into the night sky to clear her mind. She loved to sit out in the dark, the bright stars sizzling down from above. Staring at the light-splattered sky, she doubted herself. *I should not risk this madness for love,* she told herself, but her heart spoke of another tale, one in which she and Loben would live their days out together in peace and happiness. She did not know which story to believe; the voice in her mind, or in her heart. A dark figure bore down on her.

"Are you trying to escape again, Princess Varia?" a booming voice rang out. *Talow!*

"Do you never sleep?" Varia asked in an annoyed tone as the larger faery landed on the roof beside her, looming over her. "Or do you just wish to follow me all day long?"

"I have been given my orders," Talow said in a low voice. "It is because you insist on flying free that I am unable to rest at night!"

"So that's it, then, you must follow me all the time, day and night, like the future queen's pet?" Varia stood, and could see his angry features in the light of the palace around them. "Like some stray butterfly she may take in, you are her lovely trinket, until Alshea grows bored and moves on?"

Varia wasn't expecting the hard blow that caught her across the face. "You will not speak of your future queen in such a way!" Talow bellowed, startling her. She touched the sting and rose up, as did her dark fury.

"Yet you will strike me, a royal princess of Erendome, to obey your so-called queen?" She shook her fist at Talow. "What kind of warrior are you, who preys on faewomen trying to catch a breath of evening air?"

"Go inside," Talow commanded, and he grabbed Varia by the waist, pinning her wings. He did not put her back through the round dome escape hatch that marked the top of the castle as she expected. She could feel his desire for her as he flew her to the nearest balcony. Visibly upset at having to touch her, he pushed her roughly through the door and slammed it behind her. Defeated, her cheek stinging, Varia crept down the quiet hallway into her bed and sobbed. As she wrapped her wings around her body and lay there, she heard the strange sound of palace workers fastening the dome, securing it so no enemies could go inside, or for that matter, come out of it.

Varia made herself known at breakfast by coming in a moment late so that she would be seen by all. Several of the future queen's guard, a small new division of Wilhvyre at Alshea's beck and call, shot glaring glances her way. Their leader Talow in particular was in a dark mood, his bloodshot eyes tracing Varia's steps as she entered. A few of them whispered to one another. Alshea watched her sister, then the faemen, before returning to her conversation with a courtier.

Varia sat by Irea, who had saved her a seat. "Sit, cousin! The nectar is nearly gone, so drink quickly! Hurry and we can go explore some new territory today. One of the bee tamers told me that there is another grove of the foreign peppers north of the honeysuckle grove!"

Varia watched Alshea, then Talow. Talow looked haggard; his usual easy demeanor and soft eyes tormented and tight. Alshea stole glances his way.

"North, did you say?" Varia asked, now interested. "Do you think my father would mind?"

Irea shook her head. "This army nonsense is all Alshea's doing, she's feeding it into the mind of the Wilhvyre that there is an enemy on the prowl and we are on the brink of war. My source tells me," Irea looked around, "that the king himself is unconcerned with the rumoured happenings in the alleged EarthSeeker kingdom."

"He perhaps does not believe they have moved into Birkendore, then," Varia said absently.

"Perhaps not. No one has seen any evidence of it! But Alshea is thriving on the power of it, with her special forces watching you in the name of the castle." Irea giggled. "So we may have some followers, but that is no problem!"

Varia shrugged. *No problem if you are not planning on escaping to meet your enemy lover*, she thought.

"It's a perfect idea, Irea," Varia said as she chewed on some seeds that were being passed around on a stiff leaf tray. "Let us go as soon as we finish our meal."

The cousins flew easily, enjoying a stop here and there to smell a flower or dip a toe in the icy creek. For the first time in a while, Varia enjoyed herself. She felt giddy as she flew up high and then careened dangerously to the ground, stopping just in time to pull back up again, which caused Irea to shriek and drop their gathering basket. Varia laughed as Irea flew down to retrieve it. She could see Talow and now a few more Alawe Wilhvyre warriors in nearby trees, but she didn't care. Somehow Talow slapping her face had set her free; she felt no obligation to his injured heart any longer. He truly belonged to Alshea, and he could be her pet for all Varia cared. As they approached an open meadow of summer wildflowers, Varia saw jackrabbits hopping and she stopped to take in the beauty of the glen.

"It is so lovely in this meadow!" she said. "I have not been here in many suns. Why do we never come here?"

"We have not felt the need to come so far, as our gathering has always been bountiful nearer to home," Irea said. "But isn't it nice, to take a break from the castle, without fearing for our lives?" Irea handed Varia the basket as she twirled and let herself drop near the ground before exploding back up into the air again. She came back and squeezed Varia's hand in excitement. A pang of regret struck Varia as she squeezed back.

"I am sorry about allowing you to follow me, when I made that reckless decision to fly at night to Birkendore," Varia said, smoothing Irea's gleaming black hair, and she meant it. "I should never have involved you. It could have cost you your life!"

Irea shook her head. "Let's not speak of it. Come, let's find those new pepper trees!"

The two faeries flew across the field, darting into the dense forest on the opposite side.

Talow led his men to the brink of the meadow. One of them, a young faeman named Harah, spotted the rabbits.

"Watch this!" he shouted, and he sped toward the nearest one. Clutching onto the creature's ears, the startled jackrabbit panicked and took off crazily, while Harah hung on for the ride. He bounced mercilessly as the jackrabbit tried to turn and attack, but could not see what plagued him. Frightened, the rabbit darted back to its den, and Harah was bumped off as the animal disappeared into the hole in the earth. Laughing and brushing himself off, Harah flew back to the others, who also laughed at his antics. Talow pulled a long whittled stick from his scabbard and whipped Harah fiercely across the chest and face. A thin line of blood crept up on Harah's pale cheekbone. He flew in alongside the others, and the Wilhvyre nervously queued up and hovered as they were taught in training.

"You find this excursion to be a joke?" Talow said in a threatening voice as he stood before the line of warriors. "We have no time for your ridiculous games!" The faemen cowered; it was apparent they had never seen Talow act in such a manner before. "The future Queen Alshea has commanded me to follow the Princess Varia and her cousin Irea. This is a serious undertaking!"

One of the soldiers, Ledum, flew forward next to Talow and faced the line. "This is not merely a whim of the queen, faemen! For there is evidence that Princess Varia is in actuality a spy for the EarthSeeker encampment."

A murmur went through the crowd of seven soldiers.

"Is this true?" someone called out.

"It is," replied Talow. "I have seen with my own eyes that she is conversing with a hummingbird that is known to be a messenger of an EarthSeeker warrior living in Birkendore Flats."

The murmur grew again, and Talow held up his hand. "Our king would have you all believe that we are not under siege, that there is no threat! But believe me, faemen of the Wilhvyre, that is not the case! For our own princess has been in communication with them, and will be the doom of us all!"

"Then let us go and find her before she escapes our clutches!" Harah, who still glowered about his beating, said.

"You, above all, now know how dire this situation is," Talow said, handing him a leaf to wipe the blood from his face. "Never let Princess Varia from your sight! Even now they stray farther. Find them!"

The faemen flew off after Varia and Irea, and Rumendah, aged though he was, crept from the leaf he had been hiding behind as he had listened to the warriors' conversation.

"Varia, now what are you doing?" he asked himself quietly. He flew, following the loutish buzzing of the Wilhvyre army.

Varia stepped naked from the clear pond as Irea swam, dipping her wings under the cold surface.

"This was most refreshing, Irea!" Varia called, secretly glad she had time to relax and clean up before seeing Loben. She spread herself out in a warm patch of moss, and lifted her wings forward to air dry. The sun beat down on her tired body and she took in a deep breath, thanking the stone and the moss for warming her chilled skin. Soon, she was asleep, dreaming of flying across a rocky dune with Zedah. Their wings matched in time as they flew over purple gorse, free, racing. Varia laughed, they flew so fast, faster than she'd ever flown before.

An annoying buzzing sound bothered her, and she startled to find Irea shaking her awake, her damp hair tangled around her shoulders. She too had been lying on the rock, naked as she air dried, their empty basket beside them.

"The Wilhvyre have followed us! I counted three, but hear more!" Irea whispered as she stood to dress.

Varia jumped to her feet and quickly put on her petal skirt and top. "Leave it to them to spoil a lovely dream!" she spat. She smoothed her long white hair into shape with her fingers, wanting to flee the spot.

"That was a treat," she heard one warrior say to another, though she could not see them. "To be able to watch sunbathing princesses while we work. Who could ask for a better job?"

Furious, Varia searched the treetops with her eyes, but could see no soldiers. She thought the voice sounded like that of Ledum, one of Talow's cronies.

"Dare you spy on a princess of Erendome? Show yourself, coward!" Varia called. Irea held her arm to keep her from flying up there.

"Let's just go," Irea whispered. Ledum hovered away from the cluster of leaves that hid him, leering down.

"That was a compliment, Princess! And I am on duty, sworn to the king and his castle. I was told to watch you, for your safety, my lady," Ledum said.

"And when you say, 'the king and his castle', I presume you refer to my sister Alshea?"

"I do," replied Ledum in an eely voice.

"She is not queen yet!" Varia shouted. "My father will hear about this!"

Ledum looked a bit taken aback, but Talow materialized nearby, having been hiding by deliquescing into a tree limb.

"Alshea has been granted command of this branch of Wilhvyre activity," Talow said. "Her father, your father, is aware that we Wilhvyre are protecting you."

"Protecting? Harassing!" Varia said. She grabbed Irea by the wrist and tugged on her, and holding the basket together they continued on their way to the new pepper grove. Once in the familiar-smelling tree, Varia sat on a branch. Irea hung the basket nearby and joined her.

"Whatever happens, Cousin, remember that everything has a bigger reason than just you or just me," Varia said in a low voice. She rubbed her fingers along the bark lines of the tree.

"Why do I get a pit in my stomach when you say such things?" Irea asked. "Please don't lead me on any more adventures!"

"You must stay here, and let the Wilhvyre take you home."

"Let the . . ." Irea's eyes grew wild. "What are you saying?"

"I have something to attend to," Varia said. "Important business, for the future safety of the castle."

Irea gasped. "What they say, it is true! I have been defending you to the court gossips, and yet here it is, a confession! You are a spy!"

Varia shook her head. "I am not a spy, but I know a way to keep war from coming upon us! I will admit nothing to you, Cousin, for whatever words I tell you now will be pulled from you by my father's militia! Just help me escape, and I will be forever indebted to you. I promise you, this is the best for our faepeople! I would not lie to you about that."

"Varia . . ." Irea cautioned. "They will be here any moment!"

"Here," Varia said. She flew down to the ground where a large rock protruded and made a hasty stick figure about her own size and threw a large leaf over it, after tearing off a bit of her own skirt, shortening it considerably in the front. Poking bits of the fine cloth out from under the leaf, she handed Irea another leaf.

"You climb under this leaf, and pretend to talk to that one, as if it is me."

"This will never work!"

"It will long enough for me to get away, trust me. I must go!"

Varia pecked a kiss on Irea's cheek and flew off as fast as she had in her dream about Zedah. She could feel the bird's presence in the north, and zoomed to join her there.

Talow and his men found the cousins conversing while resting on a shady rock under thick leaves.

"If this is what it is to be a royal faery, sign me up!" Harah said. "For all they have done all day is fly, bathe, eat, and rest!"

"They do bring home pepperberries, it just must not take them long to do so!" Ledum said. "For now I see that their job is just so the common fae don't suspect that the royals are lazy, slovenly workers."

"Silent!" Talow said. He looked down at the two princesses. Why," he said aloud, "if the princess Varia is asleep under that foliage, is Irea continuing her idle chatter?"

"Perhaps she is singing," Ledum suggested.

"Perhaps she has tricked us all!" Talow roared. He soared down to the rock, landing lightly, his sword drawn on Irea, who shrieked.

"Don't kill me!" she cried.

"You would betray your own queen?"

"I have betrayed no one!" Irea said. Talow used the tip of his weapon to lift the foil covering the stick figure that Varia left behind. Seeing the ruse, he thrust the sword point back toward Irea, holding it close her to long neck. "Where is Princess Varia?"

"She would not tell me!" Irea said.

"Seize her!" Talow cried, and Ledum and Harah lunged at her and bound Irea's legs, arms, wings. She struggled, to no avail.

"Let me see what you know," Talow said, reaching his hand toward her forehead.   "

No!" Irea squirmed. "You are not authorized to thissell me, I am a royal in my own right! My uncle is king. Unhand me!"

"You have not been paying close enough attention to the politics at the castle, your ladyship," Talow taunted her. "I have more power now than you may realize! For I am the queen's hand, and do her bidding!"

"She is not queen!" Irea hissed. Talow caught a blow to her temple with the back of his hand.

"Quiet," he said, resting his hand heavily on her forehead, thisselling her to see what she knew. Irea struggled with the intrusion, finally bursting into tears before Talow had finished.

"I am done with her, take her back to the castle! Speak not of this to anyone, not even the queen," Talow said.

"But . . ." Harah began, and Talow held up a hand to silence him.

"Do as I say. If anyone asks, state that I will soon be along, escorting Princess Varia home for her own protection! I will bring her back to Erendome when I return, one way or the other," Talow said. The FlightSoldiers flew off, Irea their captive, to return her to the palace. Talow sniffed the air, and used the deepest of his fae senses to discover the whereabouts of Varia.

Varia found Zedah on the outskirts of a deep wood. The wood was ancient, disliked humans, and had housed many

ill-fated men over the cytons,* Varia noted upon touching the bark of a towering oak. The forest whispered its own name: *Llangdwig.* Even though the wood had been invaded by men at times, the quality of old magick was deep in it. Zedah seemed cautious and flew at a slower pace, uncertain of the path ahead through the shaded trees.

"Show me, my friend, where I can find Loben!" Varia whispered to the bird. They traveled along the base of the canopy, zipping in and out of the leaves to avoid detection from hungry beasts. Soon the tree layer lifted, and sun came through, and between the dangling mosses Varia spotted a golden pool ahead. It gleamed like the sun itself. Shielding her eyes until they adjusted to the reflected light, Varia could see an ethereal setting greet her eyes.

Colorful wildflowers, much like the ones in the meadow she'd seen before, waved in a listless breeze, but here the backdrop of soft stones and water and a tree-lined surround made the place, called Erenley Meadow, feel safe instead of exposed. There was another element that Varia couldn't place, like another world just beyond her ability to sense it. Humans had known this place, but had never inhabited it. Other creatures ruled here.

On a wet rock damp from the waterfall stood Loben. When he saw Varia, he flew to her, and they embraced. Varia felt his hard chest pressing against her and wished she could stay in his arms forever.

"I am being followed by our palace FlightSoldiers, the Alawe Wilhvyre, but I lost them," she whispered.

"We are safe here, you can speak freely," Loben replied, shaking his wet shoulder-length hair. In the sunlight, the pale brown tresses were laced with gold, and Varia admired him for a moment as she flitted back to drink him in. She noticed he had gathered an impressive array of foods for a feast for them that awaited her on a nearby boulder.

"It is good to see you, I have missed you!" she told him, her hands trailing back to him to touch his warm body.

"And I you. It is a great risk to meet, many in my kingdom

*A cyton is approximately 92 years, measured on the Feyllan calendar full moon-to-full moon from the first post-Samhain (Gregorian: November) Frost Moon suspect that I have something to do with your escape, though they cannot figure out how because I was with the royal court when you were discovered missing. Nonetheless, I too am being watched."

"My sister Alshea, the future queen, has a guard on me day and night! They no longer hide, but follow me openly."

"And so it begins," Loben said in a low voice. "The Vorku spies leave our castle at nightfall and will report back to King all of their findings. The war is upon us, as we feared."

Varia shook her head. "This is my fault! Why couldn't I have stayed put and not flown to your kingdom? Then all would be well."

Loben pulled Varia close to him, holding her. "But we would not have met," he said. Zedah buzzed nearby.

"Blessings, Zedah," Loben said, reaching his hand out. The small bird flitted close and alighted on his arm, and leaned her face against Loben's cheek. "Fly far, until I send for you. For I fear that some may know that you are my messenger, and your safety is my main concern."

Varia laid her hand on Zedah's feathered head and sent her with the fae blessing. "Be safe!" she called as the bird flew quickly to the east.

Loben and Varia kissed in mid-air before landing on a warm sandy pool bank. She stretched out with Loben beside her. Together they looked up into the canopy of trees, listening to the calm of the woods. Varia could hear a few bird calls deep in the thickets, and the splashing of fish in the lake. Clouds puffed by overhead, with the sun returning between them like a ray of hope.

"I wish we could stay here forever. No one could find us! If we stayed, we could start a new life together!" Varia murmured.

"We could," Loben said. "But our faepeople need us now. Yours need you, and mine need me, even though they do not see it yet."

"I suppose that this can never work, our love for each other," Varia said.

"It has been tried in the past," Loben told her. "And it did not succeed."

Varia sat up. "What do you mean?"

"Our Durndeng Queen Hoondeen once loved an AirWalker, an Alawe, many cytons ago," Loben said. "Their love has been sung about in songs by the valley folk, it was known to be so great, but the two tribes threatened mayhem and death if the couple stayed together. The lovers parted ways, still sworn in the eyes of the great gods, but were never allowed to see one another again."

"That is so sad! I have not heard that story before. Does the queen ever talk about it?" Varia asked.

"Queen Hoondeen never has mentioned it once," Loben said. "Not to anyone, but if you look at her, her eyes carry a great sadness to them, and you can see that even as she regally accepts her duty as King Struben's wife, her love is for another."

"That could happen to us," Varia said. "If we are discovered. More the reason to flee and begin a life anew!"

"Wild fae folk who are not living within the safety of a kingdom have a rough life, Varia. They must build their own homes, find their own food, create an existence in the wilderness without any help or protection. The only ones who are successful are those that move into human gardens, and allow humans to dote on them. But they are little more than exotic pets."

"No Alawe has ever moved into a human garden!" Varia said, offended.

"That may be true, but I could tell you many tales of our faepeople doing so, and some recent stories are even tragic. We Durndeng have a natural bond with humans, and except for those who would betray us, it has been so for many cytons. But that is not *our* fate, not for you or for me. We are loyal to our crowns! We cannot leave our homes now, even to be together. Our love may be doomed, torn by impending war, if we cannot ease this growing problem."

Varia knew it was true and a tear trickled from her eyes. "Then let us share whatever moments we have in this sacred place, and make them last," she said, turning toward him. Their bodies entwined, the sun warm upon them, as they shared their love, knowing they had to make their only day together last forever.

After a peaceful day in which the strife of the court did not disturb them, Loben held Varia's hand and looked into her eyes.

"I know what we said earlier," he told her, "That our love may be doomed. But this is the most sacred spot we could ever find, and I would like to bond our union in the eyes of the fae gods and goddesses!"

"You wish to marry me, here?" Varia asked, looking around at the evening light that now filtered through the trees, casting a brassy glow across the lake. "It is perfect!" Varia faced Loben. "I would be honored to be wed to you, bonded through time, whatever happens, Loben of Thundendell."

"And I would love to be wed to you, bonded through time, whatever happens, Varia of Erendome," Loben replied, as was the customary way. While fae weddings are usually a large many-day affair, with much food, drink, and finery, especially in marriages of those with royal lines, a mere few words needed to be exchanged to make it a true and sacred bond. They needed a witness and called upon the stone that they stood upon, and as they held hands a faint energy emitted from the rock, filling the space between them, until the couple were cast in a pale purple glow, unionizing them. And so it was.

After their wedding night together, dawn broke the darkness and the two knew they must part ways. Varia leaned her head on Loben's chest as they sat by the pool under a leaf wrap, feet in the cold silver waters.

"At least we are husband and wife," Varia said as Loben stroked her wings. "I shall go forth braver, knowing you are now truly one with me!"

"You are already very brave," Loben said. "Get back to your castle quickly, for the spies from Thundendell arrive there today. You must somehow stop the Vorku army of Birkendore from being discovered, or you will have a bloody battle at the gates of Erendome!" He fished around with his fingertips in a fine twig pouch on his belt. "I have this for you," he said. It was a necklace, full of tiny sparkling precious stones with elaborate ornate silvery swirls banding it together. "I had hoped that the opportunity would come to give this to you, and now that you are my wife, the timing is right."

He fastened the jewels around Varia's neck. She looked down, admiring the fine craftsmanship. "It is the most beautiful thing I have ever owned," Varia whispered. "My husband. But I have nothing to offer you as a gift in return."

"Varia of Erendome, your love is the only gift from you that I will ever seek," Loben said, reaching for her.

They kissed, clutching one another. The sun poked through the woods, lighting the spot where they sat. Time for more eluded them.

"I must go," Loben said, and they flew together out of the woods, staying close to the tree canopy. Once deep in the ancient grove Loben clutched Varia's hand. "Fare thee well, my love." He sped off into the south. Varia headed west, toward home, determined to stop the war before it could begin.

As Varia flew low over the rabbit meadow, she heard a thick buzzing of wings. But it was not the familiar sound of Alawe wings: It was the sound of the heavier wings of EarthSeeker SpadeWielders, what Loben called the Durndeng Vorku. They were on her, several from the sound of them, but she had lead and remembered Loben's words that she could outfly them. More than once she felt the prick of their lances on her heels, and she flew with as much haste as she could muster. Soon she felt a faery flying beside her, but she looked over to assess her enemy, startled to see Talow.

"Talow!" she called. "Help me!"

Talow did as asked and turned to face the enemy, his own blade drawn, and the sound of a terrible clash of weapon on weapon echoed as Varia sped off. The buzzing behind her was less, then none: Talow was fighting all the Vorku army alone, and would surely perish. Seeing trees ahead, Varia aimed for the nearest one and flew to the highest branch. Breathing heavily, peering to see the skirmish over the fields, she could not tell what was happening even with her keen faery sight. . . just a blur of bodies, many silver and black clad soldiers against one bright blue and gold attired warrior. Fearing the worst, tears escaped as she watched.

71

Varia knew she was witnessing the fall of the brave warrior Talow, and even though he had turned on her, she knew it was her fault. Talow must have been waiting over the long night out in the forest, spying on the Durndeng tribe's Vorku army in the meadow, anticipating his moment to save her. Varia wiped her tears and, remembering Loben's words, forced herself to be brave. After recovering a little, she flew on, pondering how to break the news of Talow to the royals. As she entered the outskirts of Ashenthorne, the Wilhvyre greeted her, and not with open arms.

"Princess Varia, we have been directed by Queen Alshea to escort you home. You are banned from roaming the countryside until it has been deemed safe by the Wilhvyre."

Harah grabbed Varia by the arm, and she tried to pull away but Ledum took her other side and they flew her toward Erendome castle.

"Unhand me!" Varia said, wondering if she should tell them now about Talow. She hesitated. If she told them, they would rush off to battle the Vorku, and the war would officially begin. She needed time to think. A lump formed in her throat from the words she withheld, and Varia nodded toward the upper story of her home. "I will go directly inside, you do not need to escort me further," she said. The warriors let go, and she flew toward her upper-story chambers.

Slipping onto the Erendome balcony, Varia opened the main doors and rushed down the hall toward her bed so she wouldn't have to face anyone from the palace. She took off the necklace Loben had given her as a wedding gift and hid it in the wooden groove on the bedframe, a hiding place she'd used since she was a small girl to keep her most precious belongings safe from Alshea's curious eyes. Her mind addled, her thoughts roamed between Talow's last fight and her wedding to Loben. Exhaustion seized her as she climbed into her comfortable bed, her words silenced by doubt.

Varia drifted toward sleep as the day turned to evening outside her windows. The chamber door opened, and Varia could hear someone enter.

"Ah!" Alshea said. "Here Varia is, after all. All of her long wanderings lately must be taking a toll on her. She has apparently survived her night in the wilds. Nothing to worry about then!" The door closed again, and in the darkening room, Varia kept her eyes closed. Tomorrow she would have to tell her father what had happened to Talow and about the Birkendore spies. Before Varia could settle back into slumber the door opened again.

"Wake, Sister!" she heard, but this time it was the deeper voice of Ezia. Varia sat up.

"What are you doing in here?" she asked her brother. "Get out!"

"I should ask you, what are you doing here? And where is Talow? Did he not find you? Where have you been?"

Varia didn't like being questioned by her brother; she was afraid she would slip up and tell him about Talow's demise. She tried to calm her jumpy mind.

"I was out too late to fly back to Ashenthorne, and slept the night in a nut tree hollow," Varia lied. "I came home, directly to bed. I have been very tired of late."

Ezia sat on the edge of Varia's bed. "I shouldn't wonder, Sister, with your long wanderings. Tell me," Ezia glared into her eyes, his own turning dark and cold. "What have you been doing in the meadows to the north? For you have been spotted there by our patrols."

"Pa . . . Patrols?" Varia asked. "What do you mean?"

"Answering a question with another question is a clever way to evade me, Sister, but since those nasty earth dwellers have been spotted in Birkendore, we are sending Wilhvyre to scan the perimeter of Ashenthorne to make sure that those dirty faeries do not enter onto our lands."

"I have nothing to tell you, Ezia," Varia said.

"You came home two moons ago with a remnant of cloth from the human dwelling, Varia. Talow found your belongings by the wading pool and came to tell me what he saw straightaway. Alshea and I sent him to follow you."

Varia's eyes lowered. It was time, she knew, to tell of Talow's fate. Tears filled her eyes.

"I feared as much, Brother, but I have terrible tidings. Talow was killed."

Ezia's eyes blazed. "Killed! What took him?"

"It was . . ." Varia knew she could not tell Ezia of the Durndeng. "A hawk. The last I saw of him, he was taken by a hawk near the north meadows."

73

Ezia looked away, and he blanched. He turned his harsh gaze again on Varia.

"Then his untimely death is on your conscience, Sister. For he was on duty, doing what the royal family asked of him, keeping watch on you. If you had stayed near Erendome and not wandered beyond our Ashenthorne borders, Talow would still be alive."

Ezia could contain himself no longer and he hovered up into the air. "When were you planning on telling us of this news?" he asked.

"My heart was too heavy with it, Ezia, and that is the truth. I needed to recover my senses. I had planned to break the news to Father on the morrow."

Ezia held himself above Varia's leaf bed. "I shall break the news to Father," he said. "And you will need your rest." He leered. "Tomorrow there will be a full inquisition." Wings buzzing, he headed for the door. Then he stopped, an imposing figure in the darkness. "If I find that your actions had anything to do with brave Talow's demise, Sister, there will be harsh consequences," he said as he exited.

Varia trembled, unable now to sleep. Ezia's words "harsh consequences" echoed in her mind as rest eluded her, though exhaustion was still very much with her. She hovered over her bed, buzzing from one side of the room to the other, her nerves rattled as outside, the moon ambled across the sky.

Chapter Seven

Varia was shaken awake by Alshea.

"The formal inquisition is ready for your presence," Alshea said. "Come now, dress. Wear your coronation clothes."

Varia, flustered as she walked to the adjoining room which housed her clothing, inspected the colorful royal gowns that hung before her. Irea flew in from the passageway.

"I'm here to help you, Cousin," Irea said stiffly. Her eyes avoided Varia's; she had been crying.

"You have heard the news then, of Talow," Varia said.

Irea nodded. "Yes, it was announced this morning, and we are all broken inside to hear of it. The inquisition is gathering, I was sent to get you dressed." Varia noticed Irea herself was wearing the long formal gown required of official palace events. "You must wear your crown, too. It is there." Varia looked at the special place where the royal crowns of herself and Alshea were kept; they rested on a crafted willow table carefully twisted into spiral shapes. Varia's crown, made of handcrafted delicate fae metal called faespell, shone with precious gems highlighting the crown's deep gold sheen. Varia fingered the tiara; she had worn it many times in her life, for weddings, and funerals, and coronations, and royal events, but never for something like this, an inquisition in which she would be forced to tell the truth. She slipped into her coronation gown and Irea laced up the back, working the old-fashioned and elaborate lacings around her wings as Varia held still and sucked in her breath.

"Cousin, there is something I must tell you," Varia whispered, desperation rising up in her. "You must help me escape the inquisition. The war we have feared will come upon us if I go before the king. I will be forced to tell the truth, and the truth is something you will not want me to share if we are to prevent a war."

"I have already told the king about our failed night attempt to Birkendore," Irea said in a sharp voice. "I was called before him yesterday myself!"

Varia hesitated, surprised by this news. "You do not know all, Irea. For you have been to the Durndeng, the EarthSeeker castle yourself, and were captured by their faefolk. They have erased your memory. I have been returning to speak with one of them, a warrior, who is working with me to keep our faetribes from killing one another."

Irea spun Varia around and stared at her. "You are desperate, Cousin! I should help you escape, and risk myself, so that you can fly free? Where would you go?"

"Irea . . ."

"No! Do not try to persuade me. There is something off about you, Cousin, and now you would have me go against our own faepeople?"

"Irea . . ."

"No!" Irea turned toward the door, and Varia grabbed her hand. She put Irea's hand on her own forehead.

"Read me now! See if I lie!"

"I . . ."

"Quickly! It is the only way."

Irea hesitated but she did as told. She concentrated and connected with Varia's Deva. Irea's eyes widened as she learned her own story about being held in the Birkendore kingdom. Varia was careful to let only those memories go, for she did not want Irea yet to know of her marriage to an EarthSeeker enemy, her beloved Loben.

Irea withdrew her hand, tears in her eyes. "How is it I have no memory of this?" she asked in a shaky voice.

"An EarthSeeker trick," Varia said. "But see? We must join in unity, not fight them! If they go to war with the EarthSeekers, our peaceful life here will be over! All will be lost."

Irea shook her head. "You show me that these barbarians kidnapped me and held me against my will, and then erased my memory! Let every Wilhvyre in this palace go to them and slay them! It is what they deserve!" Irea left, flinging the door open to the chamber, and Varia could see guards waiting in the hallway. She remembered the hammering night noises she'd heard before but decided to try and escape through the silvery domed roof one last time. Varia flitted toward the ceiling to exit when a body blocked her way.

"Your night wanderings are officially over, Sister," Ezia said. "Your moon dome no longer opens. I knew you would try to flee! Traitor!"

"I am no traitor!" Varia said, caught off guard as her brother shoved her against the wall. She slid down to the floor, wings splayed. "I am trying to save our colony!"

Ezia hovered over her in a threatening way and Varia cowered on the ground.

"The guards await you, Traitor. Get your crown, and go," Ezia hissed. Varia had never seen him so angry. She got up and returned to the willow table for her tiara. Ezia followed her, waiting as she put the ancient adornment on her head, and then he opened the chamber door and shoved her toward the guards.

"Bind her," he growled. "She tried to escape."

Varia could see the look of surprise in the guards' eyes, for they were faeries she'd known since childhood. She had grown up with Ulla and Baylo, and they looked uncomfortable as they snapped her wrists into shackles and bound her wings with a binding sack. Ulla and Baylo lifted the captive Varia up by the arms, and she was flown down to the great hall, where the inquisition would take place.

The spacious gilded hall filled, crowded with faeries pushed in wing-to-wing, as every member of not only the palace but the entire kingdom was in attendance. Varia shook in fear, remembering the EarthSeeker Druag's words about pulling off wings of spies, the ultimate faery punishment . . . an act so archaic that no one in the memories of any living Alawe faery could recall it being executed in Erendome. As Varia was brought before the throne of King Dreya in shackles, Rumendah closed his eyes and sent her a mental message: *Lift your head, Princess, lest your crown may fall.* Varia raised her chin in defiance to the stares of her faepeople. Rumendah opened his eyes and gave her a glance of sympathy before looking away, but the other spectators and even her family members, especially Ezia and Alshea, glared at her with hard cold eyes: something she had never experienced before. Her throat felt tight as she stood before the Alawe.

Her father looked like the king that he was in his formal dress and largest crown, and Varia ducked her head in the formal way, even though she was held tight by guards at each side.

Rumendah flew up above the throne and made the announcement. "Let it be known that the Inquisition of Princess Varia of Ashenthorne, Defender of Erendome, has begun!" he said. The audience held still.

"Are these shackles necessary?" asked King Dreya, obviously surprised at seeing his own kin bound. Ezia flew forward.

"I fear it is the case, Sire," Ezia said after bowing to the king. "For the Princess Varia just now tried to escape her own Inquisition!"

A murmur shot through the onlookers. Irea stepped forward from her spot next to Alshea.

"If I may speak, let it be known that she also asked me to help her flee," stated Irea, "And when I thisselled her she showed me something I did not remember, a memory that was blocked from me, that I was in honesty unable to state during my inquiry yesterday about my journey to the sunflower fields." Irea bowed and stepped backward, hiding her burning cheeks behind dark braids. To her uncle the king, she whispered, "I shall tell you what I learned anon, your majesty."

Varia's heart pumped. She didn't blame Irea for speaking up; Irea had inadvertently lied in her own minor "inquisition" with the king as the court gathered information for today's hearing. Varia knew Irea was now just trying to save herself. She wondered what would happen when the king discovered that the Durndeng not only lived just outside Ashenthorne, but that Varia had wed one of them?

King Dreya's brow creased with disappointment. "What say you about the death of the Wilhvyre warrior Talow, Princess Varia of Ashenthorne, in the land of Erendome?" King Dreya asked, omitting the word "defender." Nothing more than that could show his disapproval. His formal question meant that the inquisition had officially begun.

"Your majesty," Varia stated in a shaky voice. "I would like to speak with you and your most trusted advisor Rumendah, privately in your royal chambers."

"Why do you request a private audience with the king, when this is a public trial to learn of your recent secret whereabouts, and to learn the truth about the fallen warrior Talow?"

Varia felt weak and was glad for the moment that she was being held up, even if she was shackled. "My liege," she said in a small voice. "I wish to speak with you privately because the information I have . . . is . . . of great importance to the security of Erendome and not appropriate for public knowledge at this time."

A gasp went through the crowd, and Varia could see a few faeries looking up in fear as if a dark cloud would come and annihilate them at any moment. The king raised his hands.

"Quiet!" he roared, and the room went still. He stared at Varia, disbelief in his eyes. Hesitating only a moment, he leaned in to whisper something to Rumendah. The Elder responded with a nod and soft words, and Dreya faced his kingdom once more.

"I would advise those present to leave," he said in a strong voice, "for this public inquisition is over, and a private one will be held forthwith!"

The crowd was clearly disappointed, but they began shuffling toward the door on foot, as there was no room for flying with so many of faeries present. A commotion caused a few shouts near the door.

Varia looked up in time to see Talow, battered, part of one steering wing ripped off, but still he could fly in a lopsided way. He hovered over the audience, carrying a bulky item wrapped in a soiled leaf. Floating before the king, he dropped the package at the king's feet. A Durndeng warrior's head rolled out of the leaf wrap. King Dreya stepped back, and those nearest the throne screamed and scattered into the air to get away.

"It would appear the EarthSeekers are upon us," Talow said in an angry booming voice. "And Princess Varia has been in constant contact with them, risking all of our lives!"

All eyes shifted from the severed head to Varia, who pulled hard at her shackles, and, unable to escape, she averted her eyes in anguish. The guards tightened their grip and flew her up above the king's throne. Pandemonium arose as many faeries rushed at once to leave, and the Wilhvyre guards blockading the throne reached for Varia. Pointing toward the palace door. King Dreya shouted: "Enough! Leave us!"

The warriors stopped in mid-air and lined up in the way they were taught, ushering the frightened citizens out of the castle. Those royal fae who lived inside Erendome headed to their private rooms. Varia trembled in fear, but she made herself look at the fell head at her father's feet; it was not a Durndeng faery she recognized. Talow glowered at her, and Varia had never felt so much hatred directed toward her in her lifetime. She flinched at his glare, glad her captors Ulla and Baylo protected her. Talow could not harm her while she was held by them, though Varia believed from his glare that if he were alone with her, he would kill her. The very job he was trained as a Wilhvyre to do.

"Take her away from me!" King Dreya shouted to Ulla and Baylo. Bowing their heads, they flew with Varia between them into the next chamber. They bound Varia to the chair before the throne. She struggled again, exhausted, but was unable to free herself.

"Ulla, Baylo, you must free me! The future of our kingdom depends on it!" she pleaded.

Both ignored her calls and stood guard, unmoving, unlistening. Varia tried to free her wrists but fell into silent sobs, knowing defeat.

The Alawe Wilhvyre regained command of the room. Once the main hall was cleared, with an anguished expression King Dreya faced Talow, who bowed humbly again before his king.

"Your majesty," Talow said.

King Dreya struck a blow to Talow's chest, sending him flying backward.

"Why do you bring this scourge upon my kingdom?" the king bellowed, pointing at the severed head before his throne as Talow, flushed from the hit, turned to face Dreya's wrath.

"I was attacked," Talow said, his once-proud expression now grim. "Several of the EarthSeekers fought me. At first they claimed me, and were taking me prisoner. My opportunity was brief, and using the enemy's own weapon against him was the only way to escape. I brought the head from the falling body to prove my story to the kingdom."

"And not to claim victory as the murderous hero for yourself?"

Talow recoiled. "Your majesty," he said in a low voice, bowing again. "I do not understand. Did I not do the right thing, fighting for my own freedom, and sparing no life to gain it? For that is what I, as an Ashenthorne Wilhvyre, was trained to do, in the Alawe way. I am a warrior of your kingdom. Why do you sorrow over the loss of an enemy?"

King Dreya looked from Talow to the head near the throne.

"You are right, Talow. This is what my kingdom has asked of you." King Dreya's eyes were heavy. "This . . . EarthSeeker. He also is a warrior of his faepeople. And now two opposing warriors have battled, and the consequences will be high. War is here. And war with the EarthSeekers is something that I never wanted to see in my reign."

To a nearby attendant, King Dreya snapped, "Move this hideous head from my sight!" As the shocked attendant jumped to action, to Talow he said, "Go round the troops and have your wounds mended. I shall not make the first move to battle, but it is in my experience that the Durndeng King Struben is quick to act, and may I add, quick to regret. Hurry. There is no time to waste!"

Talow stared at the king, wondering how King Dreya knew the name of his enemy, when the court had never before admitted that EarthSeekers lived near Ashenthorne.

"Yes, your majesty," he said, bowing, and in his lopsided way, he flew to prepare for the battle that was sure to come.

Chapter Eight

"Leave me," Dreya bellowed to Ulla and Baylo. The faeries ducked their heads and flew fast from the private hall. Rumendah accompanied Dreya, and both stood before Varia, tied and prostrate on her knees in the fae chair before them.

"Father, I must . . ." Varia began. Dreya put his palm before her face, stopping her.

"I am your king at this moment, not your father! For no daughter of mine would risk the safety of this kingdom for her own fanciful whims." He lifted her head and stared into her eyes. "What do you have to say to defend yourself from the accusations of those around you?"

Varia's eyes blurred with tears, but she faced her father. His usually carefree face was lined with worry. Worry she had caused.

"I'm sorry, your majesty. I have much to explain," Varia said. "I spoke some days past with Ezia, and he told me about the Durndeng, whom we call the EarthSeekers, down by the mushroom flats . . ." Varia told her story, trying to get every fact straight. Until she came to the part about marrying Loben. She hesitated, but knew that to lie would cause bigger problems.

"I befriended one of them, his name is Loben, of the Birkendore Durndeng tribe," she said in a low voice, "but he is one who hopes for peace among us, as I do. He is a warrior, what the Durndeng call SpadeWeilders, or Vorku, much like our warrior Wilhvyre. Loben helped free me when I was captured. We communicate through messages brought by his hummingbird called Zedah. We have both tried to keep our meetings a secret to our tribes."

Varia stopped. She feared what her father would do if he discovered that Loben was not merely an acquaintance, but her husband. She avoided his gaze but he lifted her chin and looked into her eyes.

"Why did your cousin Irea not remember her journey with you to the Durndeng dwelling?" Dreya asked. "I questioned her yesterday, and neither her mind nor her body knew of her capture." Varia replied, "When Irea was captured by the warriors there, they erased her memory, my liege. It is a Durndeng trick. I was able to free her, and from my dealings with Loben I have come to discover they have not the same gift to read plants and animals as we do, but they can cause others to forget what they know."

"Ah, I feared as much, that old trick," said King Dreya. He looked deep in thought, his mouth drawn. "This could be why we have not seen them before now, and why we were uncertain of their residing in the Birkendore Flats. Our scouts may have stumbled upon their new kingdom before, and not remembered it. Alas!" The king flitted anxiously to the top of the room then landed before Varia. He turned on her.

"I feel you are hesitating to tell me something, Princess. Is that all that you have to report?"

Varia glanced from Rumendah to the king. She lowered her eyes. "That is all."

"Very well," the king said. He reached his hand toward her head, and Varia flinched, but he rested his heavy palm against her forehead and closed his eyes. Varia knew not to fight it; her father read the truth from her being, all of it, even the parts about Loben that she wanted to keep sacred for herself. As he pulled his hand away, the king looked into Varia's eyes.

"So you love the EarthSeeker, Loben," he said. "And have wed yourself to him?"

"Yes, your majesty," Varia admitted. "I do love him." Her eyes welled up with tears; for her love of Loben, and of her father, and regret for what she had caused them both.

"I see," said the king, and he had a faraway look in his own eyes. It was not the anger she had expected. "Very well. Now we have a dilemma, and it is not just the vengeance of the Durndeng tribe!" King Dreya stood tall before Varia, a menacing figure looking down on her. Varia feared for her life. She squeezed her eyes tight, waiting.

"For your safety, I will put you in our most secret dungeon cell, one that most Alawe know nothing of," the king spoke in a quiet voice. "Rumendah will escort you there, and for all purposes, it will be announced that you are in prison for treason."

Varia's eyes widened in fear. "No!" she cried out. "It's not true!" King Dreya put his hand on top of her head to calm her.

"This is what we will say, to appease our faepeople and their thirst for justice. I am hoping that the gossip and speculation of your actions will keep them busy while I devise a plan to thwart our enemy, should they attack us. For I will not open further fire on them, but shall instead send an emissary to their kingdom with apologies for this terrible grievance."

"Then you shall sentence that emissary to certain death, for they are not forgiving or understanding of our ways, Father! I mean, your majesty," Varia bowed her head, eyes wet.

"It is a risk, I understand. Unless . . ." King Dreya motioned for Rumendah to take the princess to her cell. "Go quickly, and make sure none follow you. Use all of your tricks to keep her whereabouts secret! My hall has eyes, I see, and I must act with haste to stop a faery war of the ages. Go!"

Rumendah bundled Varia against his old frame so fast that she barely noticed him grabbing her. Another moment flashed past, and they were in a separate part of the castle, one Varia had spent very little time in since she had played here with Irea and Alshea as a young girl. She wanted to ask Rumendah how he'd done it, when all of a sudden they were flying recklessly down a barely lit unfamiliar passageway. Before Varia could protest, they arrived at a mysterious chamber, the only light emanating from three small candles. Varia shuddered as Rumendah opened the sturdy gates before them.

"Here you shall be safe, for now," he said, giving her the thick leaf blankets that were strewn on the floor. He shut the door and Varia looked around: the prison cell was made of a hard petrified wood, impenetrable, and the gates appeared to be crafted of a fine iron or steel forged from a distant faery land. She could not escape. Unable to think and almost passing out from lack of food and stress, Varia pulled the blanket up to her chin and calmed her mind to deliquesce into the covers for much needed sleep. Soon Rumendah returned.

"I found this in the prison stores, mead nectars and honeys, dried nuts and seeds, and a carafe of bark tea." He placed a bundle on the floor. "Eat now, for this place shall lure you into a deep sleep, and I fear when you awaken, you may need to escape quickly." Rumendah watched as Varia nibbled on some of the seeds. "Hand me your gown, and your crown, and I will keep them safe." Rumendah turned away to give Varia privacy, though she wore a plain white tunic under her coronation gown that covered her body modestly. She lifted up her wings and tugged at the knots at her back, and was able to free the complicated dress's ties. She slipped out of the frock and it fell to her ankles, and she hovered out of it.

"The crown too, Princess," Rumendah said softly. He flew up to her and she nodded assent, and he lifted the crown ceremoniously from her head. He bowed to her before returning to the cell floor where her dress lay crumpled. He carefully folded the gown and placed the crown on top of it in a respectful way. Varia flitted beside him.

"Wear this on your body," he said, giving her a woven purse crafted of a silver thread she could not identify. She peeked inside and realized as she tied it around her waist that he had added in some of the food stores, and she thought she saw a small vial of hestus, the Light Bringer, and a short dagger.

"Because you may need to make haste, it is best to be ready! I must leave you now, my princess Varia. If you hear voices outside the door, stay silent. I shall perform ancient faerie magick to make sure that you are safe here and unseen. It will be as if this cell will disappear from this world and you will be unfound even if one of The Others stumbles upon it."

"Wait . . ." Varia had heard of such things, but in her lifetime of peace, she had never experienced anything like it before. "What if something happens to you, Rumendah? Can anyone else get me out of here? How will anyone know where I am, or how to reverse the magick? I may rot in here, dying slowly of starvation, and have no recourse!"

"I will return, my princess," Rumendah said. The door clanged shut. Varia could hear Rumendah in the passageway muttering strange ancient words, the early tongue of the fae. Varia felt lightheaded as an eerie silvery fog rose up and covered the entry to the cell. The fog mimicked the ornate steel lines of the gate, twisting and turning, conforming to its every curve before rising up and pasting itself to every wall, every crevice of the room around her. Unable to stay awake, Varia rested her head on the pile of blankets around her, overcome with exhaustion, magick and sleep, as the creeping mists stole her worry away.

In Birkendore, Loben found himself tethered prone in a fae chair before the king. While the Durndeng did not have the power to read another faery's mind, Loben feared that he would have his mind erased, and he would lose Varia forever. King Struben paced around the chair.

"So you are telling me that you have no connection with this butchery, even though you were seen flying from the sacred wood at the time of the attack?" Struben asked, his booming voice echoing in his private chamber.

"I did not know of the killing, your majesty, and was well on my way back from the wood to Birkendore when it occurred. While it is true that I was in the sacred wood, remember that my sworn oath to you and your kingdom is to patrol and glean information from the woods to keep us safe from the enemy. In this case, the enemy was behind me and I knew not of the immediate threat." It was true that Loben was caught unawares; the beheading of a kingdom guard was a war-starting act, and he knew that any attempt to show himself to the Alawe as an emissary now would fail, and he would be held captive if he attempted it, and likely killed.

"And what were you doing in the wood?" Struben asked.

"Following a lead on enemy habitation there, your majesty," Loben replied, glad that his king did not share the Alawe skill of reading his mind.

"A . . . lead?"

"Information from one of my messengers," Loben explained, not wanting to implicate Zedah.

"I see." Struben paced again. He pulled a knife from his scabbard and walked toward Loben, who braced himself, ready to meet his end.

Struben instead cut the braided ties that bound Loben. "I need you to be completely honest with me, and do not forget since you are bound to me, I will know if you lie. You are not a spy for the enemy encampment?"

"I am loyal to this throne only, your highness," Loben said. "As it has always been so. In fact I have been striving to avoid the very war that now begins, for the safety of your family and our faepeople."

Loben stood and stretched his sore limbs, deadened from being bound for half a day now. Struben leaned close, his hand about to rest on Loben's forehead. This was how the Durndeng fae could erase the mind of another faery, and Loben tensed, devastated that he might not remember Varia in just a matter of moments. He closed his eyes and waited for the searing hand of the king to place his palm on his head, but the touch never came.

"Very well," Struben said, pulling his hand away. "I have always trusted you, Nephew, and continue to do so." Struben looked Loben up and down. Loben blinked in disbelief. "You are my brother's son, and you could have been king in your own right had I not borne children of my own to take the place of my brother's pending rulership. I have watched you over the cytons, and you are now a strong, worthy warrior of Birkendore, and of our previous home in the Dunter-Gruns before that." Struben flitted upwards, hovering in the small space, making himself appear larger. Loben rubbed his arms and stared up at his king.

"Thank you, your majesty, for trusting in me," Loben said in a quiet voice.

"That being said, that I still trust you, I do know that you are not telling me all I need to know. So while I believe your heart to be pure, your methods may perhaps be befuddled and your mind may be addled. You have the look of one conflicted. Do you have anything further to report? For the safety of our tribe must be your highest concern."

"You must believe me when I tell you that it is my greatest concern, and all of my actions, even if they may seem contrary, are to achieve that ultimate goal: the continued safety of the Durndeng clan."

Struben studied Loben's face. "So be it then, you may take your leave, but remember that your brethren may not be so kind to you, for they are starting to believe you are a traitor of our clan." Loben flinched. "And while I know it is not so," Struben continued, "you must watch your wings at every turn now, for I have heard it said that we have some Vorku soldiers who have little tolerance for spies in the night, and they are rashly acting of their own accord, and not listening to the standard protocol of the kingdom."

"Thank you, your highness," Loben bowed slightly. "I will take my leave." He kept his face toward the king as he exited on foot. The door closed between them. He must find Varia! A deep voice startled him in the darkened hallway.

"I see Father freed you once again," Doon said. Loben couldn't read his tone, and spun to face his cousin and best friend, who stood between him and the hallway exit, arms crossed.

"He did," said Loben, standing a bit taller. "Are you the one who told the Vorku to arrest me?"

"Perhaps," said Doon, clapping Loben on the shoulder, harder than necessary. "Your disappearing act lately has everyone in the palace on edge."

Loben shook his head, his long hair falling over his shoulders as he smiled at his cousin.

"I have heard it said that all is fair in war," Loben said. "But I would not have expected you to be the one hindering me while I am trying to protect our faepeople!"

"Your words would seem reasonable, if I did not know that you are the one who helped the AirWalker spy escape," Doon said, rising up further into the hallway and blocking out the light.

Loben's smile vanished as he sized up Doon. "What would make you say such a thing?" he asked.

"I had you followed," Doon admitted with a shrug. "And my own spy got quite an eyeful. So you wed the AirWalker in the Llandwig forest at Erenley? That act alone reeks of treason."

The words left Loben cold, and caught him off guard. He had a sinking feeling he would not be flying off to find Varia anytime soon.

"I am free to marry whom I wish," Loben said.

"Of the Durndeng kind, yes, that is true," Doon growled. "But to marry the enemy!"

Loben felt his anger rise. "Your own mother married the enemy once!" Loben retorted, but he was sorry the moment he said it. Even in the dim light, Loben could see rage on Doon's face.

"Family or not, that is not a topic that will be discussed in my father's halls! Those words alone are enough for me to have you imprisoned, or banished to the Mysty realm!" Doon said. Loben hung his head.

"I do not blame your anger," Loben said. "I apologize. Doon, you are my closest friend, my true ally in Birkendore. I have only the best interest of our tribe at heart! My marriage to Varia of Ashenthorne will only help bring goodwill to our tribes."

"Goodwill? Talk to Brunhurn's family about goodwill! For their son's body was returned dead to the palace Thundendell, minus his head!" Doon was shaking. Loben laid a hand on his shoulder.

"His death will be avenged," Loben said in a low voice. "I too am saddened by this loss. I promise you, Cousin—" Loben looked into Doon's eyes. "Family comes first. But my wife Varia is my family now too. I must do right, by both sides. I am caught between two worlds."

Doon made a disgruntled noise before flying off into the main chambers. Once he was gone, Loben flew fast toward the palace exit. He burst through the door, startling the guards on duty there. Amid their shouts, he buzzed away, ignoring their commands to stop. He had an errand he could not delay. He had to save his wife.

Chapter Nine

Outside the dungeon gates, in the real world past the fog of spell Rumendah had set upon her, Varia could hear the rumblings of an uprising. The ground shook, the iron gates rattled, and the veil between her and the angry voices felt thin. Varia feared this may be the end; surely the Durndeng had broken Erendome's fortress walls and were looking for her, the Alawe princess who had betrayed her clan. She tried to sit up to save herself, but every movement felt impossible and she only managed to lift her head a little. She was stuck in her hazy bed behind a misty wall, doom upon her if the castle dungeon gates were breeched. From the effort of trying to lift herself, she fell back down, defeated.

How much time passed she was uncertain before Varia felt herself being lifted up, but her legs fell away, unfurling like the shrouds that surrounded her. She was not fully in her body, but in a half dream state, yet she could feel strong arms clutching her tightly about her waist. Her mind wanted to protest but she was a wisp, like a part of the dense air that promised to keep her safe in the cell. *Rumendah?* she tried to ask, but her tongue was smoke, her words vapor. The arms that bound her were too strong to belong to the old faery; she must now be held captive by a powerful enemy, one who could bypass the complicated magick set forth by Rumendah and one who knew the secrets to break the barrier spell of the ancient fae. Wishing she could rise up and fight, she remained a limp passenger in the arms of her captor, and she felt herself dropping, falling into a new place, an unfamiliar dimension, and she could sense with her very being, wherever she was now, it was a strange and dangerous world.

Fog permeated every sense as Varia forced herself to open her eyes. She could see a dark forest, though she was not in the forest, but viewing it through a misty curtain. Puzzled, she tried to lift her arm to touch the hazy surface, but her hands remained dangling by her sides. She closed her eyes, knowing that there was some strange spell still upon her, and she was helpless, bound by whatever force carried her through these unusual parts.

Time passed. Varia managed to open her eyes three more times, only to find herself in the Grey World between dimensions. Perhaps she was becoming more used to the spell, as her thoughts began to stir with stories she remembered from her childhood, stories of the in-between dimensions that led faeries to the human realm once, before the two worlds became one. She recalled tales of darker, more sinister dimensions, where evil things were said to lurk. Shuddering, Varia hoped that she wasn't in one of those places as her eyes closed again.

More time passed, and Varia felt her body being gently placed on soft, spongy ground. Pushing her will hard, she forced her eyes open. She saw a forest shrouded in murky light. A dark figure hovered over her. She felt a spark of remembrance as she saw her beloved Loben, wings spread, hovering above her. She reached up for him, and this time, her arms obeyed the command. Loben settled beside her and returned the embrace as she breathed him in, sobs of relief leaving her as she held him close.

"I thought I'd lost you forever, my love," Loben whispered as he held Varia in a tight embrace, stroking her papery wings. "We are not safe yet, but can rest awhile here, and try to regain our senses, for this world makes us jumbled and confused if we are not on constant alert."

"Where are we?" Varia asked, looking around, her mind barely able to fathom that her husband had somehow found her in the secret Erendome prison cell. Loben's face passed in and out of the mists, but she could see, above him, dank treetops and threatening skies.

"This is . . . another realm, called Drakotanith, and it is one that we must pass through to get back to Ashenthorne and our tribes. We must use care, for it is very difficult to navigate between worlds, Varia. If we do not escape soon, our opportunity will be lost, and we will be stuck here in the netherworld for cytons, maybe forever. It is not a safe place for our kind, Varia. Few who have dwelled here have survived."

Varia's hazy thoughts cleared with fear. "Then let us go now! I do not wish to stay in this place any longer than necessary."

Loben's head jerked up to the skies as a sharp cry echoed in the distance. Varia clutched at him, wrapping her wings around her.

"What was that?"

"There is much I have yet to say," Loben replied. "But we must go. Zedah will meet us at the opening of the portal. Are you strong enough to fly?"

Varia shook her head. "Not yet, Loben. I have been in a dark dream for a long time, my body is unused to movement. But I fear I will hinder you. Can you fly ahead and find the opening to our world, and come back for me? Then we can go through together."

"The portal . . . does not stay in one place long, and if we see it, we must go right through together. Let us walk a bit, until your wings awaken and your limbs are stronger." Loben helped Varia to her feet. "I will find sustenance for you on the other side, but you cannot eat here, or the vapors of this world will inhabit your body, and you will forever be a prisoner of the dragon realm."

"Did . . . you . . . say dragon?" Varia asked, now knowing in her heart what the loud cry was moments before. "We are in the dragon realm? Why must we venture to this horrible place?"

"It is the only way out, Varia. The realm that Rumendah put you in only exits here, if you do not possess the magick it takes to reverse his enchantments. From here, the fae have before been able to pass through and back again. It is a risk I was willing to take to free you."

Varia tried walking on leaden legs. "I know what you would tell me next, Loben. Our castle was overtaken by your faepeople, was it not? For I heard the sounds of an army trying to break into the dungeon before you came to rescue me."

Loben grew quiet, and helped Varia step over the cushioned forest floor. "No," he said, his eyes averting. Varia stopped him and turned his face toward her, and still he could not look in her eyes.

"What do you mean, no?" Varia tried to guess what he didn't want to say. "I heard the masses coming for me, with my own ears! I know I am right."

"They were coming for you, yes, that is true," Loben said. "But not my tribe, your own. The ones who tried to break down the dungeons at Erendome were your own kin, for they think you are a traitor, and your demise, if you had stayed, would have been eminent."

Varia stared, feeling tears threaten to fall. "Is this true? My father would never allow this to happen! For he was the one to told Rumendah to hide me in the grey dimension between worlds. I don't believe it."

Loben pushed Varia's tousled hair behind her pointed ear, and gently cupped her chin with his palm. "Varia," he said. "I have heard from many sources, that there is terrible news from Erendome. Your father is no longer king."

Chapter Ten

Varia's thoughts spun as the news Loben gave washed over her.

"No longer king?" she repeated, numb. "Is he . . . dead?"

Loben scoffed. "No, it seems his captors had mercy on him, but he is imprisoned in his own dungeon, along with a few of his most trusted court. Rumendah, Irea . . . they are all in the prison of Erendome, while the new regime takes over and prepares for war against my tribe."

"Who is it who has usurped my father's kingdom?" Varia asked, rage filling her.

"Varia," Loben said in a soft voice, as if to lessen the blow. "Can you not guess?"

Varia turned to Loben, and she could feel the blood drain from her face. "It is Alshea, is it not? My own dear sister. She has been always impatient to be queen!"

"And now, she is." Loben shook his head. "We could have had a chance at peace if King Dreya and King Struben had met, but now . . . Queen Alshea is not someone who will negotiate. She does not want what she calls 'those filthy EarthSeekers' anywhere near Ashenthorne, and she will not rest until we are exterminated."

"Then we both have no home to return to," Varia said in a whisper, heaviness filling her heart. "And yet, we cannot stay here."

"We will find Zedah. She can see the portal and call to us to direct us to it. I can sense that she is close, and we will soon find the way out and go back to our own realm. Perhaps we can still find a way to bring peace to our tribes before another battle breaks out."

"If such a war were to continue, it would be the faery war to end all wars, for we will lose too many of our fae and may never recover," Varia said, her voice somber. "Our soldiers on both sides are shallow minded and hot headed, a deadly combination of temper and ignorance." She tried her wings and lifted off the ground. "I am tired, but willing to try and follow you. Let us find our hummingbird friend who can lead us from here, and get back to our tribes, before it is too late."

"Let us go then, use care! For the inhabitants of these parts do not take kindly to outsiders."

Varia soon found she could keep up with Loben's pace, and they flew across the dim forest, deeper into dragon world.

"Are you sure this is right?" she whispered as she hovered near Loben. "For it seems as if we are flying away from the very realm we wish to re-enter!"

"I am sure, for we are leaving the way we came into Drakotanith," Loben explained. "You can never enter and exit through the same portal."

Varia nodded, although she knew nothing of portals and could not fathom how any of it worked. As if gleaning her muddled thoughts, Loben explained.

"It works this way, or at least, this is how I have come to understand it," Loben said as he held Varia's hand, encouraging her flight. "There are many worlds, as you know, such as the realm of the fae, and the human realm. Sometimes humans even stumble into the realm of their own deceased, and encounter ghosts from beyond the grave, and that is yet another world that can be accessed by a portal between the worlds. In Drakotanith, there is only a portal to the realm of the fae, not the human realm, so we can't use just any portal to leave here. We must return to the land of the ancient fae to get back home."

"I don't understand," Varia said with a frown. "Why does not this world connect with the world of humankind? For surely I have heard story and myth of human and dragon connection, in the past."

"Yes, in the past. But a very strong magick has been unleashed from the human world to keep the dragons in their own realm, and the dragons are trapped here in Drakotanith now, and no longer able to torment the humans in their realm."

"It is unfortunate that the humans have not done the same sort of magick for the fae realm," Varia lamented as they traversed the murky woods, "for I would prefer it if the fae and humankind were to no longer meet."

"Part of me would agree," Loben replied, "the Durndeng have befriended humans in the recent past, before. . ."

"Before . . . what?"

A thunderous screech filled the air, followed by dark shadow. Varia ducked down to the eely forest floor and hid behind slime-leaved plants as Loben rose up to meet the giant flying beast that searched for them overhead. Varia wanted to scream out to warn Loben, but stayed hidden. Loben was a quick buzzing spot in the sky before he disappeared up and up toward the dragon overhead.

Varia couldn't tell what was happening, but heard the loud echoing eek of the dragon and covered her ears. She curled into the smallest ball and waited, afraid when she looked up what she might see. More screeches seemed to trail off in the distance, but she could not hear Loben, nor see him flying. She hoped with fervor that he had somehow managed to escape those impossibly large claws that she had seen just before taking cover.

After a while, all was still, and Varia ventured a peek out from behind her leaf cover. The place was full of strange plants, none of which she wanted to touch, as they all had an oily shine and some even had a smoky ring along the leaf's outer edges. A large spider-like creature with eight legs clicked into her space and exposed long fangs. She shot away into the air, hovering above the creature. It moved its pendulous body side to side. In horror Varia watched it leap up at her. Its prickly long legs lashed out, and Varia barely missed being taken by its grasping front claws. She zipped out of way, heart pounding. She couldn't see the spider-beast and hovered above the blackened plants, watching. Shaking, and knowing that she needed to refuel her weak body, Varia remembered Loben's caution about eating anything in this realm. Defeat filled her soul.

A foul black insect, larger than her, whizzed by, causing Varia to crash to the ground. She stood, and wiped the grease from her knees before flitting upward once the buzzing sound faded away. She flew low over dense mounds of foliage, straining to hear Loben, looking around for other wayward insects. The air was thick and quiet except for the soft hum of her own wings. Onward, lost, she continued, wondering if she shouldn't just find a place to hide and stay put. Fear gripped her as she swooped along the forest floor until she heard, far away, the scream of the dragon once more. This cry was answered, and an absurd crashing sound filled the air, but so far off, if she had tried to fly toward the sound, she would not know which direction to go in. She ducked under a huge flat leaf for cover as dismal oily raindrops began to fall around her. She closed her eyes as she sat on a moss bank and listened to the frightening noises in the distance, wondering if she would ever see her beloved Loben again.

Varia must have slept, for she started awake when she heard a large insect buzzing above her. She shrank backward into the ground with intent to disappear but stopped herself; surely if she shouldn't eat the food here, she should not become a part of this place by deliquescing! The insect lost interest and zoomed away. Varia realized that she had found a comfortable spot; it was dryer and warmer in her green shelter than outside. She walked around on the soft moss, impressed by the space in her leafy domain. In the center of the soft mound she found a pulsing glow coming from a partially-hidden curved rock. Tentatively she approached the area and held her palms near it; it was smooth but heated, radiating warmth like embers from a fire, emanating orange light. Curious, she yearned to thissell the rock's temperate skin and learn about its origins, but she dared not. Somehow she knew the less she disturbed things here, the better. Instead she sat nearby and clutched her knees up to her chin, and wrapped her wings around her body, and listened for the whir of Loben's wingflight in the air.

She heard something, but it was not wingsong. A bird-like chirp emitted nearby. Varia jumped to her feet and hovered, trying to find its source. She heard the sound again. Focusing, she discovered that it came from the warm rock. Varia neared it and realized by looking again at its sloping surface and porous covering, it was no rock, but an egg. A very large egg, and whatever was growing within it, was hatching.

Loben dodged the showering flame as two behemoth dragons fought for dominion over the sky. The luck of the gods had favored him; as he careened away from the dragon, luring the huge blue and green beast from Varia's presence, a second red dragon, bigger and with a violent temper, had come from the shadows and chased the first. Once they were engaged in a territorial dispute, Loben was able to fly beneath them both, and now he ducked under the cover of a spiny marsh plant as Red engorged the air with flame and smoke.

Blue had enough and tried to flee, with Red in pursuit. As their crashing fight echoed far in the distance, Loben flew back to where he'd last left Varia. *I must get her out of here,* he thought wildly as he flew low to the ground, looking back every few moments to check for enemy followers. He peeked out into the valley in front of him and saw the dripping green slick trees, some large insects, but no dragons. He continued on his way. *If Varia doesn't eat soon, she will be unable to fly,"* he thought. *"I must get her out of Drakotanith!"*

He could not find her. He looked around, peeking under brush and ledge, hoping for some clue of where Varia may have gone. There was none. She had simply vanished.

Loben sat down on a pebble, shaky himself and uncertain whether he should stay or fly, while wishing he could eat from the rations in his survival pouch. The thought of forever being trapped in Drakotanith motivated Loben to continue.

As he flew and searched, Loben thought of his time spent with Rumendah after he left the wounded Thundendell castle, abandoning Birkendore and the mushroom flats he had briefly known to be his home.

It was in the same cave where Varia had hidden from the Birkendore FlightSoldiers that Zedah had greeted Loben, and with her, was Rumendah. As the hummingbird allowed herself to be held in a fond embrace by Loben, the elder sage pushed his finger to his lip and said in a quiet growl, "Follow me."

Quicker than Loben would have expected, Rumendah fled into the depths of the cave, and Loben did not have time to say farewell or thank you to Zedah, lest he would have lost the swift old Alawe in the depths. Loben's eyes grew accustomed to the dark but soon he realized that Rumendah held in his hand a small stone box full of a lighted powdery substance, like sparkling sand. *Hestus*, Loben realized, remembering stories of the Alawe dust from his childhood. The golden light filled the dark corridors of the cave until they reached a bright center, a waterfall crashing through a large opening at the top of the cave that spilled brilliant sunlight into the deep crevasse.

"Loben, I presume," Rumendah said in a calm but booming voice.

"You must be Rumendah," Loben said, bowing slightly as the older faery hovered above him, looking up into the white beam of light.

"I am indeed Rumendah, Loben." He stared at Loben in a way that made him uneasy. "We have much to do if we are to stop the destruction of our kin," Rumendah said. "War is here."

"I am aware," Loben replied. "For just today I spoke with King Struben, and he has told me of the fell deed committed by the Alawe Wilhvyre. The warrior they slayed was Brunhurn, a respected soldier from a prominent fae family. The murder has not gone unnoticed."

"I had feared it was so," Rumendah said, "although any soldier lost would have caused the same effect, prominent family or no. The trick now is to carefully plan our next moves. Because you have wed the princess Varia of Erendome, Daughter of King Dreya, I trust you. Not only because you have married one of our kin, but because I see something in you that puts my heart at ease. There is hope, here," Rumendah tapped his chest. "I am greatly relieved to see you."

"Thank you," was all Loben could think to say under the weight of so great a compliment, coming from one of the wisest elders known in faedom.

"Haste is of the utmost importance, for King Dreya's court has been overturned by his own daughter, princess Alshea," Rumendah cautioned. "She is now calling herself Queen of Erendome and has taken over the palace, and placed her own family in prison. I am, unfortunately, the next one to be arrested, for I foresaw it in the seeing pond. This is why we must meet now, for your wife is in a spelldom that is tricky to unhinge, but you must try to free her. For the special magick that is used to keep her safe in the dungeons of Erendome will diminish as I am weakened by imprisonment, and soon her own tribe, the Alawe Wilhvyre, will be able to get to her if you do not rescue her quickly."

Stirring himself out of his drowsiness and memory, Loben recalled Rumendah's words as he soared above the ground-level plants, looking for any sign of Varia: *You must venture into the dragon realm, and get out again as fast as possible, for the dragon realm has a way of luring you in, and soon you will no longer remember why you are seeking the portal, as the foul mists will steal your mind. Then you will only focus on surviving day to day the domain ruled by the ancient race of dragons . . .*

As Loben hovered over the leaf where he had left Varia, he saw several black spiky legs skitter past. Desperation seized him. Probably that foul creature had something to do with why Varia wasn't where he had left her, and he was going to find out where she went. He flew down and landed in front of the eight-legged beast as it turned its thousand eyes on him, and its throbbing body swayed back and forth.

Chapter Eleven

Varia watched the side of the egg, ready to flee should the baby . . . whatever . . . inside make any progress in releasing itself. A loud wide crack broke across the entire surface and hot liquid molten dripped out. It lit up the entire area; Varia had to flit up and out of the way lest it splash near her feet and burn her. Fascinated, she ducked behind a strap-like leaf and spied the eminent infant's hatching. A blue and teal sharp hooked beak slithered into the crack, and rocked back and forth, chipping away part of the shell. Varia watched as the hook opened into a long mouth with tiny teeth; a dragon's snout. Soon a large black eye poked out and Varia hid deeper in her foil, but the eye was too young to see, and the mouth was busy devouring hot gooey liquid. Small chirps and pecking noises emitted from the hatchling, and then, mouth smacking. Varia smiled; in spite of herself, enthralled. *I can't believe I am witnessing the birth of a dragon!* she thought, wishing she could share it with someone special. Someone like a husband.

Varia frowned, remembering Loben with a start. *I must be tired*, she realized, as she had somehow forgotten all about Loben and her need to find him. *But I don't know where to look*, she told herself. She refocused on the dragon hatchling. Its entire head was out, and Varia slipped from behind her leaf to get a better view.

The dragon's little head stood a few stems above Varia. The wide shiny eyes stared at her, and she stared back, feeling as if she could have stood there forever looking at the baby's face. It had a finely chiseled nose, and its soft scales, though wet with molten goo, shone an iridescent teal. The neck was long and also scaly, with a triangle row of ridges aligning with the creature's back. Varia stepped closer, startled when the egg broke in half, freeing the dragon, which was, she now realized, triple her size. An entire body writhed forward, nearly knocking her down. It lifted first one folded wing, then the other, and the gold and silver wings took up the whole of the small nesting den. Varia ducked as the young being flapped, spraying still-warm yolk across the thicket. To her surprise, the dragon lifted up off the ground and disappeared above the plant line. Varia flew after the newborn. The dragonlet flitted overhead, looking around cautiously, and then returned to its birthplace. Varia watched in amazement as it settled in and neatly folded its shimmering wings back into place. The hatchling noticed her, and, obviously ravenous, clacked its jaws together and lowered its head, coming nearer.

Loben dropped fast on top of the spider-beast, careful to avoid its fangs as he grasped it around the waist with all the force he could muster in the misty land of the dragon. He felt weak but whirred up and held it aloft , keeping its legs off the ground so that the creature was thrashing in midair. Loben held tight and snarled at it, *have you seen my wife, the princess Varia of Erendome?* He sent a mental picture of Varia to the spider, something his tribe did to communicate with animals instead of connecting to the Deva, and the thrashing beast stilled. It hung limply as it tried to gather its thoughts, and Loben could make out a dim picture of it going after Varia, and of her flying away. Yet he knew if he released the beast it would turn on him, for that thought entered Loben's mind too, and he realized it was the creature's plan. *We are at an impasse,* Loben sent the message to the spider, *for if you come after me, I shall kill you.*

Loben sent a mental picture of his sword piercing the beast's body and the spider falling aside, dead. The spider sent a picture back of it rising up and grabbing Loben and devouring him, head first. Loben knew he had to act quickly before his very thoughts would give him away; he flew high up in the air, lifting the heavy arachnid with him, and dropped it before flying away in the direction toward which the spider had pictured Varia fleeing, not waiting to see if the creature survived the fall. Hearing a crash followed by a screech, he knew it had survived, and he could hear it now in the underbrush, hunting him. Though he flew, the spider must have known instinctively Loben could not fly too high above the brushline, lest he attract attention to himself from the large insects he'd spied in the distance, or worse, more dragons. The spider was as fast as Loben, and it kept pace with him on the ground. An angry buzzing nearby caught Loben off guard. Almost afraid to look, he was shocked to see a wild-looking black-and-grey faery chasing him, hand-made weapon drawn. Loben could tell that the faery had once been a Durndeng fae like him, and he wondered if there would be any reasoning with this unfortunate lost kin. As a spear flew near his head, Loben guessed not and focused on the mossy clearing ahead; he only had one chance to escape, and his execution of his plan could not fail or all would be lost.

The sleepy dragon curled up after drinking copious amounts of the molten egg juices. Varia stepped close and watched as her hand reached up to touch the soft nose of the baby dragon, which seemed even larger than before, and though some nagging thought was trying to dissuade her from the act, it was as if her hand had a mind of its own. As she made contact, a million thoughts exploded through her. She had never touched a dragon before, nor known one's Devic spirit, so the connection was all-new to her. It was like touching a life form from another planet. There was nothing within her faery mind or body to compare it to, nothing that read familiar, and yet . . . she felt something, a spark, an awareness, a connection. Varia wept at the enormity of the experience. The dragon pushed its nose into her hand and entwined its tail around her foot. Varia had never been so charmed in her life.

The baby fell asleep, and Varia carefully spread herself out on the mossy enclave beside its rounded, sweet body and watched, mesmerized, as it slumbered. The tiny rumblings of its breathing delighted her, and she felt as if she wanted to get as close as she could, enamored by its soft sheen and pearl-like teeth. Tiny molten puddles of dragon drool formed near its mouth, and Varia felt a strong urge to wipe its gums in a motherly way, though she knew to do so would be folly, for she would probably be scalded. Just being nearby had to be enough, and she was grateful for the baby's warmth as she stayed nearby her new friend. For the first time since entering the dragon realm, Varia felt safe.

Loben ducked low and flew close to the ground of the moss-topped bank, zooming upward as the grey faery followed. Loben had learned that very dodging trick from Varia the day he had chased her from the shadow of the oak at Birkendore, and now found it to be most useful. A horrific collision resulted as spider and Grey Faery became an entangled dangerous union. Loben flew on as fast as he could and didn't look back, but saw enough to know that the beast and the faery who had hunted him would be fighting it out for a time. Long enough for him to find Varia, and to hopefully leave the wretched Drakotanith once and for all.

When the dragon awakened, its unique chirping sound woke Varia too. She felt strangely rested and thought she should eat something. She looked in the silver pouch that was tied around her waist; it had plenty of food in it. Why hadn't she eaten before? She felt starving and weak. Finding sunflower seeds and a bit of bark and even some dried honey drops, Varia sat down and devoured the food. She offered a honey pod to the dragon and it sniffed it, and ate it. The dragon stopped its chewing and spit out the small golden tab, and looked at Varia in an offended way.

Sorry, she sent the mental message to the dragon as she laughed. The dragon ate some more of the dried molten egg drippings nearby and crunched on its own eggshell, keeping one eye on Varia. She was delighted by the dragon's antics and clapped her hands happily.

A noise nearby startled her. *What could that be?* She could hear a crash, and the rustling of the underbrush, a clashing noise, shouts. She hid behind the dragon and peered out by hovering above him, staying in the shadows. A hideous creature, a large spider-like insect, limped toward them, its body split and damaged. A putrid odiferous slime oozing from the wounds, three legs missing. Varia shrieked and moved further back against the den's leafy wall. The dragon stepped forward, and in the blink of an eye pulled the injured beast into its large mouth, and devoured it, legs popping off and innards juices squirting. Varia shot straight up out of the leafy nest, appalled and sickened, when something large collided into her.

It was a faery. Varia flew backward, avoiding the dragon lair where large spider legs were now strewn and being eaten with a loud crunch by the hatchling. The faery regarded her, and Varia stared at him, unsure whether to flee. The faery used her hesitation against her and pinned her wings from behind, grabbed her around the waist and flew away with her, another faery now in hot pursuit. Varia struggled, trying to get free, angry that someone would have the nerve to take her away from her baby, her dragonlet, who was helpless and alone needed her.

Varia, though fed, was still weak and could not fight off the able faery, who was barely keeping ahead of the one behind. She could not get a good look at the follower but could hear the wingsong. Dazed, she called to the baby dragon with her mind for help.

Rising up from the hidden nest, the baby dragon flew. Its huge wings beat the air so heavily that it propelled the faeries forward in an uncontrolled way on every downbeat.

"Dragon!" she heard the following faery shout, and she giggled as she turned to see the baby keeping up. She felt proud of its abilities, and could see that it was having fun chasing along, going on its first outing. She could not understand why the following faery, a grey and black streaked faery that looked nothing like her own kin, looked terrified.

"He is here to rescue me!" Varia said with a giggle. "You had better stop chasing me now, or he will eat you, like that spider." Varia relaxed in the arms of her captor, forgetting why she was struggling before, now that the dragon was safely with her.

"Zedah!" came a voice, and Varia looked ahead. There was a strange wall before them, like a fog bank but see-through like glass. Varia looked at the swirling mists and wondered at the strange word "Zedah." Then she saw a frantic hummingbird on the other side of the transparent wall, as the bird dipped behind a beautiful golden light and disappeared.

"The portal!" the faery who carried her forth called. "Varia, go to the portal!"

Varia shook her head, wondering at the familiar voice, and her own name. "Varia," she repeated, and a strange surge of memory flooded her senses. *Varia is my name,* she thought in wonder. The Grey Faery grabbed onto Varia. She wrenched free from her captor's grip. She tumbled toward the ground, and was surprised when The Grey followed her and caught her before she hit dirt. The dragon growled and swooped toward them both; the Grey Faery released Varia, and she hovered in the air as the dragon did the same beside her, the air from his wings causing her white shift to blow back and forth.

"Why do you grab at me, stranger?" Varia demanded, looking at the terrified faery who now was cowering on a plant leaf.

"I . . . I . . . don't let the dragonlet eat me!" the faery wailed. The other faery, her captor, who was more green and brown in appearance, approached and reached his hand out to Varia, eyeing the baby dragon warily.

"Varia, you must come with me," he said, and Varia found him to be pleasant to look out though domineering. "We need to get back to our own land, and quickly, for this portal will not stay in one place long."

"Leave!" Varia said, smirking. "As if I could leave my own child, my baby!" she stroked the dragon's neck and it chirped in a satisfied way.

"You have allowed the dragon to cast a spell on you, my love, but it must stay here, and you must come with me, for you are faekind and the dragon cannot survive in our world."

"Then this is the world I choose," Varia said in her most forceful voice.

The Grey flitted upwards, and eased toward the portal. The Brown faery saw him and grabbed The Grey around the legs.

"The portal only works one time! Do not steal the chance of the Princess of Erendome!" he thundered.

The Grey and Brown scrapped as Varia turned to fly with her dragonlet back to their den, for she cared not about the other world or the two strange faeries who seemed only to desire a fight. She was about to fly away from them both when she was grabbed hard by the hand; she was yanked away from her hatchling, and had no time to protest. She clutched blindly for her dragon friend just before a sudden tight sensation covered her body, a feeling of crushing as she was pulled into a tunnel of light. Then darkness, and she knew no more.

Chapter Twelve

Varia felt her body being hurled as if down a long narrow tube and she could feel others nearby. She struggled to open her eyes. *What foul deed is this?* she wondered, as she could see naught but a strange grey sleet all around her, blurred edges leading to a faraway shaft of light.

The light neared until she dropped out of the strange tunnel and hit the ground, and heard thudding sounds all around her. Moaning, she opened her eyes, but the brightness of daylight stung her. She pushed herself up onto her knees, shaky and unsure. Blinking, she allowed her eyes to become used to the sunlight. She stood and looked around.

There were others; two faeries and, she realized with a hop of her heart, her beloved dragon. She rushed to the stunned creature and knelt beside him, but he did not stir. She stood and glared at the other two, who were getting to their feet and looking around warily.

"What have you done to him?" she demanded, pointing to the still beast.

One of them, the brown one, carefully stepped toward her, his arms extended as if taming an angry bee.

"Varia. Listen to my voice and no other, for I am your ally and will help you through this confusing time."

Hearing her name, Varia tensed, wishing she'd tested her wings in case she had to fly away quickly. The stranger approached her, in a steady and slow way.

"Stay back!" she said. "For I do not know you, and I do not know where I am!"

The Brown edged closer. "Then read me, as your kind can do, and you will know all."

The other faery, The Grey, stepped backward, looking up and around at the tall and majestic forest where they had landed. Sunlight filtered down through the canopy of ancients, filling the undergrowth with a soft yellow beam, speckling the green foliage as The Brown stood before her and reached for her hand, and placed it on his own forehead. Grey crept away and flew off when Varia closed her eyes and pushed her energy toward the brown faery. Her Deva mingled with his, and pictures popped into her head; she saw a great castle in a tree, with glittering gold domes, and knew in her heart it was home. Then another castle, underground yet exquisitely detailed, and realized it was the home of the enemy living there, but still her heart filled with love. And then she saw why; the very faery she was thisselling, The Brown, was her own, and he was from the enemy castle. She sensed the sweetness between them, and realized that they were wed, and then —the dungeon. News of her sister Alshea overthrowing Erendome. In a rush of horror and relief, the story missing from her addled mind came flooding back. She pulled her hand away as if burned as tears streamed down her face.

"Loben," she said, and she reached up for him and held him close to her. "Then we are back in the realm of the fae now? We are home?"

"We are," Loben replied, his own face flush with relief. "You were under a dragon-spell, and I fear that we may have a small problem . . . a large one, actually, for I believe that the dragon saw you first, before any other creature, when it hatched."

"Yes," Varia said, looking over at the poor beast. "I watched it hatch, and it saw me when it emerged from its egg."

"I thought so," Loben said, shaking his head. "Did it stare at you intently after it was born?"

Varia nodded. "Yes, and that must have been when it cast its spell on me."

Loben sighed, looking over at the lifeless form. "I have heard of such things occurring in the bird world. This unfortunate being believes that you are its mother."

Varia gasped as she looked over at the blue-tinged scales, the delicate golden wings. In the sunlight the dragon's color was iridescent and shimmering, and Varia felt that dragon-spell tug at her heart as she watched it slowly stir.

"This is a mere hatchling!" Varia said as the dragon sat up on its haunches, blinking in the unfamiliar world. "Dragons grow to be enormous! How can we keep a dragon hidden in the faery realm?"

"It is not just the fae realm that concerns me," said Loben thoughtfully. "For remember, because the fae have traversed into the human realm, our two worlds are connected now. Passing between our worlds is as effortless for us as breathing, and I fear that it may be the same for this poor fellow. We may have inadvertently just unleashed a dragon into the world of both faeries and humans."

Varia rushed to the aid of the addled baby and put her arms around his scaly neck. The dragon leaned against her and she struggled to stay upright, resting her hand on its head in a comforting way.

"He cannot stay here! The humans will do foul things to him if they discover him, as they do to their own animals, and our faepeople will not understand him and will shun him. We have to find a way to send him back!"

"There is only one I know of who can tell us how to do that," said Loben. "But I fear that he is imprisoned by your sister the Queen Alshea in the prison of Erendome, and cannot help us now."

"That may actually be a rumour," said a deep voice. Varia and Loben startled and turned to face Rumendah, while Zedah the hummingbird hovered above his head.

Loben grinned and approached Rumendah, and they grabbed upper arms with a nod in the fae custom of greeting. Varia also nodded in reverence. Zedah seemed wary around the large beast Varia rested against, and flitted behind Loben, peeking out to assess every so often.

"I am most glad to see you, Rumendah. How did you escape the prison?"

"I did not escape, for if you were to go to the dungeons of Erendome now, you would find me there, a mere sleeping old faery. Even the Queen Alshea would not disturb an old fae's rest. At least, I hope that she would not, for then my ploy would be discovered, and I have much work to do, as do you, Loben and Varia."

Rumendah looked at Varia and the dragon. "I see we have another complication," he said. He closed his eyes and focused on the baby, then he smiled. "Smote," he said. "I think that is your name." The dragon shook, his loose scales lapping against his hide. Rumendah reached his hand out gingerly to the baby dragon. Smote pushed his tiny snout into the elder's palm.

Zedah obviously had enough of being in the strange creature's presence and sped away.

"Smote may yet be an ally, but hiding a dragon in this world has failed in the past, and more than once." Rumendah looked around. "Did I not see another faery, a strange-looking one who came through the portal with you from the other realm?"

Loben looked around for the other. "He was but a lost soul from the dragon realm of Drakotanith, and he has chosen to flee. I do not think that he will cause us any grief. He is of no importance to our mission."

Rumendah looked in the direction where the Grey Faery had disappeared. "You never know what part anyone has to play," he said under his breath, "until all of the parts have been played out." Rumendah handed out honey tabs and a vial of nectar to Varia and Loben. "Quickly drink and refresh yourselves, and Varia, I see that you still wear the silver pouch I give you. Empty the food stores, for they are tainted with the craft of the other world, but keep the hestus, for dark times are ahead."

Everyone nourished hastily and flew after Rumendah toward the mountains in the north. Smote, though small for a dragon, was now nearly four times larger than Loben, the tallest faery in the group. Smote seemed to enjoy the flight, and tried to lift himself from the forest floor up into the sky, but always one of the fae stopped him and made him return, staying low.

"Smote will need to eat," Varia said to Rumendah and Loben as they flew. "And I fear he does not eat fallen twigs and grass."

"He will have to hunt," Loben said. "He will fend for himself."

"But he will kill innocent creatures!" Varia said, great emotion filling her.

"Perhaps he will eat some of the food in our pouches," Loben said, laying his hand on her wrist to comfort her as they continued on their way.

"He will not eat fae food! And I have noted it, he has grown already after just one meal," Varia said.

Rumendah gave Loben a stern look and Loben seemed to understand that this was not a conversation to venture into now, for the dragon was already becoming a problem. Loben surged forth, leaving Rumendah and Varia behind.

Onward they flew, until late afternoon. They arrived at the cave where Loben had met Rumendah before.

"There is much magic at work here to keep us safe and unseen," Rumendah said. They ventured into the cave center, where sunlight trickled in from the waterfall's opening, illuminating the sheet of water that noisily fell. The lake water sparkled faintly. Varia stripped off her tunic and silver bag in a tired way and jumped into the pool, and while underwater she felt an enormous splash beside her. She knew Smote had followed her into the drink. The dragon swam underneath her in the dark depths of the cave lake and she was amazed at his prowess. As she pointed her wings and swam, the icy water cleansed her, stripping the last remnants of Drakotanith from her very soul. She climbed out and found the faemen had already set up a makeshift camp for them.

"Varia, we have stores for you," Loben called out. He came to her and handed her a bundle and pulled her, wet from her swim, against him. She leaned into his warm embrace and they stood together a moment, their first deep breath since leaving the Erendome prison. In the water, Smote rose up suddenly, looking like a strange sea creature as he breached the water's surface. Several large fish flapped up above the lake with him and Loben laughed at the dragon's antics. Varia looked inside the woven package and was delighted to see her own clothing, much more suited for living away from the castle than the white thin coronation underslip, now stained with the oils of the grey leaking plants they'd encountered in the dragon world. Loben kissed her gently on the forehead before returning to Rumendah. Varia dressed in heavy leggings and a warm tunic and joined the two around their small hestus fire. Smote climbed out of the lake after a time too, dripping with his mouth full of flopping fish. Varia cringed and looked away as he stole over to a far corner to gorge himself in his slurping, crunching way.

"Our next moves are of extreme importance," Rumendah said after they ate a relaxed meal of dried fruit slivers, flower nectar, honey drops, and bark tea. For the first time since she could remember, Varia felt warm, full, and rested. She leaned her head against Loben's strong shoulder, and folded her wings around her. She wanted to doze off but forced herself to pay attention to the elder's words.

"The king is safe, for now, and so is your cousin Irea," Rumendah said. "But Alshea a has tight control of her faepeople. Those who disagreed with her uprising have left the castle and are living in exile in the far reaches of Ashenthorne, staying in the faery woodland houses with friends and neighbors. Our tribe is split now, and our numbers are few as the Birkendore soldiers gather for war. It is a war the Alawe will not win, for Alshea has put your brother Ezia in control of the army, and he has neither the skill nor the heart to take a troop to victorious battle."

Varia sat up, realizing that her very tribe's fate rested in her hands now.

"This is disturbing news, Rumendah. What do you think, Loben? Can we stop the Vorku from attacking Erendome?"

Loben stared at the ground in a thoughtful way before slowly shaking his head. "No," he replied. "Our soldiers are built for war, and our king is proud. He must avenge the death of Brunhurn, our fallen soldier. His family will insist on it, even if the king does not."

"I fear there is little we can do then, except help the king and Irea escape, and those of his court who are also imprisoned."

"Then we shall have a war within our own walls," Varia said. "For Alshea will not easily step down from the throne! With Ezia as commander and Talow as her captain, we are up against the most desperate and strong-willed of our kind." Varia stared into the mesmerizing black eyes of Rumendah. "Does this . . . mean . . . that we must go through the dragon realm again, that wretched Drakotanith, to help them escape Erendome?"

Rumendah smiled a bit as he shook his head. "No, my princess," he said in a reassuring voice. "Your father is simply in jail, not nested between two worlds for his own safety as you were. For while Alshea may be a mad queen, she still loves her father. She will not allow harm to come to him. My reasoning is that in her mind, she has put him and your relative Irea in prison for their own good. Alshea truly believes that she will thus save the kingdom."

"I doubt it not," Varia said. "She has always thought that father was weak, and had a soft place in his heart for the enemy."

"Your father does indeed, and that is what has made him a brilliant king for cytons. There has been peace for a very long time."

"Before now, there was peace because our faepeople believed the EarthSeekers to be extinct," Varia said. "How is it that the Durndeng could be living just beyond Ashenthorne, and we had no knowledge of it?"

Loben shifted and cleared his throat. "Your father may have known, and thought it best to keep our tribe a secret from your clan."

Varia nodded. "Perhaps. I remember you told me of your Queen Hoondeen loving one of the Alawe before she married King Struben," Varia said.

Loben rubbed his hands over the hestus flame. "It matters not. We must find a way to break into Erendome and free your father, for I have an idea."

Varia reached over and clutched Loben's arm. "What is it?"

"We are busy thinking of ways to thwart warriors, but your mentioning Queen Hoondeen made me realize that there may be a better way. She loved an Alawe once. Perhaps she can help us save our faepeople if we can get the queen to manage peace talks with your sister Alshea. For surely, your father must know, or may even be related to, the one she loved. For that Alawe was a member of your clan, and has lived in the Erendome court."

Varia stared disbelieving at Loben. She had no words upon hearing this news.

"Well suggested," said Rumendah. "Although, freeing your father is not necessary to glean that information, for do not forget, there is one who is older even than your father, who may know of such things as secret romances and their outcomes."

Varia stared at Rumendah now, watching the shadows from the hestus flame cover his intent face.

"Ah yes. Many think I am just an elder of the court, whispering information about where the best honey hives are to the king, but I have been here all along, since the days your great-grandparents ruled, my princess. And I remember when Hoondeen, who was a Durndeng lady in the court of the Dunter-Gruns, met and fell in love with that Alawe so long ago. For they had a difficult time, as you two do, keeping their love affair a secret, and the distance they had to travel to find one another was far greater than the distance between Ashenthorne and Birkendore."

While Smote snored smoke peacefully in his corner, Loben and Varia sat at the edge of the fire, rapt as Rumendah shared his tale.

Chapter Thirteen

"In the great age of the Durndeng, the faeries lived a bucolic life in the forests outside of countryside estates of humans. Learning to appreciate strange human treats such as sweet sugared cakes, the fae of the Durndeng soon developed a relationship with certain humans, allowing them to pass into the fae realm as the faeries would pass into the human realm, thus breaking down the barriers between worlds and creating a permanent portal. Sometimes, if a human were particularly favored, the fae would use their ancient faery magick to help maintain the household. The faeries were nicknamed Brownies by the humans, and thus they peacefully co-existed for many cytons.

"And so it was until man began to build great machines, and replace the humble horse with motorcars, and a war broke out that sent all men to their hell and back, and now they were broken and traumatized, or dead. But just before the turn of mankind caused the fae folk to shy away from their former friends, the Durndeng were at the height of their days, with faery song and good food filling their halls in their intricate underground castles, and in every house in the faery village lived the happy, content Durndeng faepeople.

"Around that time, some members of the Alawe tribe were on the move, looking for goods to trade on their way to their relatives' summer castle in the north. A mishap involving a predatory fox broke the group apart, and several of the Alawe were separated from their party. One of them was a handsome and brave faery, a member of the royal court. His name was Prince Dreya."

Varia gasped, forgetting she was in a dark cave listening to Rumendah's tale, so transported had she been by his words.

"Dreya . . . my father? The king?" Varia said, covering her mouth with her hand. "But what are you saying, Rumendah?"

"Listen more. The prince was lost, and having trouble finding nectar to keep his strength so he could fly. He lost his flight ability, he was so malnourished, and found himself walking through unfamiliar woods, with many great perils all around him. He saw humans, and their strange animals, and their homesteads. He stayed hidden, for that skill did not abandon him, but even after a few days of wandering, he had a hard time keeping himself one with the plants of this new strange area. Eventually, he fell, and lost consciousness. All would have been lost, but he was found. And the person who found him, was a lady faery of the high court. It was your own Queen Hoondeen," Rumendah looked to Loben now. "And she was but a princess then, but took pity on the lost Alawe prince. She hid him, and nourished him, found him the nectar he needed to fly. And during this encounter, they fell in love."

Varia was surprised to find a tear on her cheek. "Just like us!" she said to Loben. "He must have had such a hard time leaving her! Why did they separate? Did they know one another long?"

Rumendah looked up at the ceiling hole to the sky. The outside light was turning orange with dusk. "Oh yes. They did. They loved each other for longer than you have known Loben, Varia. They spent the entire summer together, until King Hirth, who is King Struben's father, and Loben's grandfather, I believe . . ." Loben nodded in agreement and Rumendah continued. "The king began to hear rumour of an enemy in his midst. He flushed Dreya out, and he was to have his wings plucked and to be cast out into the wilderness, but from my understanding of the tale, Queen Vorteen, Struben's mother, took pity on the Alawe prince. She helped Dreya escape, and arranged for the broken-hearted Hoondeen to marry her own son. That is how Hoondeen became queen of Loben's tribe, with the help of her mother-in-law, Queen Vorteen herself."

"I've not heard this part of the tale," Loben said, listening as raptly as Varia. "My own sister, now departed, was named after Queen Vorteen, so I find this part of the tale of utmost import."

"And well you should, for there is even more to tell. A darker, more sinister part of the tale. For what King Struben doesn't know is that . . ." Rumendah looked up through the ceiling hole again, distracted by something only he could hear, for though his ears were old, they were the ears of a faery elder, one who could wield the ancient magick of the fae. Rumendah closed his eyes, and when he blinked them open, they were wide. "Hide!" he commanded, and he tapped his staff against the hestus flame, blackening it before disappearing.

Loben turned into a stone, and Varia faded back into the wall of the cave, blending herself with the craggy surface. Over the sound of the waterfall a thousand wing beats drew near, and soon the opening grew dark with the arrival of the Alawe Wilhvyre, the AirWalker FlightSoldiers.

"We must make an encampment near this water for the night, for there is fresh nectar nearby, and we have stores of seed and nut. Rest now faemen, for tomorrow we will stop those dirty earth dwellers from crawling out of their nasty hole once and for all!" Ezia shouted from above to his faesoldiers.

Varia shuddered, nearly losing her connection with the stone wall that hid her, when she heard her brother Ezia's words over the dull roar of the waterfall. The Wilhvyre army began setting up an encampment, clattering their weapons to the stones and barking orders to build hidden tents in the underbrush. In the cave's corner, Smote the sleeping dragon opened one eye, and looked up at the cavernous hole where the activity of hundreds of fae warriors disturbed him.

It was fortunate indeed for Rumendah, Varia, and especially Loben that the Wilhvyre were preoccupied with their setting up of an encampment, and that they were loud about it. The waterfall gurgled over the noise of the three fae tiptoeing over to Smote to console him, for though the dragon was less than a day old, he obviously did not take kindly to strangers in his territory. Especially strangers who seemed to threaten his mother, for that is who Varia was to him.

"Good Smote, good baby!" Varia cooed in a quiet manner. "That's my wonderful boy. Rest, do not let those noisy faemen bother you." Varia rubbed the infant's snout, which seemed to calm him, for his growling deep in his throat, (a growl that sometimes threw forth tiny sparks), was lessened now. Rumendah stood before the dragonlet and waved his staff, mesmerizing the beast, until Smote belched a small flame and turned to face the wall to sleep once again.

Varia breathed a deep but silent sigh, and the three moved to a far corner to converse.

"I guess it's a boy we will be raising," Loben said gamely.

"Yes, it's a boy, but not the type of child I expected to have with you! I am sorry, I did not mean to let Smote attach himself to me! What a way to begin our wedded lives, with a dragon hatchling in tow who has no manners, knows nothing of this world, and is growing larger by the moment!"

"I will certainly vouch that the infant has grown since this very afternoon," Rumendah said, "for every meal he eats, he halves up his size."

"We cannot stay here, but how will we get Smote to stay put?" Loben asked.

"Can you put a spell on him to sleep?" Varia asked, looking over as the baby's glistening scales heaved and fell with each sweet breath.

"It is not safe to do so," Rumendah said. "For if the Wilhvyre find this cave and explore it, they will come across him, and soon as not would probably slay him. He must come with us. It is the only way."

"We will never get him out of here unseen!" Varia whispered in a high voice.

"There is a passage, but it is a long trek to the outside. Quickly gather your things and follow me."

The company of three packed up all their belongings, taking careful care to cover up the evidence of their camp. Varia woke up Smote, who shook his head in a confused and tired way.

"Come, dear Smote. Come with us!" Varia said, and she followed Rumendah toward the far end of the cave, where a dark crevasse, barely large enough for the dragon to fly through, led to unknown depths. Smote narrowed his eyes and crept toward the opening as Varia pointed to it. Varia flitted through the opening following Rumendah, who was leading the way with his hestus-tipped wand, and Smote brought up the rear as they all strayed from the minimal light of the cave and into the dark mountainside.

"We must be wary," said Rumendah in a low growl of a voice once they had traveled far enough from the earshot of any Wilhvyre sentinels, "for there are creatures that dwell in these parts that no faery has lived to describe."

"That is all you need to say, I will heed your warning," Loben murmured as he flew through the cavern ahead of Varia. The cave walls were cold and damp, and Varia shivered, reminded of her time in the dragon realm. There was something comforting about the steady flap of Smote's wings behind her as he followed along, until the crack they traversed narrowed and the dragon was forced to scamper behind on foot.

After they had journeyed awhile in their quest to reach the other side of the cavern, Rumendah stopped suddenly.

"What is it?" Loben whispered as Varia strained to see ahead of her in the vast darkness. She thought of the hestus in her pouch and was tempted to light it, but something told her she may need it another time.

"Shhh," Rumendah said, as all the fae listened intently. In the distance ahead, a muffled chafing noise could be heard. Rumendah sniffed the air.

"Slow worm," he muttered under his breath. "We'd best fly up to the ceiling, follow me." Rumendah flitted silently to the topmost part of the crevasse, although it was not high and only brought the group three times their length away from the cave floor. Smote, on the other hand, was still walking on the slick cave rocks, as his wing span was too large for him to fly in the cramped space. The fae continued to move forward, Loben with his sword-like Vorku weapon drawn and at the ready, Rumendah by his side. Varia too pulled her blade from its scabbard, and held it aloft, gulping. She had never harmed a living being in her entire life, and hated that it could happen now, in self-defense.

Rumendah lifted his light higher and they saw it, the strange square lizard-like head, followed by a writhing, legless body.

"That is no worm!" Varia whispered when the beast stopped, and flicked its tongue in the air, as if tasting strangers in its realm.

"A slow worm is not a true worm," Rumendah agreed, "but a legless lizard, a carnivore no less, and careless with the lives of the fae it may come across. Proceed!" The fae flew quietly above the blind "worm," as it turned its head and listened for the faint whir of faery wings. Then it leapt straight up toward them, gaping mouth open.

Loben jabbed his sword at the beast, and the lizard clamped its cavernous mouth down hard on the flat of the blade, wresting it from Loben's grip as he struggled to hang on. The force dropped Loben from the sky, and he landed hard on the cragged rocks beneath him, momentarily stunned, giving the worm the moment it needed to find its prey. The sword clattered loudly to the cave floor as its snake-like head lunged at Loben, who held up his hands in defense. Varia shrieked, certain she would witness the death of her husband, but the quick chomping action missed Loben by a stem as he rolled away from the creature. Varia was ready to fly down and take action when a low growl emitted from Smote. Smote came forward, head low to the ground, breath steaming with anger and revenge. The blind worm stilled as if trying to decipher this new menace, giving Smote the only opportunity he needed. Smote was so quick that Varia could not see the young dragon's head dart forward, but the worm squealed its last gasping breath, as Smote engulfed its head and torso in its mouth. The legless lizard shook violently as the life left it, and then, with a chomp of sharp teeth, Smote bit through, leaving the decapitated torso on the cave floor. Varia retched at the smell of blood, and Loben grabbed his fallen blade and flew up and put his arm around her and pulled her away from the carnage.

"He did save us," he said as the fae moved further up the cave, away from the splatter and crunch of Smote's candid eating habits.

"He is an impossibility!" Varia moaned. "How is it that I, a mere gentle fae of this world, could care for such a violent, unkempt creature? I do not understand my own heart, for part of me is proud of him, and more of me is repelled by his actions."

Rumendah chuckled. "That is dragon-spell for you, Varia. For you two have discovered each other in Smote's first look, and will forever be connected, in this realm and beyond. There is no cure for it."

Loben smiled too as Varia whimpered and leaned into his arms, their wings beating slowly as they hovered high in the cavern. Soon the bone-splitting noises diminished, and Varia called softly to her charge. "Come now Smote! We must continue."

The dragon emerged from the fissure's depths and they went forward, the dark crack in the cave brightening ahead as the orange light of sunset filled the cavern.

"Not much longer! And then we shall rest and eat," Rumendah said, his voice cheery now. Varia felt relief at the thought that she could finally be free of the dank slit and see the last moments of the day's sunlight, and perhaps find fresh water, sweet nectar and clean air. She sighed. Smote, now bulging and larger than the faeries by several stems (and growing by the moment, Varia noted) had to squeeze his way through some of the tighter spots of the cave. At one point, he stopped, something Varia noticed when his scuffling gait grew silent.

"Wait!" Varia called ahead in a whispered voice to Loben. "Tell Rumendah, the dragon is having trouble keeping up."

"How is that?" asked Loben. "For he is swifter in every way than all of us." Loben turned back, and Varia saw his eyes widen. She turned to see that Smote was helplessly stuck behind a narrowing of the rocks. Varia gasped. "Oh no!" she said, for Smote had grown considerably in just a matter of moments and could now no longer navigate the narrow crack.

"It is that slow-worm that he ate," Loben spat. "It has already made him grow larger!"

"I have heard that a baby dragon reaches full size by the age of just a moon or two," Rumendah said, nodding. "That may be why our friend here has grown so."

122

The three looked helplessly upon the young dragonlet, now wedged between the cave walls, frantic as he tried to free himself. Even as he flailed, he seemed to grow larger still.

"Why, he has grown twice his size!" Varia said.

For it was true; poor Smote was now doubled in size, and the soft rounded hatchling look about him was gone, as his features had become more chiseled, which gave him an adolescent appearance.

"He is but a day old! How can he change so much in just a day?" Varia asked.

"I do not know," Rumendah said, shaking his head. "Perhaps there is a time difference from our world to his, that is causing him to age at a faster pace. For while I have heard that dragons grow quickly in their own realm, here, the rate seems increased."

"And now he is stuck completely!" Loben said. "How will we get him out?"

Varia went to him, and tried to overlook the slow-worm innards that had stuck to his nose as she reached up to pat him on the head to comfort him.

"Easy, dear Smote. We will help you," she said in a soothing voice. "Do not despair."

Smote struggled and began to roar, his loud voice echoing off the cave walls.

"Shhhhh!" Varia said, looking around. "The fae have keen ears, if they are in the cave on the other end, they will hear you!"

Smote did not heed the warning, but let off another deep smoking howl, this one shaking the very walls that bound him.

"Quiet!" Rumendah demanded, and the dragon for some reason clamped his mouth shut. "That will draw every enemy within a crow's flight to us! Blasted beast." Rumendah flitted around the dragon's snout nervously, pacing in the sky, deep in thought. Loben joined them and looked carefully at Smote, trying to decipher where he was wedged. Loben touched the place on Smote's shoulders where he was being crushed by the stone he had grown into, and pushed on his scaly hide.

"I think he could go backward," Loben said finally. "There is more room behind him than in front of him."

"He could not get out the way we came in, remember how narrow the opening of the crevice is?" Varia said, a wail at the edge of her voice. "And, he cannot turn around in such a tight spot."

"At least he will be more comfortable while we solve this riddle of how to free him," Loben said. He flew up and pulled on the spiky green horns atop Smote's head, lifting with all of his strength until the now twenty-stem long dragon moved his head up to the sky. As if understanding, Smote stretched his neck, and his shoulders raised up out of the stuck place, and he was released from being crushed between the rocks, although now caged in the very walls of the cave itself.

"There!" Loben said. "Now he is not hurting."

"Perhaps we can leave him for a while and try to set up a camp, for he is certainly safe here, for now. Nightfall is coming," Rumendah said.

"Leave him! Do you think he will stay silent if I leave him? We need to set up camp here, so he can see us. He cannot even lie down in that tight place! We must stay with him so his spirits are not dashed. He is sensitive, and still very young," Varia said.

Loben nodded in agreement, and upon activating the extra hestus Rumendah provided, the cave was brightly lit. There was a shallow hole below them that Loben explored. "It has a wide flat surface beneath; we can all sleep there," Loben said. "And Smote will still know that we are nearby."

Smote tucked his legs under him, and although he couldn't curl up, he slept upright, his snores emitting a steamy smoke from his nostrils as he slumbered. Loben went over and removed the offending lizard goo from his nose so Varia could get closer to him.

"Thank you," Varia whispered, wondering how Loben could stand to touch the stuff. She leaned against the cave wall with her hand resting on Smote's nose, careful to avoid the scalding exhale of breath. "My poor dear Smote," she said, and she must have dozed off curled up around his nose, for soon Loben was shaking her awake.

"Come and stay warm with us by the fire," Loben said, and he pulled Varia over to the craggy drop into their encampment. Varia flitted in front of the fire, and watched as Rumendah, deep in thought, smoked on his narrow reed pipe, silent and far away in his mind.

Varia leaned her head against Loben's warm chest and the two pressed together under a thick lambsear leaf blanket he provided for her from his pack, and she was grateful to be in his arms again. The weight and worry of her day took her and she could no longer keep her eyes open as she watched the fire dance inside the black mountain, warming her as she fell into a deep sleep.

Chapter Fourteen

Varia awoke with a start, wondering where she was. Looking around, she could see a small hestus fire before her. Sparks flew and snapped in bright hues of orange, yellow, blue and red. Varia watched the show a moment and remembered: Loben, Rumendah, the dragon Smote. The crevice in the cave. She flitted up above the shallow divot line; it was very dark but she could see the shadow of the sleeping Smote and make out the slumbering figure of Rumendah as he leaned against the cave wall in the flickering light.

At her action, Rumendah woke.

"Where is Loben?" Varia whispered, for even her wingsong seemed loud in the cold dank night.

"He has left us to warn his faepeople of your brother Ezia's plan. We are at the dawn of battle," Rumendah said, his voice heavy. Varia sat beside him, looking through the slit in the wall where Smote slept, his nostrils glowing red and warm as he breathed in and out.

"Any suggestions about how to get Smote out?" Varia asked, hope waning within her. Loben gone, Smote stuck, her father and cousin imprisoned, and her sister gone mad with her newfound power . . . Varia's simple and peaceful life was turned upside down. She shuddered with the cold and dampness and Rumendah put his arm around her in a fatherly way.

"I have figured out how to release Smote, but I must wait until the first stroke of sunlight, for it will be loud and your brother's army will be on us like gadflies to sheep."

"Ah," Varia said, wanting specifics but then again, the rare quiet moment seemed too precious to waste. She leaned her head against Rumendah's sinewy shoulder and closed her eyes, and sent out a thought to her father: *Father, I am safe, I am coming for you, I will do my best to save your kingdom from destruction,* but even as she thought it, it felt like a lie.

𝔇awn touched into the cave with golden red fingers and Varia found Rumendah hurriedly packing up their belongings. "Much of this I shall hide, for we must fly as lightly as possible," Rumendah said. Varia put a few items of food and a nectar flask in her belt pouch, after drinking as much as she could quickly down. Rumendah picked up the vessel he carried the hestus in, and took some honey from the food stores. He began mixing the two ingredients into a sticky paste.

"What are you doing?" Varia wondered aloud as she put her sword in its scabbard and tied it to her waist. Rumendah nodded toward Smote, who was beginning to wake, his sleepy eyes opening.

"I am going to free him! Now please don't pester me with your questions, Varia, for this trick shall take all of my skill to master, and I am not even sure that it will work. I must concentrate." Rumendah was focused on creating his mixture and Varia clamped her mouth shut, feeling like a scolded faechild. She watched as the old faery flew up and began placing large dots of the stuff on the cave walls that held Smote captive.

"Now, timing will be everything, Varia. When you see sparks turning white, call to Smote and begin flying out toward the sunlight. Do not hesitate. This part is important; save yourself! Do not return for heroics, not to save me, nor to save Smote. That one will be fine on his own, and as for myself . . . I am old and wiser than a fox. Do not worry about me, do you promise? When the moment comes, flee!"

Varia's bottom lip trembled in fear but she nodded.

"Very well. Onward!"

Rumendah picked up his wand and dipped it into his stores of sparkling hestus powder, the sandy grit sticking to the honey he had smeared on the tip. He flew up to one of the spots where he had smeared the sticky faery dust pile and inserted his wand, and muttered an incantation under his breath. Varia's eyes widened as suddenly the potion caught fire and blazed amber gold. Rumendah lit all of the honeyed areas and Varia saw the plan; he was going to blow out the cave wall in a fiery explosion. The hestus burned hot white with sparks careening from the source.

"Fly!" Rumendah commanded, as Smote stamped behind the wall. Varia flew toward the exit calling "Come Smote!" As she stopped and turned, her silver purse Rumendah had given her banged against her body, and her small sword released from its scabbard and hit the rocks, clanging loudly. Varia looked down but couldn't see the blade in the dark rocks, and the dragon bellowed, his own smoke and flame barely missing Rumendah, who hovered nearby. Varia knew she would have to leave the only weapon she had behind as Smote charged against the cave wall, and with a crack and thunderous clap, the walls gave way to the dragon's girth and Smote was free. Varia flew for the cave opening with all her speed, followed by black smoke and a mountain of dust, hoping somehow Rumendah had gotten out of the way as the hatchling sped after her.

Varia broke free into the light, and it was fortunate dawn had barely shown itself, for even at this early time the sun was too bright for her unaccustomed eyes. Trying not to think of Rumendah and her lost blade, she sped toward the west, toward her home Erendome, when she heard Smote's yelp behind her. A thousand angry bees is what she heard, but she knew it was Ezia's FlightSoldiers, for the Wilhvyre had felt their noise deep in the cave from the next valley over and were already on her, weapons drawn. She flew fast but they were gaining on her in a way that surprised her, and she understood that she was not fleeing from the fae she had grown up with but an army that had been in training since the time she had been put into the hidden prison cell at Erendome, and they were now after her as an enemy.

Behind her she felt a heavy swift wind and recognized the sound of Smote's wingsong, and she felt him flying beneath her as she was uplifted by his heavy air. Knowing he was trying to save her, she dove down and clutched onto his hide, holding on to the horned scales on his head. She could see from the corner of her eye a spear raised by one of the Wilhvyre and she ducked her head, flattening herself against Smote's neck. As soon as she was well-seated, Smote took off with a speed Varia had never experienced before, not even when playing with birds in her youth.

Smote left the army behind him and flew her swiftly toward Erendome, and Varia realized as the frigid morning air whipped across her face as she rode that Smote understood where she wanted to go, and could somehow sense her plan, and that they truly were one.

Loben stood before King Struben, his arms and wings bound by a golden prisoner's rope. The king flew back and forth before him.

"I have done as you asked," the king said, "and have sent the faewomen and children to the temporary shelters in the Rhysgollen forest, deep beyond the oak root, and have my warriors at the ready surrounding Thundendell's castle walls. My question for you is, why would you return here if you had an opportunity to leave with your wife, and start a fresh life away from this horror?"

Loben looked around the king's private chamber, and he admired its high ceiling, ornate art, and the finely woven fabric drapes created by dozens of fae artisans. Musical instruments, used nightly by the king's musicians, rested against the wall, which was glowing with a golden hued swirl painted over the opalescent plaster.

"This is why," Loben gestured to their surroundings. "Our faepeople are an advanced, wondrous civilization! And while I am beginning to understand..." Loben wanted to add, *as your wife Queen Hoondeen once did,* but he refrained from bringing up the old memory, ". . . that the Alawe also are not the tree-dwelling thugs we once thought them to be, I cannot allow us to be defeated by an ambush. And I cannot yet stop this fight. Some will be lost, yes, but our new colony will stand a chance at thriving, and perhaps if the Wilhvyre armies come to understand that we are willing to fight for our place here, they will think twice about their attacks on us and somehow we can come to an agreement."

"That is optimistic thinking indeed," King Struben sighed. "Loben, you are my kin, and while I trust you, this is not the first time of late that you have been brought to me in shackles! I shall release the prisoner's label on you and make you one of my trusted advisors. I do believe that you truly have the best intentions for our faepeople, even if your methods may be somewhat skewed." The king floated to the ground and tapped the gold bindings, which loosened at his command. Loben slipped the rope from his body and stepped out of it.

"Thank you," he said, rubbing his arms where the grip had him.

"Now tell me once more about the Grey Faery; he was once Durndeng?"

"I believe so," Loben replied.

A worried look crossed Struben's face, and the king seemed deep in thought. "I have some recollection of a story like that," he said, mostly to himself, "but in my memory of it, the faery was exiled to the Mysty island prison for treason. I do not understand how he could have found his way to Drakotanith." As if in a fog, Struben shook his head. "Never mind now, we have other problems closer at hand!"

"Your Vorku army is ready for battle, your highness," Doon said as he entered the room. He scoffed when he saw the golden bindings on the floor in front of Loben.

"Tied up again, Cousin?" he asked. Loben clapped Doon on the shoulder.

"I am sorry about our earlier disagreement," he said. "I still hold you in highest regard, as my friend and relative."

Doon gave a sheepish smile. "I have been lectured long by my father about inter-tribe relations, so I am the one to apologize." Doon put his hand on Loben's shoulder. "I support your decision to wed the AirWalker. The Alawe," Doon corrected himself, using the more respectful term.

Loben smiled and waved him off. "As I said before, family comes first, Doon. I am glad to be back in your good graces."

"Enough of this sentiment. Line the Vorku up, tell them I am coming," Struben said to his son. Doon nodded dutifully and took his leave.

"I fear a blood bath," the king said to Loben in a sad voice. "First, we are forced from our first home, in the Urunhem Downs palace in the land of the Dunter-Gruns, by a few reckless human children with newfangled contraptions called . . ."

"Cameras," Loben interjected. "I believe that is what they are called."

"Yes. Whatever those wretched machines of men are called, that can capture an image of the fae whether they be caught physically or not! The humans have forced us from our very home, with their stomping about in our woods, damaging our structures, scaring our faepeople in their mad pursuit of us. And the fae who allowed that . . . abomination to occur, the ones who had their . . ."

"Photographs," Loben interjected.

"Yes, photographs taken, have been banned to live their lives in exile in the woods! They are now no better than the wild fae of the mountaintops, living outdoors like common birds or insects. Disgraceful!"

King Struben walked over and sat on his nearby throne, his wings slipping through the back of it and resting in place behind him.

"None of it matters now, any new place we go, we will have to make peace with the native faeries. I opt to stay here, to try and find our peace with the Alawe, since . . . well, since we have a certain history already."

Loben nodded, opting not to speak, but knowing that the king meant his own wife's previous love affair with a member of the Alawe tribe, King Dreya.

"We have a battle at our doorstep, Loben. Will you stay and fight?"

Loben shook his head. "I must help Varia release her father, for their true king regaining the throne is our only hope at stopping the Wilhvyre from their task to destroy us and roust us from our home. Queen Alshea is unstable at best, murderous at worst. I must help restore the Alawe kingdom quickly. Our plan was to ask the queen to help with negotiations, but now we have a battle on our doorstep instead."

"Very well," Struben said. "Guards!" he called, and two sentries blocking the door entered, bowing to the king. "Escort Loben from here, and do not let any harm come to him. Get him as far west away from our own militia as you can but return quickly, because we are awaiting our company, the AirWalker raiders, and we will need all the help we can get."

The faemen flew off toward the main doors of Thundendell castle, with Loben flying right in between them.

Chapter Fifteen

Varia sent her thoughts out toward Smote and asked him to stop flying. She was sore from riding his neck, and her face was cold and flushed from the wind of haste. Smote relaxed his gait and moved his wings in slow strokes, until he glided effortlessly above a lake and landed in it, floating toward shore. Once they reached the sandy bank, he lowered his head and Varia stepped off. She tried her own wings, as she had to tuck them in tightly behind her so they would not fray with Smote's speed, and she felt the strain as she flapped them a few times to release the pressure of holding them still.

"I fear I am not meant to ride you!" she said. Worry about Rumendah began to plague her now that she was at rest and not fleeing for her life, but she knew there was nothing she could do for him. She sighed. "I must leave you here, Smote, and I wish I could make you understand. But my tribe needs me, and I cannot very well go back to my home riding on the back of a dragon!" Even as she said it, Varia could picture herself doing it, and the image pleased her. But for Smote's safety, she had to make him stay put, at least for now. She sat down and patted the sand, and the beast, now about twenty-four stems long, bounded toward her like a gigantic wolf pup. She felt small under his enthusiastic exit from the water, and braced herself, but he carefully avoided harming her as he curled himself next to her on the warm beach. Putting his damp snout beside her leg, he breathed gently and began to fall asleep. Soon the dragonlet was snoring, and Varia moved back out of harm's way as small flames periodically emitted from his nostrils.

"I do love you, you crazy dragon," Varia whispered. She quietly crept away and flew toward Erendome, now with a considerable flight ahead of her. No sooner had she reached the nearby wood when she heard the familiar stroke of Smote's heavy wingfall.

The hatchling caught up to her and flew happily beside her. Varia turned around, and fluttered back to their beach once more.

"Smote!" she said in an exasperated way. "You must stay here, without me! For I must go alone."

She sat down on the sand again, and Smote joined her and fell asleep for the second time. Varia tried to sneak away, but this time his thick eyelid opened, his silver and gold eye peering at her as she tried to escape.

"It's no use trying to outsmart a dragon," she said aloud, frustrated, feeling in a rush to get out of there. Ideas came to her but she couldn't restrain him or bring him with her; both would be dangerous. Varia put her forehead in her hands, stumped. In the distance she heard a high pitched noise, one she recognized as a hummingbird call. Her heart leapt. Could it be Zedah?

The call was closer now, and Varia looked up to see the iridescent ruby head of Loben's most beloved friend. Smote eyed the bird in a tempted way and Varia glared at him.

"NOT FOR YOU," she said in a loud and firm voice. Smote looked away, as if most uninterested in tiny little birds. Zedah perched herself on a pine branch and awaited Varia's approach. Varia backed away from Smote, scolding him. Since Smote could still see her, he did not try to follow and slept once more as Varia reached out for the hummingbird.

"Lovely Zedah!" she said, and she held the bird close to her. Zedah nuzzled her, careful with her long pointed beak. Zedah made a low noise which meant she had a message, and Varia placed her hands on Zedah's heart, listening for it.

"Loben is coming! Oh, dear Zedah, please tell him where to find us! For I am lost with this dragon in tow, I have no means to accomplish anything, it is quite like bringing a fallen tree along wherever I go, so cumbersome a beast is he."

"So he is," said a low voice, and Varia turned, expecting to see Loben. But it was not her husband who emerged from the pine thicket, but the strange grey faery who had followed them through the portal from the dragon realm. Varia flitted backwards as Zedah zipped into the sky.

"What are you doing here?" Varia asked, remembering now strange details of her time in that eerie realm, about being chased, and Loben and the grey faery fighting. She felt her belt for her weapon, and remembered her blade had been lost. She hovered just out of the other faery's reach, on guard.

The other seemed unused to speaking, and he tried his words in a careful way. "I am the dragon's guardian," the grey faery said. "At least, I was meant to be. I am guardian of this one's mother, Evara y Bliw, or in the common tongue, Evara the Blue, and I have promised her I would care for her newest young one. But then . . ." the grey faery's face turned red, whether with anger or shame Varia couldn't tell, "then you came, and he put his dragonspell on you, not me, and so I am lost. For he cannot align himself with more than one being! My very purpose is destroyed."

Varia looked around and noted an escape route through some thistle should the faery become violent, so distraught was he.

"I did not mean to be the one he chose," Varia said in a hushed voice, "and in fact, though my very heart sings for him, I find I am at a crossroads, for he is a hindrance to my plan to save my kingdom!" Varia relaxed a bit as she watched The Grey fixate his gaze on the sleeping Smote. "But perhaps you can help me after all," Varia said, "and help dear Smote."

"Smote!" the Grey said. "Is that the name you have given him?" Grey looked miserable. "His name was to be Fletheroth y Gras, Fletheroth the Green, but I cannot rename a named dragon either. Woe is me!"

Varia could see The Grey was full of emotion, and she hesitated to say more, for their conversation had only proved to upset him thus far.

"I need you," Varia said, speaking to him as she would one of the palace faechildren. "You know dragons, you can communicate with them, can you not? I need you to look after him, keep him hidden and out of trouble. For Evara the Blue would be most grateful to you, as will I, if you could do this thing for the faepeople of my kingdom."

For the first time The Grey looked Varia up and down. "You are no . . ." his addled mind fished for the word, "Durndeng. You must be an AirWalker! You are enemy of my tribe that I once was a part of long ago. Why should I help you?"

Varia's mind raced as she tried to come up with an answer. The Grey hovered menacingly above her, and looked as though he might strike her. Smote lifted his big head and his eyes narrowed in a hateful way, but the Grey raised his hand and muttered some strange incantation, and the dragon crumpled back to the ground. Varia screeched.

"What did you do to him?" she asked, trying to go to the fallen one, but Grey grabbed her and held her back. She thrashed, trying to free herself, but Grey was wiry and strong, probably from fighting all the horrible beasts in the oily dragon realm.

"He is not harmed!" Grey said, finally letting Varia go when she calmed herself some and quit struggling. Once free, she flew some distance away, wanting to go to Smote's aid, but afraid of what Grey might do to him with his secret spells if the dragon awoke again.

"I am wife of Loben of Birkendore, formerly of the Dunter-Gruns, and he is a Durndeng warrior," Varia said in an attempt to convince Grey to help her. "And we are both trying to prevent a war of our kind. What I say to you is true, and Smote needs watching. Won't you help save your former tribesclan, as that is my only intent!"

Grey hesitated, sitting and resting his dust-colored wings on a nearby hosta leaf. He looked at the sleeping hatchling.

"My allegiance is to his mother, so for that reason alone, I shall help you," Grey said. "I care not for the troubles of the fae, for I was abandoned by my own kinfolk, and tricked by the elder of my clan and sent into exile, and there I found the portal to Drakotanith, where I have remained forgotten and alone for cytons beyond my reckoning, never aging, not remembering who I was, only focused on the day-to-day life of dragons." Grey had a wistful gleam in his eye. "So used to that wretched place am I that I cannot stand the beauty here; the sun is an abomination that hurts my eyes and skin; the food is sweetened to nearly kill me with its sugary substance; the soft beds of fragrant leaves spoil my hide, now used to hard stone and spiky, poison-tipped plant life." Grey spat his words. "This world is too perfect. I would long to go back and fight daily for my life in my defense of Evara, who must be frantic with worry about me, and her missing beloved hatchling."

Varia felt a pang of guilt that Smote had been ripped from his mother before they met, and her heart went out to the mourning mother dragon, Evara the Blue. But a sense of urgency told her not to remain any longer.

"I must fly out. Stay with Smote and use your charms and tricks to keep him subdued, for he will wish to find me if he awakens," she said, feeling strange about giving orders to a true dragon tamer.

"I know what to do, and it is not because your words tell me so," Grey replied. He floated over to the sleeping Smote, and he stood before him, his scrappy handmade weapon drawn. Varia nodded to him and was about to fly off when a pair of brown arms grabbed her.

She recognized the embrace immediately; it was Loben, and in the distance, Varia could hear Zedah's call to them. Grey hovered menacingly, showing his pointed wooden weapon to Loben, who held his bare hands out, offering peace.

"I mean no harm," he said in the fae way, and Grey relaxed some. "We must go now," Loben said, assessing the situation, somehow understanding the Grey was watching over Smote. "Thank you for helping us." To Varia he nodded. "Let's go. We must free your father, the true king of Ashenthorne!"

Varia gave a final glance back to the resting Smote, hoping she could trust the grey faery. Grey was silent as Varia and Loben sped off toward Erendome.

They flew fast and it wasn't long before Varia saw the edges of her homeland. There was the cool, still pond she and Irea visited on hot summer days, the meadow her mother took her to as a child to play with the rabbits, the forest where she and Ezia and Alshea had learned to collect honey and where Ezia had learned to tame bees. Her heart welled with the emotion of return when she saw, and then could smell, the peppertree grove, her favorite spot, her beloved trees. Varia was home.

But now she could sense danger, and fear. Things were not as they once were in Ashenthorne. Varia flew to a familiar peppertree and asked its Deva to offer her and Loben secret shelter. The tree, though alarmed, agreed, and the two hid in a hollow that she sometimes napped in if it wasn't occupied by a squirrel or other creature. Loben flitted beside her, his arms embracing her waist.

"I wish that we did not have to go closer to Erendome, for I fear you will be caught," Loben said.

"I must free my father! I wish I knew what became of Rumendah, for I have barely had time to worry about him, but he freed Smote with this magicks and I do not know if he escaped! Do you suppose he made it out?"

"I would place a wager on my very life that he did," Loben said, "for he is full of cunning and guile. Did he ask you to meet him here?"

"No," Varia said, a frown creasing her brow. "He gave me no direction at all, except to keep going toward Erendome, which now I have done. Do you suppose he means to find us here?"

A buzz of wings filled the air, and Loben and Varia ducked further into the dark tree hole. A small army of Wilhvyre flew past, Varia saw as she spied out the hollow. She gasped; these were mere faeboys, barely a cyton old, not yet ready for battle but dressed like Wilhvyre in the formal blue and gold uniform of the Alawe warriors. There were less than twenty of them, and Alshea recognized some of them as children of her woodland friends. Her heart lagged at the sight of it.

"Those are no soldiers!" she told Loben when they had passed. "They are just faechildren. What is Alshea thinking?"

"She is thinking that she will win this war and annihilate my kinfolk, whatever the cost to yours," Loben said grimly. "Let's go, I know the back way to the prison cells, from having rescued you from there."

"I will follow you," Varia said, her heart racing as they flew up to the top of the tree canopy.

Once in the bright sun, Varia motioned for Loben to imitate her. "We shall tree-walk, or airwalk, it is why we are called such by other fae," Varia said. "Follow my example." She grabbed a bit of tree branch and pulled down hard, and let go; as the branch swung upward, she grabbed it again and allowed the tree to fling her up into the sky, where she tucked in her wings, and as she began falling back to the earth she grabbed another branch until it was stretched, and then she let go, and grabbed it once more and was flung high again, and thus silently campaigned the distance over several trees at once, more silently and less strenuously than flying. Loben imitated her, and they made good time and quickly arrived at the outskirts of Erendome, where a sea of warriors wearing blue and gold awaited final instructions from their new queen.

Varia and Loben hid in the treetops and watched as the wounded Talow emerged from the front platform of Erendome castle.

"We have an army already making those Earthworms who have taken over Birkendore miserable and sorry they have come near our borders of Ashenthorne!" Talow shouted, and a rousing cry was raised by the warriors as they lifted spears and fists in the air. "And now it is our turn, to go to Birkendore and reclaim the land that is and has always been rightfully ours, to regain control of all of Ashenthorne, and to rid our lands of the faepeople who have come to invade our kingdom! Fly, Wilhvyre, and do not stop until we reach the enemy, and do not rest until none are left living!"

A cheer went up as the makeshift army fell into place, gathering into straight lines and looking menacing as they left Erendome castle and flew in V formation toward Birkendore. Talow was not yet capable of joining them due to his injuries and he stayed, shouting orders to the guards at the castle door.

"Kill any EarthSeeker you see on sight, do not ask questions or let them talk to you! For we have learned that they have powers that differ from ours, and they can erase your very memory and make you forget why you are standing here to guard your Queen Alshea of Erendome, Land of Ashenthorne."

The guards, about a dozen, bowed to Talow before he re-entered Erendome. Loben stayed back and nestled further into the tree canopy where he hid.

"Perhaps you should leave," Varia whispered. "For your very life is in danger here. I can go quietly by myself to the prisons, and see if I can free my family. I do not think they would kill me if I were to be captured, but I fear they will kill you."

"No," Loben said. "We may need both of our sets of skills. I will continue on with you. Let's go."

They slipped back up through the tree branches and made their way in a stealthy manner to the underground prison cells of Erendome, where lucky for them, the remaining guards were not on sentry, as all Wilhvyre eyes were focused to the east, where the soldiers knew the enemy EarthSeekers would soon arrive from Birkendore.

It was Loben who led the way, quickly finding the hollowed rock that led to the underground prison cells. He pushed it aside and they flew into the closed dark. Varia reached into the silver bag Rumendah had given her and found the hestus. Using his own trick, she felt for a loose root sticking out of the earthen wall and silently asked the whitebeam tree to let her have it. She pulled gently and the root broke free, and Varia placed the hestus powder on the end of it and blew on it, activating its powers, and held the lit stick aloft as she flitted behind Loben, worried that they were being followed.

"I don't trust this!" she whispered when they stopped in a deep recess in the stone walls, gaining their bearings. "I cannot believe my sister will not have guarded this route to the prison."

"This is not the route to the prison, at least not one that anyone knows about except Rumendah, the king, me, and now you. This is the king's own passageway to escape in case of war. Aptly we shall use it as such now, if we are able to free him from the cell, for I fear that guards will certainly be on duty there."

Varia's heart fell. "I must fight my own kin, then?" she said in a quiet voice. Her insides wrenched at the thought.

"You have lost your weapon," Loben said, looking down in the sparking flame at her empty belt loop where her dagger had been. "Here." Loben opened the leaf-stitched satchel he wore on his back under his wings, and pulled out a small lance. Varia took it, and held it up to see it in the hestus-lit tunnel, dappling the channel with an eerie light.

"In just moons past, if anyone had told me I would be about to fight my own kin with a Vorku blade, I would have thought them mad," she whispered, wondering if she had what it would take to push the weapon into the pale blue luminescent skin of someone she cared for to free her father. She hoped it wouldn't come to that as Loben rested his hand on her shoulder.

"We both have been pushed beyond our comfort Varia, I in my clan, and you in yours. But we must get your father back to my kingdom to negotiate a treaty, so that we can all live together in Ashenthorne and Birkendore, as one peaceful kingdom."

Tears threatened, a luxury Varia had not allowed herself of late, but Varia knew she too was a warrior now, and she pulled herself upright.

"Let's go," she said in an even voice. Loben nodded in the weak light and flew on until they reached the end of the burrow to find a small wooden door lit from behind, beyond which would lay the main hallway of the castle's prison cells. Loben carefully pushed it open. Varia followed, and was surprised to find they were standing in a large store room. Loben walked on tiptoe to the cave-like entrance of the warehouse. Varia recognized ahead the passageway that led to the main prison cells, just down the corridor from the secret cell where she had been placed just half a moon before. As they listened silently in the darkness, Varia realized Loben was right; they were not alone.

Chapter Sixteen

As Varia and Loben were about to enter into a confrontation with the guards at Erendome castle, far to the east another mêlée was beginning, for Ezia and his Wilhvyre army surrounded the castle doors at Birkendore, rushing the palace Thundendell. The clash of blade upon blade, the whir of a thousand wings, the screams of the fallen tore through the peaceful wooded glen as the fae struggled in combat, each one willing to lay down his life for his own tribe. The very trees shook in fear at the loss of each immortal faery, for the trees could feel each lethal stroke as if an axe were permeating bark and branch. Animals from the smallest beetle to the timid deer fled. Rocks hunkered down, grass bent away, flowers shied. Such a battle had never been fought between the shadow of two realms, and it was an experience for the natural world no living being had ever expected, nor would ever forget.

Casualties were few, however, as King Struben had already led most of his fae folk away from the castle, and the last guards gave a stand and then flew away, quickly losing themselves in the familiar woods around them, as the king had instructed them to do. Ezia stood at the castle door, pounding to be let in.

"Cowards!" he cried, smacking the wood with his Wilhvyre weapon, a sharp lance used for spearing the enemy. Some sort of faery magick had been used to protect the door, Ezia noticed, as he could see that while the door shook, there was a slight space between his spear and the door that emanated with a violet vibrating light each time he made a blow. Angrily, he threw down his spear, and stood on the leaf-littered ground.

"They think they are clever, hiding and using magick protections from the ancients to keep themselves safe! We will find a way in . . ." Ezia eyed the tree standing tall above him, and he flew up to its great root that bent away from the trunk and rambled over the ground. He laid his hands forcefully on the shaft, and without bothering to ask its Deva for permission, he read the tree. Ezia closed his eyes, and lifted his face, shining with exertion, toward the treetops. He pulled his hand away and a thin eel-like smile crossed his lips.

"Ah," he said, and only the closest fae to him heard. "No tree, no castle."

Varia flew up to the top of the storage tunnel and peeked around the corner. There were seven guards. Three were on the move, restlessly pacing as they flew from one end of the prison lobby to the other. Four were in a far corner where they had opened a box of stores. They were drinking mead, she noted, for she could smell the fermented honey wine as it permeated the air. The four were obviously drunk, as none flew, and all were lounging on top of bags of grain and nuts, laughing as they passed the mead around in its large flagon.

Varia held up seven fingers to Loben, who nodded. She showed him with her hands where they were in relation to the cell door. Loben nodded again, and then shrugged. Varia's face burned. They had no plan other than freeing her father. *Outnumbered* . . . Varia for a moment wished that Smote were there, as he would certainly cause a distraction. Something told her not to wish it, because she guessed that he could sense her thoughts. Varia closed her eyes and envisioned him sleeping peacefully on the beach, with Grey standing guard, and hoped that was enough of a vision to make it so.

On a rash whim Varia flitted out to the main corridor and back into the keep again. She heard shouts and at least two sets of wings coming her way, and she darted toward the back of the cave-like room toward the exit as Loben pressed himself high up against the rock ceiling. The two guards flew right under Loben, and kept after Varia.

"What's happening there?" called the third, non-drunk guard. Neither of the pursuers answered, because just as the two sentries grabbed Varia, Loben hovered above and laid his hands on their heads, and erased their memories. As they stood before Varia, befuddled, they gasped and released her when they saw they held one of the princesses of Erendome. Varia gently took their hands and opened the tunnel door and led them down the cavern's path until they could see light out the other end. She gave them a bit of a push and they wandered, as if drunk themselves, toward the sunny meadow surrounding the whitebeam tree that housed the castle.

Varia flew back to join Loben.

"Hullo?" the third Wilhvyre guard called out, searching for his cohorts. "What is happening in there?" The soldier, who Varia recognized as Ledum from her inquisition, poked his head around the corner. "EarthSeeker!" Ledum shouted, seeing Loben, and he ran at Loben with his lance-like blade held ready to pierce his hide. Varia could hear the drunken ones laughing at Ledum near the prison cells, and she was relieved they thought their comrade was fooling them. Varia flitted up against the ceiling and pointed at Loben as if in fear for her life, and Ledum nodded and took off after him.

Loben flew down the passway with the Wilhvyre just on his wings, and Varia took the moment to slip into the main hallway of the jail. The drunk ones were still laughing, until one spotted her.

"It's Princess Varia!" he cried, and he swooped into the air ungracefully, coming after her. Varia easily dodged him by flitting aside, as it is well known in faery lore that it is unsafe to fly while drunk. The loutish warrior crashed into the wall behind her. Varia spotted the cell key, which was wooden and shaped like a round spiral cylinder. It rested on a small shelf near the prison door. With as much speed as she could gather in the tight quarters, Varia flew down and grabbed the heavy object. She sped off around the corner back into the passageway, the three remaining faeries, two she recognized as Ullo and Baylo, flying drunkenly after her.

Varia used her best trick and flew directly to the ceiling and deliquesced, melding herself into the stone. She clutched the key tightly to her chest and closed her eyes, hoping she had disappeared before the warriors followed her. Ullo and Baylo crept into the room and looked around

144

before they opened the cellar door leading to the tunnel and continued their search. Varia opened her eyes, and if the remaining Wilhvyre warrior had looked up, he would have seen two eyes peering at him from the stone walls, but he was poking his lance into dark corners on the ground, still looking for Varia. For a moment, Varia thought she was alone with the faeman, but she spotted a small stone in the corner of the room, a stone that had not been there before. It was Loben. She held her breath and waited.

Ezia lined up his Wilhvyre army in a clearing near the Birkendore oak that housed the castle Thundendell.

"In times of war, we must do desperate things," Ezia shouted as the faemen hovered at attention. "And in this case, our very home, our palace at Erendome, is at risk! I would ask you that you would do this thing, and while many of you may find it to be . . . an abomination . . . it is the only way our lands will be clearly ours again, free of the earthworm faeries that have polluted our home with their presence!"

The Wilhvyre soldiers looked at one another with uncertain expressions.

"We must kill the tree," Ezia said, and a hush except for the thousand wings beating stilled the land. To kill a tree was a heinous crime, for it was the fae themselves who could commune with the trees, and understood their needs, their stories, their song of leaves in the wind and their roots in the soil that remembered ancient times. Not one faery moved or spoke.

Ezia went on. "If we take this one life, this simple tree's life, then the fae will lose the home they have been so actively building, and their very reason to stay here will dissolve! It is the only way to destroy this enemy, these fae who have locked their front door with magick and who hide from us instead of facing us and fighting to claim their land! This is a war we cannot afford to lose, for if we allow this one tribe to move into our territory, we have opened the door for all other undesirables to inhabit our lands."

Still not one faery reacted, and Ezia proceeded as if they were in agreement. "Take your weapons and begin as a team to cut the treetop from its trunk. Slay the tree!"

Reluctantly the fae soldiers flew in formation to the old oak and surrounded it, looking up into its broad canopy to assess the giant, small were they compared to its great height and girth. One soldier known as Fawkes hovered before the pack, his sharp blade drawn. With a great wrenching heave, he laid his weapon into the hide of the ancient oak. The oak screamed in pain and astonishment, its Devic spirit hid, and all was lost as the Wilhvyre called their battle cry and began to hew the tree in earnest.

Loben unfolded his gold and black veined wings and stood up behind the Wilhvyre soldier. He reached his hand toward the back of his head, but something, perhaps the crinkle of his stiff silver Vorku uniform, gave him away. The Wilhvyre turned quickly and fought Loben. Varia sent a message to Loben's Deva to keep him safe, and sped down the tunnel, key in hand, to release her father.

Hands shaking, she fitted the spiral key in the lock, and tried to swivel it into position. The key fit but the door would not open. She tried again, to no avail. Was there another part of the puzzle, an incantation, a secret word? Frustrated and worried at the clashing sound of her husband's fight in the next room, Varia tried to think. She closed her eyes and connected with the Devic energy of the lock, of the curved key. *Intent,* she heard the word whispered in her mind. Varia had heard of such things, that certain magicks required the right intent to use them. Varia took a deep breath and sent the words: *I mean no harm* to the lock, to the key, to the prison cell itself. She sent a mental picture of freeing her father and Irea, of their happy reunion, of the good it would do for the kingdom and for the very race of the Alawe. She fixed the lock and key together and pushed. The door opened.

Though many Wilhvyre worked at chipping away at the tree's trunk, their progress was slow, as their weapons were made more for piercing the enemy than slashing down trees, as such an instrument did not exist in the fae world. Still

Ezia hovered above them, shouting commands to continue the deed as the fae flew in a dozen at a time, chipping away until the crisp bark sprayed into bits on the ground, creating a sawdust pile near the door of the grand castle Thundendell. The tree pulled its energy inward, becoming slow and quiet like stone, accepting defeat at the heinous act. The warriors' faces were grave as they hacked and splintered the rough skin, one small piece at a time. The tree, and Thundendell palace with it, would surely fall by nighttime.

Varia creaked open the door and peered into the darkness. She could make out figures, but was uncertain who lingered there. "Come!" she whispered into the pitch, and saw her father King Dreya try his wings and near the cellar door. His usually luminescent pale blue skin was dry and tight, and he looked older, and Varia could read shame on his face, but he held his head high as they embraced.

"Father!" Varia cried out louder than she meant to. "I am so glad you are safe!"

"I am not safe here, in my own castle," King Dreya said. "A sad but true fate. Ah, come now, dear one. Here is your cousin . . . Irea."

Irea came forth from the dim prison, her usually perfect dark hair tangled. She smoothed it as she emerged from the jail. She too looked different, Varia noted. Wiser, somehow. Calm and composed. Like a queen herself. Varia flew up to greet her and held her close, and Irea returned the hug with fondness.

"I apologize, Varia . . ." Irea began, but Varia shook her head.

"No time, we must flee! Even now Loben holds the last guard at bay."

A groan came from the corner; the first guard who had crashed into the wall was coming to. He opened his eyes and saw his prisoners escaping, but then his eyes rolled up into his head and he lost consciousness once again.

The fighting noise of Loben and the last guard had ceased, and Varia's heart bumped with fear about the silence. She was about to lead the way when she noticed inside the dark prison cell a sitting figure leaning against the wall. She flew into the chamber to tap the sleeping Rumendah on the shoulder to wake him.

"Come, Rumendah!" she said, relieved he was not harmed in the blast to free Smote. When she reached her hand out and touched his bony shoulder, a mist rose up from his body and he disintegrated. Varia hovered backwards to get away from the disappearing wise elder. "Rumendah!" she called out, alarmed.

"Pay it no heed, it is but a trick! The old faery himself has not been here in a half moon," King Dreya said. Varia left the jail behind and joined Irea and her father in the vestibule. Just then from around the corner came Loben, who bowed upon seeing the king of all the Alawe.

"Your majesty," said Loben, resting on one knee. Dreya brightened at the sight of Loben.

"My son, it is good to meet you at last," the king said. He reached for Loben's arm and pulled him to his feet. "You have treated my daughter well and have come to my aid in my darkest time, and for that I thank you. You do not need to lower yourself in my presence, for you are family to me now."

"I am pleased to see you safe," Loben said. "We haven't much time, we must get you out of this prison and away from Erendome, for your own kin have turned their allegiance to your daughter, Princess Alshea, the one who now calls herself Queen Alshea."

"So I have heard," Dreya said, his eyes conveying his sadness. "Let us fly!"

The passageway was cleared thanks to Loben's fighting ability; the last guard was tied and mouth-bound in the storeroom, Varia noted as they flew above him. Upon seeing the king, the faery looked up with wide eyes. Through the narrow escape tunnel they flew, barreling out the other side at their top speed. Varia, Loben, Irea, and King Dreya aimed toward the human house, the last place that Ezia or Talow's forces would think to look for them now. It was with a deep sense of gratitude and satisfaction that Varia followed her father, who led the way as the rest of their small group followed.

Though the human dwelling was far, it did not take them long before they neared it. King Dreya stopped flying as they approached the outlying tree line and he hovered, holding up his hand.

"Listen," he said. For in the distance over the field they could see the dwelling they sought, but there was a loud crashing noise, and the yelling of men.

"Humans!" Varia said, seeing tall forms working in the fields there. Though she had never seen a human before, something else caught her attention more: A stack of murdered trees, stripped of their foliage and branches, took up a great portion of the area. Human men were stripping the bark from the dead trunks. Varia blinked back tears and looked away.

"We have been so concerned about the problems of the fae that we have not been on guard," Loben said through gritted teeth. "For it appears humans are coming to inhabit the very center of Ashenthorne!"

"This cannot happen!" King Dreya bellowed, and Varia started. She had not seen her father so upset before. "We cannot allow these humans to return here!"

"Look!" Irea spoke for the first time, her eyes narrowed as she assessed the strange beings and their inflicted devastation from afar. A clunky loud device on round legs rolled across the newly dug path that led to the previously abandoned home.

"That is called a motorcar," Loben said in a quiet voice. "They are a machine of man. They use them to transport themselves and their belongings from place to place. They are dangerous devices. In our former home in the Urunhem Downs, we lost one of our own who was struck by one while flying across an open path."

"What is happening, Father?" Varia asked as the motorcar rumbled down the new access trail to the house.

"It appears the humans are moving back into their forgotten home," King Dreya said. "As if we could afford a new menace!" He glanced at Loben. "No offense, lad. It is just that things have been peaceful in my kingdom for a long time, and now we are affronted by new forces at every turn!"

Loben nodded but said nothing. The group of faeries flew to a nearby tree and rested on a branch. Loben broke out stores of nectar and seed he had gathered in the jail warehouse for them to feast on while they decided what to do next.

"I have some experience with humans," Loben said as he cracked open and ate a sunflower seed. "They are different than you might expect. Some are decent, but they are greedy for power, and for belongings. In our dealings with them, we have lost much."

"You have met a human?" Irea asked, her coal eyes wide.

Loben looked at her, and his gaze held her for a moment before he continued talking. "No," he said. "I have not personally met one, but part of our clan had involvement with some human children, and it ended badly. We had to leave our beloved palace. They stole our —essence. It is difficult to describe, but they had a device that could create our image on parchment, and they told others of our existence." Loben looked shaken as he recalled the tale. "We had lived in the Urunhem Downs for many many cytons, and there were always a few humans around, but mostly the fae kept to themselves. A few of our clan . . ." Loben's eyes darkened, "befriended the young ones and played with them, as if they were mere pets. The child-humans took something called a photograph, a very image of us that they could carry around on a flat sheet, like a leaf scroll, and show to other humans. Soon word got out there were faeries in the Urunhem Downs, Cottingsley was the human name for it, and we were hunted and forced to leave our home, our castle that we had lived in for generations. That is how we came to live here, to build Thundendell in the mushroom flats in Birkendore."

Varia's heart grew heavy at Loben's tale. She now knew what it was like to be forced from her home, and her determination to save Erendome and Birkendore grew strong within her.

"We must get rid of the humans! But, we will need an army, an army that we do not have separately, but that we have together!"

"What do you propose, Princess?" King Dreya asked his daughter. "You have seen that we have no control of our own army, let alone the army of the enemy fae tribe! How do you expect to confront a group of fae warriors and ask them to come together to eliminate a larger threat?"

Varia hung her head, not having an answer. Irea cleared her throat.

"Perhaps it is time we found Loben's King Struben," she said. "And the Queen Hoondeen. For when they realize that we can truly be of one mind . . ." Irea gave King Dreya a meaningful look.

"Yes!" Varia said. "That was our first plan, until we heard of the ambush. If Struben sees that we can work together for a common good! Once they hear about the killing of the trees that the humans have committed, they will rally with us! No faery, regardless of tribe, would allow such a thing to happen on our land."

Loben shot straight up into the air, and made a call Varia recognized. "I hear Zedah!" he called down to Varia as he hovered above the tree line, answering the hummingbird. He returned to the group with Zedah following him; so quick was she that none had seen her approach. Zedah seemed shy around the king and Irea, and stayed behind Loben as he cupped her feathered breast with his hands. His expression grew grim.

"There is bad news in Birkendore. Thundendell is under siege!' he said. "And Ezia is leading the forces. The battle has begun!"

King Dreya flew upright. "No!" he said.

Varia's eyes misted. "Are you sure, Zedah? It is my brother who is attacking?"

"Zedah is certain of it, for she was sent here with this message by King Struben himself. Come, we must go and help them!"

Together the fae launched themselves into the sky and followed Zedah, for only the hummingbird knew the secret whereabouts of the Durndeng king.

As the four neared Birkendore, Varia could smell the mushrooms growing on the river bank and she breathed in the earthy scent. Yet something all-new permeated the air; a stillness she had never felt before. She slowed and then stopped in midair to hover noiselessly and take in the sensation.

"Father!" she called ahead where the king was continuing to follow Zedah. "Wait!"

King Dreya and Loben halted in mid-flight and Irea stopped as she caught up to them, breathless.

"What is it, Daughter?" Dreya asked. Varia held out her arms, trying to sense the energy.

"The trees . . . their Devas are hiding," Varia said. "Listen." With all of her being, Varia sensed the forest around her, and could feel the despair. Loben did not have the same way of reading the air, but he too could feel a difference.

"It is as if the wood feels dead," he said. "Is it because of the humans killing the trees in the meadows?"

"No," said King Dreya in a deep, gruff voice. "That is not what I sense. I sense something far worse, a crime against Nature herself."

"It is Ezia," said Irea suddenly, who tended to read things more quickly than Varia ever could. "He has attacked with an intent to kill the tree at Birkendore!'

"He wouldn't!" Varia said, aghast. "Even with his reckless ways, he was raised an Alawe! He would never harm a living thing!"

"We are at war now," said Dreya. "During times of war, all rules change. For I sense it too, Irea. An army of my kingdom is doing grievous harm to the Birkendore oak. We must quickly find King Struben and stop this madness!"

"Alshea would not stand for this," Irea said quietly. "For even though she wishes to save Erendome from the EarthSeekers, she would never allow Ezia to murder a living being! I fear he has gone rogue, now even disobeying Alshea's orders. Ezia must be stopped!"

King Dreya looked at Irea, and reached over and brushed back her black hair. "It may be time to implement the plan we discussed. Let us fly straight and fast to the hiding place of King Struben!"

The four fae flew off, and Zedah, who had rested in wait on a slender nearby branch, led the way once more.

Soon the faeries flew into a deep wood. "I've not been to this place before," said King Dreya. "We have long avoided this wood, for this is one of the ancient forests of the

Wildlands, and may be the type of forest where the portals to other realms are often thin and dangerous."

"I know the wood that you speak of," Loben said. "It is the Llangdwig forest to the north, where we journeyed through the portal. This wood is called Rhysgollen by our kinfolk, and while old, it is a friendlier place than the other."

"That at least gives me some cheer," said the king, with a cautious look around.

"Are you sure our king is here, Zedah?" Loben asked the bird, who also had slowed and was hovering, looking uncertain.

The hummingbird continued to fly in answer, and the group wove through the elderly oak grove covered in hanging mosses and vines. Under a tall stretching tree, Varia spotted a large boulder at the base that seemed out of place, and Zedah flew right to it.

Within a moment Irea, King Dreya, and Varia were caught by Birkendore guards clad in the same silver and black uniform as Loben.

"Unhand the king of the Alawe!" Loben said fiercely. The guards, whom Varia recognized as Gurhook and Druag, though she knew not the third guard, released them. Gurhook glared at Irea and Varia.

"It's the prisoners we lost!" he said, an astonished expression on his face.

"They are emissaries of their tribe," said Loben. "Lead us to King Struben, for he is expecting us!"

Gurhook glowered but did as he was told. He flew to the heavy stone and tapped on it. The door sprung away from the tree roots and opened easily, an action Varia couldn't fathom as she watched the heavy boulder swing toward them. Inside was a lit passageway, smelling heavily of deep earth. It seemed to be a temporary shelter for the Durndeng in times of crisis. And, Varia noted from the still-crumbling soil, hastily built. Soon they entered a large hallway on foot. Many tapestries of fine cloth had been placed against the bare dirt walls there, and the atmosphere was warm and regal, lighted with resin candles. King Struben was seated on a makeshift throne carved of a block of wood. He nodded to King Dreya, who bowed his head in reverence. Next to King Struben was his wife, Queen Hoondeen. The Queen, dark haired and exquisite, rose up when she saw King Dreya, her eyes searching his, a misty faraway look taking her. When she saw Irea, the queen covered her hand to her mouth.

"Is this . . . the one?" Queen Hoondeen asked, in a shaking voice.

"It is," said King Dreya. Irea bowed to the queen of the Durndeng.

"My daughter," said Queen Hoondeen, reaching out for Irea. Irea nodded and fell into the queen's arms, and both of the faewomen cried. They stood in an embrace that spanned the lost cytons between them, the missing words, the never-touched upon feelings.

"Daughter!" Varia whispered to Loben. "My father and Queen Hoondeen had a child?"

"It would appear so," said Loben in an even quieter voice.

"That would make Irea . . . my sister!" Varia said.

"It would appear so!" repeated Loben. The two stared at one another in disbelief. "This must be the story Rumendah was trying to tell us before he was interrupted, when we were in the caves," Loben said to Varia in a whisper, as all within earshot looked away to give the reunited pair a moment of privacy.

"I have already loved Irea as a sister and I welcome this news! Though now that you mention him, I am very worried about Rumendah," Varia said. "I hope that we will discover he is safe soon, he should have turned up by now."

King Dreya was still looking at the earthen floor to give the newly reunited mother and daughter a moment between them, but King Struben cleared his throat.

"There is time for catching up later," said King Struben, taking the surprise of the reunion in stride, in royal fashion. "But now, we must stop the AirWalker warriors that are destroying our tree at Birkendore even as we speak!"

"How can we stop an army," asked King Dreya, "without losing one?"

Varia's mind raced. What could stop the faemen from cutting down the ancient oak at Birkendore? If the Vorku were unleashed on the Wilhvyre, many would perish. A thought occurred to her.

"Father, I must go. Please trust me, I have an idea," Varia said to the king.

"What is it child? We cannot behave rashly, many lives are at stake!"

"There is one piece of the puzzle that you do not yet know. I know what to do!" Varia insisted.

"My army is at the ready, King Dreya, though I know that our faepeople do not want to a battle. But I must send them now, to save our home. I cannot hesitate," King Struben said.

Even as he spoke, the warriors of the Durndeng came out from another tunnel, silver clad and armed. As they marched past the throne, in groups of two they flew out another tunnel that led to the outside world.

"They are already called to battle," said Struben. "I fear whatever plan you have, you are too late."

"It is my wisdom they follow," said a raspy voice behind Varia. She turned to face Rumendah. He was injured; his face and neck were red and burned from the cave blast, but he was alive. Varia fluttered to him and hugged him.

"I have been so worried about you!" she said.

"Worry not," said Rumendah. "1 will accompany you, Princess Varia, as I think I know your plan. Loben, come with us." Nodding toward King Dreya, Rumendah took flight. Varia and Loben had no choice but to follow.

Chapter Seventeen

As they exited the hiding place of King Struben, the sky above them filled with Durndeng warriors hovering in formation, waiting for all of their troops. It felt strange to be the enemy in their camp, Varia thought, but being with Loben comforted her. They acknowledged him as he approached.

"Hesitate as long as you can," Loben said to the troops. "We will try to get the Wilhvyre army to leave Birkendore and return to Ashenthorne!"

"You cannot reason with them," said the leader of the Vorku, the brave warrior named Wurdu whose appearance was marred by a scar across his cheeks and nose. "They seem to have taken leave of their senses."

"It is true," agreed Doon, who flew up to join the two. "Cousin," he said to Loben, "we have discovered that the Alawe king's children have taken over their own castle. They are renegades."

"They are my wife's kin," Loben said. "And we do not wish to harm them. Hold back as long as you can, and we will try to remove them from our realm."

"Every stroke of their weapons against the oak weakens the tree!" Wurdu said. "We cannot wait, I am sorry Loben. We are flying out the moment all of our Vorku are aligned for battle."

Loben, exasperated, flew away and Rumendah and Varia followed. "We are late! We cannot implement any plan, there is no time!" he said as he hovered above the Vorku army, watching them line up under Doon's firm leadership.

"There is one thing that could work," Varia said, and Rumendah nodded. Varia flew to a nearby limb and sat on the rough bark, the others joining her there. She closed her eyes and concentrated.

"What are you doing?" Loben asked.

156

"I am calling forth Smote," Varia said. "He is in tune with me, as I am the one he imprinted on. He will heed my call and come to me."

"How will he escape the grey faery, even if he does try to come?" asked Loben. "For that one seems as if he will not allow the dragon to leave his side, and that he would stop Smote should he try."

Varia knew she hadn't thought her plan through thoroughly, but she had to do something. She pictured Smote, and saw him in her mind's eye lift his sleepy head from the beach. She saw him then stretch out his wings, first one, then the other, and saw the grey faery scold him and try to hold him back. But Grey's tricks didn't work, and within moments Smote was in the air, and Varia could feel his yearning to be with her. She too felt the strange connection she had to the beast, and without warning she flew quickly toward the north where she had last seen him. He was coming, she knew, and she rushed to greet him halfway.

Loben stared after his wife as she flew off in such an unexpected hurry.

"You and I have other ways to slow the process of the annihilation of that oak," Rumendah said. He flew toward Thundendell, Loben following close behind. They hid in a tree as they arrived at the eerie scene where Ezia's men took turns hacking away. A large chunk was missing out of the tree. Rumendah reached out his hand and closed his eyes, sensing the devastation.

"This tree is still alive, but barely. It is not far from losing its balance and falling. If they don't stop now, the castle will be ruined and the tree will perish. We must stop them quickly!"

"We know not if Varia's plan will work," said Loben. "What else can we do?"

"We will use you," said Rumendah. "As bait."

Varia flew toward the pine forest of Hammershins, a place she had visited as a child for family outings when her mother was alive. As she approached the wood's edge, the sight before her filled her with pride. For there, zooming out of the forest like a blue tidal wave, was Smote. He had grown considerably since Varia had seen him a mere day ago, and to her, it felt as if it had been a cyton. She wondered at that; she had barely had a free moment to think of him in her quest to free her father, but upon seeing his majestic blue head as he careened toward her, his golden wings catching the filtered sun, she felt as if she could never leave him, not even for a moment, again. *Dragonspell,* she reminded herself. Smote slowed as he approached Varia, hovering in midair as she kissed his delicate nose.

"Dear Smote, how I have missed you!" she cried as she climbed up onto his neck and assumed her riding position there, glad she wore her thick tunic and leggings and not her usual flower petal skirts she dressed in at Erendome court. "I need your help, to save a tree! For a crazy wind has taken over my brother, and he harms it as we speak. Fly!" she commanded the dragon, but without warning Smote's body heaved in an undulating way, and he crashed to the ground. Varia hung on, falling with him.

Loben eyed Rumendah suspiciously. "Truly, you want me to fly out there? You do realize your kind is faster than I am?"

"I do," said Rumendah. "Under normal circumstances. But I offer you this . . . advantage, something to aid your speed and get you away from the Alawe warriors quickly." Rumendah made a chortling noise deep in his throat, and Loben knew he had called upon the service of a bird. Apprehensive, Loben looked into the sky and saw a large raven soar toward them.

"This is Krahbane," said Rumendah. "An old friend of mine, one I have known since he was a mere nestling."

Loben reached his hand out to pat Krahbane on the neck. The bird's black eyes followed his movement; the corvid was at least double the size of Loben in height, nearly two feet long, but much wider and sturdier, with a huge wingspan. Loben felt the bird's energy and mentally asked if he could climb onto his back. The animal bent his legs to lower himself, and Loben hopped on. Krahbane adjusted himself to the new weight of his passenger and vaulted to a nearby branch. Loben squeezed his knees tighter to hold on as the bird flew to a further limb. They were balanced and ready for flight.

"Go, lure the Wilhvyre far from the Birkendore oak! Krahbane will take you fast away, and your presence will be enough of a distraction to buy Varia some much-needed time."

"We are off, then," Loben said to Rumendah. A heavy space fell between them, but no words could fill it. Krahbane lifted himself and Loben into the air on their way to save the wounded tree.

Varia would have been crushed by the weight of the careening dragon if she had not let go and soared up into the sky to escape just as Smote was about to hit earth. Her cries did not wake him nor stop his fall; Varia knew the grey faery must be lurking about and she searched for his slender form from her hiding spot in a leafy tree. He approached, flying to the collapsed Smote and laying his hands on him, deepening his slumber.

"How dare you!" Varia scolded as she swooped down to where The Grey hovered over the dragon. "I am about to take Smote to war, to help me save a tree from destruction and frighten warriors away from the new home of the Durndeng!"

"Help them!" The Grey faery said. "I have heard how the AirWalkers would help my tribe, by cutting down their castle's tree!"

"Your tribe! You have already said that you renounce them, that the Durndeng sent you away as an outcast. Why are you concerning yourself at this late time with the battle of the fae here on earth?"

The grey faery looked up at Varia, shaking his head.

"This dragon is one of the most noble creatures in existence in any realm, rare and true, and you treat him as humans treat their cart ponies! He is not a pet for your whims but a unique being with special needs. Your bond to him does not give you permission to use him like a human would use rented mule."

Varia did not know what any of that meant, and it disturbed her some that The Grey would know so much about humans. Her anger and worry grew.

"Release him now!" Varia yelled. "Or bring on the wrath of all of the Alawe, for when all is said and done, your moment in which you thwarted the only way to stop this battle will surely be the thing that all the fae discuss from this day forth!"

Whether it was her tone of voice or her words, Varia didn't know, but Grey raised his hands above his head and looked up to the heavens, and Smote stirred and sat up abruptly. Varia went to him; he seemed dazed but aligned himself with her so that she could climb aboard his neck. Varia returned to her seat, and flipped her long white braid behind her neck, glaring at Grey.

"If you want to keep an eye on him you may join us," she said in a calmer voice now. "But you must stay out of the way and not hinder my actions."

Grey girdled the dragon's neck right below Varia. Smote sniffed the air, and took flight.

Krahbane soared above the treeline, and the blue sky above seemed huge to Loben as he contemplated his next move. *Surely this will be the end of my immortal life,* he thought as the giant raven made his descent toward the Birkendore oak and the Wilhvyre army. *But it will be an end worth giving.* Using the high undulating warrior's call of the Durndeng Vorku, Loben dove riding on the back of Krahbane toward the hundreds of Alawe, who heard his cry and turned, weapons at the ready, anticipating his invasion.

Krahbane crashed directly into the front line of Alawe, sending them flying, and some, knocked unconscious by the blow, fell. Loben sensed the bird's second attack and he rode gripping tight as a swarm of Alawe hurled upon him. Beating them off with his weapon, Loben could feel every blow of his own lance not as an enemy killing an enemy, but as a brother killing a brother, for that is what these fae warriors were to him now, his kin. Not that any of them knew that.

Krahbane was a beat of black feathers and an angry cah as he dived after the faery horde. They had stopped cutting the tree to fight him, Loben noticed. From the corner of his eye he saw a white-clad figure floating like a beacon within the blue and gold army: Rumendah was behind the Alawe, hands up, putting an enchantment on the wounded oak tree so none could further harm it. Relief spread through Loben as he realized that they had stopped the attack on the oak, and Thundendell palace. His relief was short-lived as he felt a spear strike through his wing. Pain permeated his body, and he fought to stay conscious through it. *So this is my end,* he thought, as blackness engulfed him, and the last thing he saw was the feathered head of Krahbane before him as he clutched the raven's neck, trying to hang on as a hive of blue and gold opposing warriors surrounded him, until he knew no more.

Varia could see the Thundendell tree ahead of her, even though her eyes stung with the fast wind of Smote's flight. She did not see Loben and was glad of it; hopefully he had not had to join the fray. Her eyes scanned the area and soon she found it: Ezia held Rumendah at spear point. Varia's wrath took her, and envisioning Smote lowering his head like a battering ram, the dragon did exactly that, as they sped toward the Wilhvyre army.

"What kind of monster is this?" Ezia asked in a horrified voice. As if he figured it out not a moment too soon, he shouted, "Dragon! Flee!" Ezia himself dropped the spear he held, a shameful act for a Wilhvyre warrior, and flew straight up into the sky, a trick Varia had seen him do when he would evade an angry bee hive. Rumendah ducked behind a tree, and the dragon sent a hundred fae scattering into the air with his forceful blow. Many crashed, and those who still had wits about them fled in the direction of Ashenthorne, following the first one out, Ezia. Pitiful shouts of "Dragon!" filled the forest, as if no one could believe what they were seeing, and saying it over and over might make it real. Smote chased a few lingering warriors off, writhing like a snake in the air, but soon enough all the Alawe were gone, none sturdy enough in body or spirit to take on the beast from another realm. Varia laughed as she approached the hiding place of Rumendah. She flew to him as Smote and the Grey landed on the ground, where Smote crept upstream toward the river with the Grey at his side.

"Our plan succeeded!" Varia called to Rumendah. "We saved the tree of Birkendore!'

"That remains to be seen, and there is one other we must try to save," said Rumendah in a quiet voice. He pointed to the ground where a large raven, Rumendah's Krahbane, stood over the fallen Loben, guarding him. Varia swooped to him, her wings tucked back so she would drop to the ground more quickly. Krahbane acquiesced, backing away as she went to Loben's side. He did not stir. Varia clutched Loben close to her as the buzz of the Vorku army filtered in from a distance. She listened to his chest for a sign of life; there was none. Varia sobbed as she clung to his limp body, her mind reeling. Feeling strong arms pull her away, she fought to stay by Loben's side but was too weakened with sorrow. Her father held her firmly beside him, and he spoke into her ear.

"My other children have usurped my kingdom, and you are my final heir, Varia. You will someday be queen! There is time to mourn your beloved later, but now, this is when you must rise up! You must rally the forces, and create unity! Loben's death will be in vain otherwise."

Varia only wished to be by Loben's side, but she stayed by her father, his words washing over her as she stared at Loben's motionless body on the forest floor. Soon the wood was filled with warriors, and the king of the Durndeng, King Struben, floated down beside her and King Dreya. Varia gave a pained look to the Durndeng king as he stared in horror at the sight of his slain nephew.

Rumendah joined them on the forest floor. He knelt and put the blade of his slender knife under Loben's nose. "No breath," he said, his expression grim. The elder lifted Loben's body into his arms and listened to his chest. "His heart is still, I fear he has perished," Rumendah said in a low voice. Rumendah called Krahbane to his side and the bird lowered his body so the elder could place the fallen Loben on his back.

"I shall take him back to the ancient forest Rhysgollen and see if we can revive him, but I am afraid the fall has killed him," Rumendah said to Varia. "I am sorry, my princess." Varia cried out in anguish, unable to contain her grief as Rumendah flew off alongside Krahbane, carrying Loben. Varia looked at the Vorku hovering above, at her father and King Struben floating side by side.

She felt raw energy and despair course in her veins and flew up to face the army. "My brave husband died so that our tribes would have peace!" she said, her words potent. "His life is the price that Loben was willing to pay, so that our tribes will know one another again, as it was cytons ago when your Queen Hoondeen and my father, King Dreya, were two fae in love, not merely two members from opposing clans. We are strong faery tribes separately, but together we can be even stronger! Right now my own palace is in jeopardy from the jealousy and strife within our own Alawe family, but our two tribes must unite, for a bigger threat has come upon us!" Varia felt another wave of emotion hit her but she forced her words to come. She flew back and forth, addressing the Vorku, noting Doon's crestfallen expression. "Now, even as I speak, a human family has moved back into the dwelling in the meadows between our castles. They have already murdered many trees, and are killing the landscape to create . . . paths . . . for their . . . machines. It has been said that, like herd animals, humans never dwell alone, so my intuition tells me this is the first step of a human being invasion! We must rise together to stop it from happening! Together, we can make a difference! Separately, we will perish one by one as humans kill the flora and fauna around us and steal our very homes."

Varia fought the tears that threatened to fall as King Struben held up his blade to show support of the union. Loben's cousin Doon looked at his father the king of the Durndeng, and followed suit. One by one, the other Vorku mimicked the action, and soon a thousand lances pierced the air, showing the unity that could bring the Alawe and the Durndeng together for a common cause.

"My father and I must leave now to reclaim the castle of Erendome from my reckless sister, the former Princess Alshea," Varia said. King Dreya flew next to his daughter and hovered beside her.

"We have left with you with our Princess Irea, for she and her mother Queen Hoondeen have much to say to one another and are reuniting," King Dreya said to the crowd.

"The Princess Irea herself is a symbol for our faepeople to how we can fight our prejudices and become one nation. We will contact her when the time to bring our tribes together has come. In unity!"

King Dreya held his sword abroad, and the others lifted theirs higher, and a shout rose up in unison as the fae of Feyllan brought together their tribes for the first time for a common goal, to save their castles from the human invasion.

Chapter Eighteen

The Vorku army lined up to prepare for their return flight to their own temporary palace as King Struben and Prince Doon joined Varia and King Dreya.

"We shall look after Loben, if there is any hope," King Struben said to Varia.

"Thank you. My heart desires to stay with him, but my head is telling me that our situation is urgent and that I must go. I know he is in capable hands."

"Yes, we have skilled healers in the Durndeng tribe, although gathering our kin from their various hiding spots may prove a time consuming task. You sort out your affairs at Erendome while we reclaim Birkendore."

"The tree will live then?" asked Varia.

"Sadly, I am unsure. We are staying in our temporary dwelling in Rhysgollen forest until we are certain, and we won't move back inside until our most adept palace flora consultants have checked it and we know we won't further harm the tree by moving back under its roots." The king sighed. "After this atrocity, it is likely the tree won't allow us to live there again, even if it lives." King Struben had a grim look on his face and his normally sparkling eyes were dull. "Never in my lifetime did I expect to see an Alawe attack an innocent tree! I have concern for the future of all of fae kind."

"As do I," said King Dreya. "And my own son led the attack! I know what I must do about it, and I am not looking forward to the task."

"I have been told by my Vorku sources that a dragon was brought forth by your daughter," said King Struben. "This also concerns me greatly." He gave Varia a disapproving look.

King Dreya's eyes grew wide. "I have yet to see this dragon, but I too was told by Rumendah that my daughter brought it from another realm and has tamed it. It seems our problems are not over yet!"

"Or the dragon could be a solution," said King Struben. "For what humans would want to live in a place inhabited by dragons?"

"'Tame' is a strong word," interjected Varia. "Let us say that I have found a way to control it, and not alone. There is a strange grey faery who follows it wherever it goes, and considers himself to be its guardian." Varia looked at Struben. "He says he was once a Durndeng, before he was banished to the dragon realm."

"Banished to the . . ." King Struben had a faraway look in his eyes. "I recall something like that occurring during my grandfather's reign. He must be very old indeed, if it is the same faery I have heard tell."

"He does not look old, but he has alluded to being so. The mists of time work differently in the dragon world. But it matters not. We must go now. I will leave the dragon here to fish in the river and The Grey will watch him until my return, for Smote will only add chaos to our errand. Kindly ask your faepeople to stay away from the dragonlet, for while he is friendly enough, and playful like a fox pup, he is growing steadily and does not realize his own strength."

"I will send a few Vorku guards to secure the area while the beast hunts. Fly safely," said King Struben.

"Please . . ." Varia choked up. "If there is any hope for my beloved Loben, please take good care of him." Varia knew she did not have time to dwell on losing Loben now, as her sister needed to be de-throned and Erendome restored, but her mind reeled with the idea that he may never return to her, that she had lost him forever. So deep was the pain of it that Varia made herself put it aside as she dealt with the task at hand.

"I promise you, Princess Varia, he is my nephew and my main concern too. We will do all we can, and then more."

King Dreya and King Struben clasped arms in the fae farewell of warriors and Varia and her father took to the air. *"For Loben,"* Varia whispered to the wind as she surged forth with renewed energy. They had a castle to save from a mad queen.

As it happened, Varia did have time to mourn Loben while she flew to Erendome with King Dreya, for she was able to cry privately and grieve. Her heart ached at the thought that they would never be together again, that he had died trying to save his home from her own brother. Soon after they passed the human dwelling, all of these thoughts began weighing heavily on her mind.

"Do we have a plan, Father?" Varia asked. "What is to become of Ezia?"

King Dreya looked stern as he flew alongside Varia. "I must regain control of the throne, my daughter. I hope no more bloodshed will befall us, but I must fight to become king once more. Alshea . . ." Dreya looked sad as he said her name, and Varia knew it was because he had such high hopes for her reign, now lost. "She must be brought down. And I fear a worse fate is in store for your brother Ezia."

Varia's throat tightened upon hearing these words. She felt that she had caused all of this pain by being so inquisitive, by flying to the Birkendore mushroom flats to find the fae they had once called EarthSeekers. If she hadn't discovered their dwelling, could the tribes have existed peacefully side by side for cytons, without knowing any better? Varia wiped a tear that fell. She remembered her promise to cry no longer and lifted her chin, pushing aside all thoughts, as her iridescent wings carried her home.

Soon the king and Varia were on the outskirts of Erendome castle in Ashenthorne forest. Zedah appeared, and Varia's heart ached upon seeing her. She held the hummingbird in her arms and they shared a moment of loss together before Varia released her.

"She summons me," said King Dreya, tapping into the bird's Devic energy. "Wait here." Varia rested in a nearby tree as her father followed Zedah to the north. She ate a few seeds and drank some nectar, nectar Loben had given her just that morning, from her flask. In the distance Varia could see the glittering domes of Erendome through the leaves of the whitebeam tree. Soon the tree would lose its leaves to autumn, and while Erendome would seem exposed, few could see the castle, if they were not expecting to find it. Again Varia was reminded about intent. It was such a powerful force in the world, she thought. She asked herself, *what is my intent now?* And she realized the answer was to right a grievous wrong, to restore order in the kingdom, and rid the human dwelling of its new inhabitants so that Ashenthorne would be safe again and her cousin Irea could return home, and they could be fae princesses again together. Sadness filled her as she realized even if all of that somehow happened, it would never be the same. Irea was no longer even her cousin, and Loben was dead. The faepeople were divided, her sister and brother would be no longer welcome in Erendome. Everything was already changed forever.

Soon King Dreya flew back to the tree where Varia reclined. "Look," said King Dreya. He pointed to a stony crag below them and there marching on foot was an army, the Wilhvyre. Varia started and jumped to her feet.

"Fly!" she called. King Dreya smiled.

"They are with us now," he said. "They have abandoned Ezia's leadership and will help us free the castle. Your brother and sister are barricaded inside of it."

"Do they yet have any followers?" Varia asked.

"A few traitors. Talow, Harrah, Ulla, Baylo, and more who did not turn back to the proper reign. But not enough to fight, we must overthrow them without bloodshed." King Dreya sighed. "They are my family, after all." The king flew down to greet his army, and Varia followed. As he landed before the hundreds of Wilhvyre, they all dropped on one knee and lowered their heads out of respect for their true king.

"Arise!" said King Dreya, and it was the same voice Varia remembered, and a thrill went through her to see that things were returning to how they once were, with her father in charge. "Any indiscretions in the past season shall be overlooked once Erendome castle is returned to order! Fear not, my faemen, for while many of you abandoned me . . ." he looked carefully over the crowd, and some looked away, and could not face him, "you did not abandon Ashenthorne or its faepeople, and for that I am willing to forgive you all. For now, the task at hand is to capture any rebels remaining in the castle, but do not harm them! For we have lost many in the past days and it is now time to heal from our own transgressions and rejoice in our newfound allegiances! Fly!"

The Wilhvyre, now a well-trained entity, arose in a cloud of wingbeats and flew in formation toward the castle, King Dreya leading the way. Varia stayed back. She only wore her Vorku blade and she wished not to fight her own siblings with it. Intuition and her own Devic spirit told her to wait instead by the secret exit from the Erendome prison where she had escaped with Loben only days before. Quickly she flew there, and hid in a tree and watched the rocky hole as darkness fell.

In the Rhysgollen refuge castle, Rumendah watched over the body of Loben, holding his old hands over him and chanting an ancient fae incantation to heal him.

"His wing is badly damaged," said Irea, who stood nearby. "But other than that, he does not have any injuries that I can see."

"It was the fall that took him," said Rumendah. Queen Hoondeen was directing her faepeople to gather aids for healing Loben; soft petal cloth and hestus-warmed water, and the small chamber where he lay was lit by softly scented resin candles and a quickly carved-out hole to the surface of the earth, where sunlight now filtered inside, filling the room in both shadow and brightness. Rumendah stepped back.

"It is up to him now," he said. "For there is naught we can do. His wing is wounded, yes, but it is a clean hole and can be patched. For now, we must wait and see if he recovers, for while I find no life in him, I find no death there either."

"It is strange," said Irea. She looked at Queen Hoondeen. "Have you seen anything like this occur before, Mother?"

"I have," said the queen. "But not for three cytons. That warrior did pass. It was during the time of strife when you were born, my darling."

"It must have been difficult for you," said Rumendah, "being apart from your child these many suns."

"It has," said Queen Hoondeen, and a flicker of emotion filled her voice. "But I knew that your father's sister Liope would raise you as her own, and she did so."

"She was a good mother to me," agreed Irea. "And Dreya a kind uncle. I now know why others wondered about the fact the king spent an extraordinary amount of time with me, his mere 'niece,' when I was young. Now I know that he understood I was his daughter."

"You should have been his heir," said Rumendah with a slow wing beat. Hoondeen stared at him.

"I suppose that is the case," said Hoondeen. "As she would have been the first heir of both thrones."

Irea laughed. "Perhaps it is lucky for all it did not happen, for I am no queen," she said. But none others laughed. Instead, they stared at her with a deep reverence. Her smile ceased.

"We have two kings now," Irea said in a meek voice. "There is no need to talk about what has happened in the past."

"Our needs are as yet unknown," said Rumendah. "For now, it is enough that we reclaim Erendome and rid our Ashenthorne lands of the human element!"

As Rumendah spoke he looked down on Loben's unmoving form to see if the enchantments had worked. Still no breath came.

Varia could hear the cries of her sister Alshea and her small entourage at dawn as the Wilhvyre invaded by breaking into and entering the very moon dome she used to escape from at the top of the Erendome palace. Her hunch proved correct; soon Alshea, followed by Talow and Ezia dressed in their Ashenthorne Wilhvyre uniforms, fled from the tunnel exit.

"Stop!" Varia said, flying down to them, her heart thumping. "You must stop now, Alshea! We have a bigger dilemma than your fall from grace! The humans have moved into the mid-plains. We must band together to stop them!"

"You!" Alshea shouted, her wrath seething through each word. "You are the cause of all of this strife! If you hadn't flown off to meet the enemy! If you hadn't uncovered those foul earthworms dwelling on the edge of the land of Ashenthorne! I would not have had to rise up as queen and usurp father's position as king, as the fae-king is addled, and did nothing, even though we were under attack!"

"Addled is a strong word, Daughter," said a voice behind Varia. She turned to see King Dreya and a dozen Wilhvyre, who had soared in silently upon the small group.

"Father!" Alshea said, surprise on her face at seeing King Dreya returned with his own army. "Oh, dear Father."

"Dear father?" King Dreya scoffed. "Am I not the same 'dear father' that you imprisoned a mere fortnight ago? Am I not the same 'dear father' that you abducted from my own bed and put in shackles, leading me to my cell before the eyes of my own faepeople? For that is the same faery that I am, and yet here you would call me a term of endearment! You are impossible, Alshea. To claim that you care for me when clearly your actions show otherwise!"

"I have only acted for the safety of the Ashenthorne Alawe!" Alshea said. She lowered herself to the ground and stepped toward her father. "I acquiesce, and give you my crown. For now that you have returned to your senses, it is clear to me that you may be able to stand in the position of king once again."

"Now that I have . . ." King Dreya repeated, as he stared at Alshea. "Truly, you are a magician with words, my daughter. Guards! Seize them!" He pointed to Alshea and Talow, but Ezia was quick witted. He zoomed up into the sky so high that he was a tiny speck against the blue before any could catch him.

"Leave him be, for now," said Dreya as the Wilhvyre guards put Alshea and Talow in shackles, and lined the others up at spear point. "Quickly return these . . . malcontents to the castle, and put them in my prison. We have much work to do in a short amount of time if we are to organize a siege on the human encampment. Jail all of Alshea's treasonous affiliates and then have the Wilhvyre report to the great hall!"

Talow glared at Varia as warriors restrained him. When guards shackled Alshea, she held her head high even as she was led away by the true Wilhvyre army. The warriors flew off with their prisoners, following orders and leaving Varia and Dreya behind.

"What of Ezia?" Varia asked, looking up into the empty sky.

"He is a liability, certainly, but not of immediate concern. First we must gather our troops and make a plan to reclaim all of Ashenthorne."

Varia stepped closer to her father and leaned her head against his shoulder. "Father, I am glad that you are safe, but my heart is broken. I feel I must return to Birkendore and tend to my husband. I cannot bear not knowing his fate!"

"We would have received word if there were a change, my princess. And I have need of you yet."

Varia turned and looked into her father's worn face. "What is it?"

"Your charge, that dragon. Call him forth. His services are needed by the fae of Ashenthorne and Birkendore!"

With that, King Dreya flew up into the air and winged his way toward Erendome palace. Varia stared after him in disbelief.

Chapter Nineteen

Loben opened his eyes, and found that he was stuck; he could not move his body. Before him the air was hazy and his vision wobbly, and he sensed that he had somehow slipped into the realm of the dragon once more. Though he could not see clearly, he could make out a shape before him; a large silhouette loomed closer until an impossibly large and serpentine head grew nearer. *Dragon!* he said to himself, but his mouth did not work, his body stayed still. Knowing that if he hadn't died already, he would now, Loben braced himself for the end.

I cannot touch you, said a voice, and yet it was not a voice in his own tongue but he understood it, much like when Zedah "sent" him a message. *I see that you are injured and as long as you are in a dreamstate, I can speak with you.*

Who are you? asked Loben, again with his mind as he could not move or speak. The great slitted eye of the dragon stared at him as if stealing his very being.

I am Evara y Bliw, said the dragon's silky voice, *and heed my words Loben of Birkendore. I know that you and your wife Varia of Ashenthorne have stolen my newborn dragon, and that you have also taken my faery guardian, Barghest the Grey, from my realm. I demand to have them back. I shall not release you unless we first strike a deal.*

Loben's mind spun. He tried waking himself up out of his troubling dream, but he could smell the strange air, taste it on his tongue like a spoiled seed. Somehow he was trapped between the dimensions of Feyllan and Drakotanith, and somehow Evara the Blue knew how to control him, and the passageway between worlds.

If I am to come through the portal, it will shatter if I choose not to return to Drakotanith, and the world of dragon and fae will never be separate again, said Evara. *Because the fae have already broken the portals between mankind and faery, we shall all three types live together in one realm. Dragons will prevail, Loben of Birkendore, for dragons always win.*

I shall do whatever it is you ask of me, Loben sent his thoughts to the angry mother dragon. *For we did not steal your baby on purpose. He was merely caught up in our journey and brought to Feyllan mistakenly when he followed us through the vortex.*

Return him now, said Evara. *Or the consequences will be beyond anything you can possibly imagine.*

Loben recalled the dragon realm, its horrible air and oily leaves, and he imagined its hideous creatures loose in Feyllan, connected to the human realm. Life as all had known it would cease; darkness would take over the land and dragons would inhabit the earth. The faeries and humans would forever perish.

I will do what you ask of me, Loben sent his thought to the dragon. *I strike this bargain with you.*

So be it, it is so, the dragon sent. *Go now back to your world. This is the only task that should be of any importance to you, Loben of Birkendore. For the entire fate of Feyllan and the human realm is now in your hands.*

In the makeshift Durndeng shelter in Rhysgollen forest, Loben's eyes opened wide and he took a deep breath and sat up. Those around him flew backward in alarm, but Rumendah went forth to him first and grabbed Loben as he struggled to regain his lifeforce.

"Rumendah!" Loben said, his eyes wide but unseeing. "Is it you? Am I back from that other wretched place?'

"You are," Rumendah said, resting his crinkly claw of a hand on Loben's forehead. "Rest a moment, now. Do not try to rise up yet." Rumendah looked around the room where Hoondeen and Irea hovered nearby. "I realize this is your home, Queen Hoondeen, but please spare us a moment alone. I have grave concerns about Loben's condition and wish to clarify his health."

"We leave him in your capable hands. Come, Irea, with me." Hoondeen rose, and her entourage followed her, but Irea glanced back before leaving the chamber to give Rumendah a meaningful look.

Loben regained his senses and looked around the tapestried room. His eyes were wild and he tried again to sit up.

"I have an errand of utmost importance! I must take your leave, I must find Smote and his keeper!"

"Smote?" Rumendah closed his eyes and put his hand out in front of him, feeling the universe before him.

"Ah. The dragon flies now as we speak to Ashenthorne, with the grey faery riding his back. He has been summoned by Princess Varia."

"Varia!" Loben started, as if only now remembering his wife, so distracted by the dragon was he. "Varia is like a far-off distant dream, a pleasant dream. She is at her home in Erendome then? Did the plan to usurp her sister's reign work?"

"It did," said Rumendah, sensing the answer on the air. "Why are you concerned with Smote? For you were not dead, nor were you alive. All breath had left you, as had your heartbeat, as if you were but a fallen tree branch waiting to rot into the forest floor. Where did you go?"

Loben stood, still groggy, and tested his wings. He could feel a shot of pain course through him and air going through the hole in his left wing. He turned his head to assess the damage.

Rumendah cleared his throat. "I will patch that for you, now that I know you are not a corpse! It may pain you some for a few days, but you are lucky you weren't further injured. Now as to where you were . . ."

Loben sat down and put his face in his hands. "I cannot stay here to molder! I must be away, but my own wings are failing me. I must fly!"

"Loben!" Rumendah laid his hand on the younger warrior's forehead. "Calm yourself. I shall have to read for myself what distresses you so." Loben nodded assent, and Rumendah listened to Loben's Devic spirit tell the tale of Evara the Blue, of Smote and the grey faery Barghest, and of the agreement he had made with Evara the Blue.

"Ah . . . a deal. You made a deal with the dragon," Rumendah muttered after pulling his hand away.

"Is that not what I should have done?" Loben asked, worried. "For she would not release me from her mindhold until I struck a bargain."

"No, no, there was little choice to be made. It is just that . . . dragons sometimes cheat. They make deals, but usually there is a trick in the language, a word with double meaning, something that puts the odds in the favor of the dragon, and makes the one on the other side of the bargain become a most delicious meal when the agreement is not met."

"I am at risk of becoming a dragon's meal!" Loben felt faint but shook his head. "I was cautious, I do not expect there to be any problems other than now I must perform this impossible task of returning Smote to Evara the Blue in the dragon realm."

"Alas, it is no small task, indeed," said Rumendah. "But since your own wife Varia is in control of the fledgling, it is not as impossible as it may seem." Rumendah motioned for Loben to turn so he could examine the wounded wing. Rumendah closed his eyes and held his hands near the injury. He opened his eyes and looked at Loben, a grave expression on his face.

"This wing was shot straight through, which means the hole has no connecting points, nothing I can use to heal it. I fear your only choice is for me to repair it artificially, though the recovery time never works out well for a restless warrior."

"Fix it, then, Rumendah, for I need to find Varia and Smote."

"I cannot, at least not in a hurry. It will require several days of rest to repair it for proper flight, and then you must learn to fly once more. I am sorry, Loben, but you must stay here and recuperate."

"Recuperate! There is no need for me to do so, for by the time I am well enough to fly the world will have been overtaken by dragons! I must go now! Seek out Krahbane the raven, he will help me on this errand."

"There is nothing more dangerous than flying on a bird when you are incapable of flying yourself!" Rumendah said. "That's a reckless plan, but I see your options are limited." The elder looked around the infirmary room, and spotted a fine soft roll of tree bark leather, used to make slings for the injured.

"Take this and tie yourself on the bird, for your plunge will be the death of you . . . and if you don't make it back alive, Loben, none of us will survive what will befall the world."

Rumendah closed his eyes and the same strange noise he had made when summoning Krahbane before, but quietly, sending the call onto the plain of the cosmos. He opened his black eyes and stared at Loben.

"One further thing, since none of us know how quickly King Dreya's redemption of the castle is progressing, nor do we know how large that dratted dragon has become, or whether . . ." he lowered his voice " . . . we truly can rid Ashenthorne of the humans . . . I fear that a mere string to tie yourself onto a fast-flying bird is not protection enough." Rumendah reached for the large reed pouch that he always kept on his hip. He opened it and fished around for a moment, and pulled up a small ornately carved box.

"What is that?" asked Loben.

"It is a lofting ointment, we Alawe call it lucene," said Rumendah, and Loben shook his head, not recognizing the glittering white oil when Rumendah opened the lid.

"Ah," Rumendah held it up. "You may not have need of it in your clan, being ground dwellers as you are. When our Alawe babes learn to fly for the first time, we, living in trees, find it necessary to rub this onto their bodies. It is a potent, but magical salve that keeps them aloft even if their wings are not strong enough to support them. Because faeries are immortal and therefore seldom have offspring, it is a very rare substance, and takes many moons to concoct even the smallest dab of it. Yet I do not hesitate to offer it to you, Loben of Birkendore, for we are in need of your flight skills now more than ever."

Loben lowered his head in deference to Rumendah's gift.

"Stand up, then," said Rumendah. "I am going to spread it on your body before Krahbane lifts you to your destiny."

It is often said that faeries are iridescent, sparkling creatures, and that myth is based in some truth. Young fae in their early flying moons are often covered with lucene, and thus do glow, even at night. Since fledgling fae are also the most likely to be seen by a human, it is often assumed that faeries are luminous. It is also usually believed that faeries are much smaller than they are in reality, and that too is because it is the youngest ones who are most spotted by outsiders. Loben was a glittering sight to behold once Rumendah had covered his body with the luminous gel, confirming that faeries can sparkle.

"I look ridiculous!" Loben said, examining his arm. He tried rubbing the ointment off.

"Lucene will not be so easy to remove," Rumendah said. "It wears off slowly, thus giving a faechild time to learn to fly, and giving a fallen warrior time to recover from his injured wing." Rumendah had skillfully patched Loben's wound while Loben ate a quick meal of dried mushrooms and drank honeysuckle wine for the pain, and while the area was not the iridescent gold and black like the rest of his wing, the color matched well and one would have to look very closely to see the repair.

"Now your ride arrives," Rumendah said as Krahbane entered, hopping into the room, uncertain. Rumendah gave a chortle and Krahbane visibly relaxed and approached. Upon seeing the dazzling Loben, an expression that could have only been amusement filled his eyes, but the raven lowered himself so Loben could easily mount his feathered back.

Loben used the bindings to attach himself to the bird as Rumendah whispered to Krahbane's Devic spirit.

"Away with you both on your duty! For now I see that keeping an angry dragon content is of far more importance than chasing humans away from our lands."

Loben held on tightly as Krahbane tensed for flight. The bird leapt forward, wings shattering the still air as he flew down the wide hallway to the bright outside world.

Varia heard the snapping of branches and the sound of tremendous airsong and she cringed, knowing what was coming next. Smote crashed from the forest, twigs and branches flying off his thunderous wings. The Grey held on tightly to the dragon's neck, a mere small speck against the huge girth of the maturing dragon.

Varia braced herself, flapping her wings hard against the approaching dragon wind, but Smote, sensing her danger, slowed his beat to a petal soft flutter and landed feather-soft on the ground before her.

"Oh my darling Smote! You have grown ridiculously large!" Varia said, as both the emotion of being a proud parent and relief at seeing him well filled her. She approached with her hand outstretched, and he gently placed his face near her palm. They held the position, and she transferred her sore heart into his soul; her pain for Loben's lost life. Smote hung his head and she climbed up onto the bridge of his nose and held on to the spikey ridge between his eyes and rested her body against him, giving him a hug.

"We must be strong for Loben," she whispered to Smote.

"You must have summoned the dragon," The Grey said, "for my charms did not work on him whatsoever."

Varia shook free of her moment with Smote. She flew backwards and up to meet The Grey face to face.

"I did summon him," she said in a voice that would remind any around her that she was a true princess. "I was asked by the kings themselves to call on Smote to assist in the retaking of the lands of the mid-plains from the humans that dwell there."

"I thought as much!" said The Grey. "Why you cannot leave this poor creature alone is a mystery to me! I am still his guardian, whether you are under dragonspell or not. And while I have no knowledge of how to get him back to his world or how to find his mother, I will still stand by him every moment he is stuck in this wretched place."

"Our tribes need him," Varia said in a calm voice. "And I am his true master, not you."

The Grey shook with anger. "I refuse to let him go on this frivolous errand with you!"

"All the fae are in jeopardy, our very lands are in danger if we allow the humans to stay here. For never do they come singly, according to the Durndeng. They are like flies, buzzing in first one, then more. We must act now, and if you do not stand aside, I will be forced to take further action against you!"

Smote shook his head and the Grey let loose of his hold on his neck and floated in midair.

"The humans cannot see us if we do not allow it anyway! Why waste your energies on those lowly life forms?" The Grey rose up and hovered above Smote's ears, and the dragon twisted his head to see where the faery had gone.

"It has been many cytons since you have lived in this realm, Grey. Some humans can sense the fae now, as our world and theirs have converged, and those people with a special gift of sorcery can see us, whether we allow it or not."

The Grey lowered himself to the ground. "Then there is no hope left for this world," he said, his head hanging, "if the realms of fae and mankind have meshed into one."

"I refuse to give up! Mount Smote's neck and we will go and meet the reunited Wilhvyre army, and we shall join together with the Vorku army of the Durndeng and stand together to fight the humans!"

The Grey looked defeated but did as he was told, and Varia joined him, noticing that Smote's neck was more than double the size as it was last time she rode on him. She sent a thoughtwave for Smote to go to the clearing near Erendome castle where the convergence of armies would await their arrival. The enormous beast lifted his golden wings, dropped them in a fury of wind, and took flight.

Chapter Twenty

Smote had barely flown from the wood when a black speck dotted the horizon. Varia strained her eyes and could make out a bird, but when she saw a fae warrior riding upon the animal, she tensed. Was this a rogue soldier out to harm her and Smote? She thought of turning away to hide when she felt something tug at her, a familiar presence. *Loben's Deva!* she thought. Smote directed himself into the energy between the connecting Devas of Loben and Varia, and the dragon and raven grew nearer to one another, all energy fields pulled together as one. As they neared, Varia could see that Loben was sparkling white in color, like an Alawe babe, covered in the child's flying aid, lucene. *Rumendah*, Varia guessed where the ointment had come from.

Varia swept herself up from Smote's neck and flew to Krabane and ushered the pair into the nearest tree as Smote landed on the ground, Grey still astride him.

"Loben!" Varia was overcome with joy, and disbelief. "How is it you survive? Nay, survive enough to ride on the back of a soaring bird to return to me?" Varia hugged him as he struggled to untie himself from Krahbane. The bindings pirouetted to the ground like falling snakes. Loben gave her a tight and desperate hug, as Krahbane shook himself, fluffing his feathers and preening. Loben looked into Varia's eyes.

"I was not dead, but called forth by the mother of the dragon Smote!" Loben said, his manner wild, ignoring Varia's attempts to now touch him gingerly, her fingers needing to feel his flesh beneath them. "I was brought to a half-realm, not Drakotanith, not Feyllan, and Evara the Blue demanded that she must have her offspring back anon or she will break herself free from her realm and destroy the portals, and combine the dragon and fae world forever!"

Varia's eyes widened. "She cannot! For none will survive here if dragons roam freely."

"That is exactly why we must stop her by sending the baby dragon and the grey fae guardian, whom she calls Barghest, back to Drakotanith."

"Barghest?" Varia tried the name on her tongue. "That is The Grey's true name? We must hurry, for my father has called upon Smote to take our tribes to victory over the humans! Then we will return him to his distressed mother."

Loben shook his head. "There is no time for that, our mission is late already. We must go now and do the dragon's bidding, or we will have a problem much bigger than a few stray humans moving in nearby."

"Loben! You know the damage the humans cause, their cruelties to tree and beast! How can you say that it is not a problem that they move here?" Varia felt anguished; here her beloved Loben had come back to her, against all odds and in a way she didn't understand, and they were arguing over who would use the dragon to better the cause.

"My darling wife," Loben held her gaze, his own gold eyes full of pain and concern. "Trust me. Please. This is of the utmost importance. I . . . made a bargain with Smote's mother, Evara the Blue. And Rumendah assures me, a bargain with a dragon usually doesn't end well. We must hurry!"

Varia felt shaken to the core. "You bargained with a dragon, Loben? They are slippery with their words! What did she say, exactly, this Evara the Blue, Mother of Smote?" Varia used the full dragon name with contempt.

"She said . . ." Loben fought to find the correct wording. "She said that I must bring Smote back or she would come through the portal and break open the division between the worlds, and that dragons will always win."

"Those exact words?" Varia questioned.

"I . . . don't recall," Loben admitted. "I was not myself at the time, but in a strange realm I did not know. I do understand that there is no time for further bargaining, however. Take me to the portals of the ancient forest, so that I may send this one back to his home!"

"Faery!" came Grey's warning voice, and Varia and Loben looked up in time to see a blue streak barreling down on them from high above. Varia held onto Loben's wrist when Krabane jumped away and soared off unexpectedly. Loben hung in the air, lifted by the lucene, but the blue faery's blast of wind as he hurtled past caused Loben to trail away from Varia and float to the ground.

Varia saw that it was her own brother Ezia who had interrupted them. He landed on the earthen floor, his weapon in hand, and demanded The Grey leave the dragon's side. Smote lowered himself, pressing his ear scales back, looking like a puma about to pounce.

"Smote! He is my relation," Varia said quickly, sure she would see her brother devoured like the unfortunate meals she'd already witnessed the dragon consume.

"So nice of you to save me, Sister," Ezia said, fury leaking from his voice. "I see that you have taken up with dragons and other enemies."

"The tribes are now united," Varia stated, flying down to Ezia but keeping Loben in her sight, putting herself between them.

Ezia pointed at Loben. "That one wears the precious sacred oil of our tribe, and has stolen enough lucene to assist the flight of twenty Alawe babies! I see how it is now, that the EarthSeekers will come into our lives, first taking our lands, then taking our females . . ." he looked directly at Varia as he said this. "And then our most protected belongings, taking these things out of our own faepeople's hands."

"Enough! Why are you here?" Varia asked. "Be gone, before we get the armies to take you to the prisons with our sister Alshea!"

Ezia laughed. "You . . . and who else? This injured foreigner, or the freakish one who lives on a flying lizard's neck? I think not. I am here to take . . ." he pointed to Smote . . . "the dragon."

Ezia reached into his pouch and pulled out small black ashy lumps and crushed them in his hand, and blew the smoky contents toward Varia and Loben, and then The Grey. The last thing Varia saw before she swooned was Loben and The Grey fall backward, and Ezia leap onto an angry Smote's back, and hide his wings from the fierce wind of speed as they flew away.

When Varia awakened, Loben lay crumpled beside her, but The Grey, Barghest, was gone. Her head hurt and she felt the strong need to eat, knowing that she could not fly until she did so. She tapped on Loben's shoulder and he roused himself as she reached into her pouch and pulled out some seeds and dried rosemary for them to share.

"What trick did your brother play to cause us to fall?" Loben asked as he sat up and tested his wings, first one, then the other.

"That is a powder reserved for use in war, sauma powder. I have only heard of it, and have never felt its consequence before now. It is a powerful sleeping potion used to distract the enemy. As we now are to my brother, it would seem." Helpless, Varia looked around for Smote and Barghest.

"Where do you think that Ezia took the dragon?" Loben asked, holding his head. He drank nectar from his belt flask and handed Varia some, and she consumed it in one swig.

"My guess is that he went to the castle to free my sister and Talow and their followers! I hope Smote is not harmed by the guards there!" she said, wiping her mouth with the back of her sky-colored hand.

"I saw him, and believe me, our small spears could not pierce his hide, so much has he grown. How could Ezia control him, I wonder?"

Varia thought a moment as she stood up, and brushed dirt off her tunic and leggings. She tried to help Loben up but he stood on his own. "Ezia is a bee tamer, he is trained to calm angry animals. He must have used his skill on Smote, who is yet young and impressionable."

"Ah." Loben looked up; above them the trees were lit from the west and the blue horizon paled as the day waned. "We must find them," he said. "Although I cannot go on foot."

"Lucene will lift you if you just hold on to me, I will not feel your weight," Varia said. Loben shook his head.

"I am a warrior of the Vorku council, and now I am to be towed around by my wife like some Alawe baby? This is of great humiliation to me, Varia. I cannot do it."

Varia faced Loben and pushed his usually tidy but now scraggled brown locks behind his lucene-covered pointed ear. "My darling, we have many lives to save, and this is no time to argue. Hold on to my hand." Varia flapped her wings hard to get momentum and she clutched on to Loben's hand, and he spread his wings, flapping his uninjured one, and soon they lifted off together in a lopsided way, heading in the opposite direction from the human dwelling where two kings awaited the dragon's arrival, far south from the ancient wood where behind a hidden portal awaited a livid mother dragon. Instead they flew west toward Erendome, Varia's birthplace, where neither of them could know what awaited them.

King Dreya shielded his eyes from the western glare as he faced the human dwelling, where the people, tall and strange, were packing up the strange device King Struben had called an automobile.

"Truly, this is a contraption unlike any we fae know about! Do you understand its machinations?"

"I do not," said King Struben, who hovered beside the king, a thousand troops wearing the black and silver uniform of the Vorku behind him, just as King Dreya's faemen wore the gold and blue of the Wilhvyre beyond. The two tribes merged, ready to attack the humans, but they awaited Varia and her dragon to come assist in the purge.

"These apparatus plague us, and are a new invention of mankind. We have lost members of our clan to them, as they chug about on their paths, once reserved only for their carts and ponies. So fast do they go, faster than a runaway horse, that if we are struck by them, we shall perish."

King Dreya stared at the automobile with a new look, akin to fear. "These are dark and strange times indeed for our kind," he murmured. "Let us surround the perimeter of the human house, and as soon as I catch word of Varia's arrival on the beastly dragon, I shall call forth a single note . . ." the faery beside him handed the king a fanciful horn carved of seashell from the Mysty Island shores. "And this call shall signify the moment we attack!"

"It has been long since our troops have warred," said King Struben. "And our last wars were on other faeries, not mankind. This may be folly, for the humans, though dull-witted, are large and sometimes can catch us if they can see us. We must have a secondary line of attack in order should we have any unforeseeable problems."

"Well said," King Dreya noted. "Let us meet with our warriors and plan an invasion, with my daughter and her dragon leading the fray!" King Struben and King Dreya flew up above their armies, and all who witnessed the two mighty faery kings soaring together were struck with amazement; the Durndeng because they were taught not to trust the Alawe and would have never believed a union was possible, and the Alawe because they did not even know the Durndeng still existed until a few moons previously. The kings raised their swords to the air. The warriors responded with a resounding cry, but to a human passing by, it would merely sound like the wind rustling in the tall late summer grasses.

As they neared the clearing where the Erendome whitebeam tree stood, Varia could see in the distance the huge outline of Smote, now nearly half the size of the castle itself. He was upset, she could tell from this distance, and her heart clutched at the sight of her brother riding him, using the same bindings that Rumendah had given Loben to control the dragon's snout. Ezia hovered above Smote, his weapon drawn, the reins in his hand as he shouted to the castle guards. As they neared, Varia could make out his words.

"Free the queen Alshea of Ashenthorne and her companions, or I shall release this dragon upon the castle and none here will have a home to go to at nightfall!"

Varia couldn't believe what she was hearing; such threats coming from her own brother, her kin. She knew Ezia was hot-tempered and vain, but she found seeing him mad with power and revenge too much to bear. Heart heavy, she pulled Loben to the same tree that they had hidden in once before as she watched the scene from the shadows of the tree limb.

"Ezia! Go away with that beast, and do not disturb us here!" shouted Heldah, one of her father's hands. The pale blue faery shook his fist at Ezia.

Varia could sense Smote's pain at being bound and wondered how Ezia had discovered the only weak spot on her beloved dragon so that he could physically control him.

"Smote is being harmed," Varia said to Loben.

"And I have searched as far as my eyes can see, and I do not find The Grey. For that concerns me even more," Loben replied. His eyes darted all around the castle's tree and beyond to the meadows toward Craggyrock Lake. Varia looked as well, and Loben was right: The grey faery, Barghest, was not near.

"His only loyalty is to Smote, where do you suppose he went?" Varia wondered aloud. She too now felt a deepening concern about Barghest, but her immediate thoughts were to protect her charge Smote. Making a rash decision, she laid her hand on Loben's wrist in goodbye and flew toward her brother, and her dragon.

In the darkening of night Barghest the grey faery laid his hands against the ancient oak trees, and felt a pulse emerge from the tree, a vibrating air that told him that the dragon realm was near.

"My queen Evara! If you are nearby, please tell me how to free you from this vault!" Barghest cried into the dense forest. The still wood remained thus, but a small thornprick of light emerged from between two trees far up in the wood before him. The circle of light wavered and wobbled, and then grew. Barghest flew fast toward it and held out his hand to the opening. Behind it, he could feel Evara the Blue's presence, the dragon he had followed and cared for in his more than six cytons of banishment in Drakotanith. A tear rolled down his cheek as he sensed the huge dragon moving forward, and he felt her thoughts as she "spoke" to him.

"*Come forth my faithful Barghest,*" Evara the Blue dragon said in her silky way. "*How my thoughts of late have concerned you! I do not feel my child is with you. What fate has befallen Fletheroth the Green?*"

"The dragon child has been stolen by a rogue faery," Barghest said. "A relative through marriage of Loben of Birkendore."

"*Ah,*" said Evara, though she thought her words. "*I see that my presence is needed on the other side of this portal.*"

Barghest, you must help free me from the dragon realm. My child needs me."

"Yes, your highness," Barghest bowed even though Evara could not see him. "I suppose this means that Loben of Birkendore failed to keep his end of the bargain?"

"*He had failed from the moment the bargain was made,*" said Evara. "*For the deal clearly made was that he would return my child to me 'now,' and now has long since passed. Release me, for I have much to do in the fae kingdom, my trusted Barghest. I only need you to enlarge this portal and I shall come forth and claim my child, the young dragon king Fletheroth the Green.*"

Barghest reached forward and slipped his hands into the small lit opening, and though the purple light burned him, with slow deliberation he widened the vortex by pushing the wavering energy out with all his might.

Varia flew up to Smote and touched his face. The bindings were tight and she realized with horror that the dragon was having trouble breathing as small puffs of smoke emitted from his nose.

"Release him, Ezia!" Varia screamed up at her brother.

"Never!" Ezia returned defiantly. "He is a prize of war!"

Varia's ire took her and she zoomed up to her brother, barreling at him with all of her force and knocking him away from the bindings. Once free, Smote dropped to the ground and used his front claws to easily snap the fae ropes. Ezia swung his weapon at Varia, the Wilhvyre blade barely missing her torso.

"Ezia! Regain your senses, for you are quite mad! You must stop this now, we must unite to cleanse Ashenthorne of the humans! For they are the true threat, not the EarthSeekers as you so believe."

Smote rose up in the air with a single wingbeat and opened his cavernous mouth, ready to devour Ezia. Varia held her hand up to stop him.

"Enough!" she said. She sent Smote a mental message to desist, and the dragon huffed out a lick of flame, his first in anger, which Ezia dodged, before retreating once more to the ground. Smote waited, looking up, in case he should get lucky and Ezia should fall into his jaws. Ezia hovered and still held Varia at the end of his blade.

"You have ruined everything!" Ezia spat. "Our entire lives are destroyed because you followed your heart to the enemy's encampment, because you chose their kind over our own."

"I chose no such thing! Ezia, you are finished here! Give up your weapon, you are outnumbered and your small sword will not stop you from being taken by father's prison guards."

Ezia held the sword up over his head, and Varia realized he meant to kill her with it. She heard Loben shout "No!" from where he was helplessly waiting for her in the tree. Releasing her wings to the sky, she dropped to the forest floor just as the weapon whizzed past her head. She looked up in time to see Ezia fly off, again a mere spot in the deepening heavens.

Night fell, and Varia and Loben were forced back to their tree hiding place, where they took turns fitfully sleeping, while Smote ate, then slept. They shared stores of nuts and nectar and when the earliest hint of dawn emerged, they were tired but could see well enough now to fly to the portal of Drakotanith to return Smote to Evara the Blue. They were preparing for their journey when shouts from the castle distracted them.

What Varia didn't know was that Ezia's dragon-stealing had been a ruse to distract the guards at the Erendome castle door. It had bought Alshea, Talow, Baylo and Ulla the time they needed to plan their escape. Talow was the one who masterminded the plan.

"Guard!" he said to the only one watching them, a large but slow Wilhvyre soldier named Armba. "The queen Alshea has taken ill." Alshea was splayed on the ground, wings spread, her chest heaving, her eyes rolled back into her head. Armba looked into the cell, and stood before the prison door, uncertain.

"I will go and call for help," he said hesitantly. "She looks not well."

"If you do not assist her now, she will die, and the wrath of the king Dreya will be on your shoulders! For while the king and queen . . . princess . . . have had a bit of a . . . disagreement . . . Alshea is still the king's favorite child and he will be devastated if you do not save her. Open the door! I will step back."

Talow nodded for Baylo and Ulla to lean up against the walls, their wings pinned against them, and their hands clasped behind their backs. It was a faery position that marked good will and no wrong intention, and as Alshea's condition seemed to worsen, Armba must have recognized that his options were slim. He took the ornate key from his belt loop and inserted it into the lock. The door clicked open.

Alshea looked to be consumed by a dark fever, and her body writhed. Armba kept one eye on the prisoners who lined the wall, and they were keeping their word, with wings pinned and hands joined. He was watching them when Alshea herself rose up and pinned the guard by the neck, a blade resting across his heart.

"One slight wingbeat and it will be your last one, Armba," Alshea said as Talow rushed to the stores to find fae wing binding bags and used them to pinion the guard's wings behind him. Talow threw Armba in the cell and shut the door, as Ulla and Baylo led the way out, collecting as many weapons as they could from the prison antechamber. As a group of four, they flew down the tunnel and out the secret exit once more into the night, into freedom.

Chapter Twenty-One

"How did they escape?" Varia asked the guard on duty upon hearing the news Alshea was gone, looking at the embarrassed-looking Armba in the dim morning light. Smote waited beside her, and Loben seemed grateful to be riding on the back of his proud blue and green steed instead of being pulled along by his wife. "Never mind," Varia said as the guard seemed at a loss for words, and Armba hung his head. "It matters not, the castle is reclaimed! Send word to my father, and we shall continue on our true business."

Varia summoned Smote to her and he flapped over to the castle entrance, creating a blustering wind that caused the castle guards to tuck their wings behind them so they would not be taken by the breeze. Varia mounted his spiky long neck, settling in front of Loben, the two of them ready to embark on their journey to the northern ancient forest, Llangdwig, to find the dragon realm portal leading to the murky world of Drakotanith. With a tight throat, Varia realized that she was about to say goodbye to her beloved Smote, or leave the fate of her loved ones in the claws of an angry mother dragon.

For every one up, one down wingbeat, Smote could fly as far as a hundred faery wing beats. Both Loben and Varia had to duck behind the large scales that protruded on Smote's neck, to hide from the violent wind of dragon flight. They were nearing the north wood when Loben lifted his head, hearing the air.

"Ask Smote to stop," he said, his voice low. Varia sent a mental message to Smote to land on the ground, which the dragon did with utmost grace.

A faint high-pitched chirping noise sounded in the distance. Loben answered it from the back of the dragon's neck where he stood on Smote's grand scales, holding on with one hand to balance himself. It was there Zedah found him.

"Zedah!" Loben said, and the bird flew fast toward him, darting in front of him for a moment before nestling into his chest for the embrace that he offered. Her enthusiasm knocked him off balance, and Varia hovered close, watching them. Varia realized with a choked breath that Zedah, like she had, still presumed Loben was dead. *How wondrous for her to see him alive again,* Varia thought as the shimmering ruby head of Zedah bobbed in Loben's arms. Only for a moment did she seem put off by his new sparkling white appearance, but their Devas connected, and they found themselves one again.

"She sends a message that the combined fae tribes await aid of the dragon," Loben said in a grim voice.

"Tell them we were detained on an important mission, and that the dragon is returning to Drakotanith by way of the portals of Llangdwig forest," Varia said, placing her hand on Zedah's breast.

Varia spoke as Zedah preened. "I wish it were not so, but I realize now our actions must be for the greater good. And unleashing a dragon on the humans, as much as we may fear and dislike them, is cruel. They know not that such beasts exist. We still have the ability to hide as we need to. We will find our way with them, if we must deal with them at all." Varia looked toward the thick hollow of trees where she had been tossed from a portal less than a moon ago. She sighed. "I do not like this next thing that we must do, but let us return Smote to his mother before it is too late and she charges the vortex."

Loben turned in a quick manner and pointed toward the forest glen ahead. "I fear we are already too late," he said, as there in a tower of sunlight, stood a dragon so large that only the front of her long, blue iridescent body could be seen. And standing with arms crossed over his chest on her head between her tall pointed ears was a tiny little figure, the grey faery Barghest.

Varia flew to the ground and dropped to her knees in deference to the enormous creature, but Loben, because of his lame wing, had to stay put on Smote's back. Zedah took flight and was gone before any could see her leave. Evara the

Blue took one step and was upon them, her serpentine face coming quickly toward Loben as she turned her eye toward him. The unblinking golden orb consumed him in a wreath of light, and he held his hand up over his face, trying not to fall into the dragon's spell.

Evara's teeth were larger than Loben himself. He would not even be a satisfactory meal for a creature so gigantic. His immortality meant nothing at this moment, so exposed to those dangerous razors was he.

"We return your dragon hatchling to you unharmed," Varia said, her voice shaking.

I see, sent Evara the Blue, her thoughts so immense that trees shook and late summer leaves fell like raindrops to the earth. Varia covered her ears in pain and put her head on the ground, agony consuming her. Loben soared lopsidedly down to the forest floor beside Varia, and grabbed her in his arms and pulled her behind the cover of young saplings where they peered out to keep an eye on the huge beast. Smote gave Varia a last look before he sidled up to his mother, squirming about and leaping in her shadow. He twisted and turned like a grey squirrel puppling, as if understanding that this impressive dragon was his mother, exuberant in their reunifying. The tiny figure of Barghest stood triumphant at their union as he rode the crested head of Evara the Blue.

Evara glared at the two spying faeries, and without another thought she lifted her heavy wings, and then lowered them, easing into the sky with a wind that knocked both Varia and Loben flat to the ground. They were pinned by her gale until she, with the much smaller Smote flapping behind her, disappeared over the treeline.

"She heads to the southwest," Varia said, jumping to her feet as the gust stilled.

"At least she left us in peace," Loben replied, standing and joining her.

"No, I mean—the portal to Drakotanith is north in the depths of Llangdwig forest! She is going the wrong way!"

Loben shook his head, not comprehending. Varia reached out and clutched his arm.

"Loben, she is heading directly toward Erendome!" Varia said.

The kings Dreya and Struben awaited a dragon ally that never came. It was Zedah the hummingbird who arrived instead.

"There is Loben's emissary, the hummingbird Zedah," said Doon, who hovered alongside King Struben.

"Ah, so it is. Bring her forthwith, and allow me to see what news we have from my nephew Loben."

Zedah followed as Doon led the bird to the king, who held his arm out for Zedah to land. She did, and nodded toward the King of the Durndeng. The king bowed his head, as was the customary respectful way to address a loyal bird messenger. King Struben placed his hand on Zedah's breast and closed his eyes, their Devic spirits connecting. His eyes flew open.

"This is a grave situation indeed!" said Struben. "For Zedah brings news from the fae, and from the trees. It seems the dragonling's mother, a fully-grown dragon from Drakotanith, has come through the portal, upon finding the deal she struck with Loben to be void. This creature here . . ." King Struben rubbed Zedah's ruby head, "tells me that the trees speak of the beast that is heading for Erendome now to seek her revenge!"

"Aye," said Rumendah, who had mysteriously appeared before the kings. "I have come to bear the same message. Erendome will soon be under attack by Evara y Bliw, the ancient and wretched dragon released from her oily portal! The trees are speaking of it, as the whole western Hammershin wood is ablaze!"

King Dreya reacted at once. "Gather all of our forces, these mindless humans are the least of our concern! Armies, westward toward Erendome!" King Dreya commanded. In V patterns, the Vorku and the Wilhvyre armies flew up together and swarmed as one, wings humming as they veered toward Ashenthorne to save Erendome castle from the wrath of the angry mother dragon.

Smoke furled deep and dark as the Hammershins woods to the northwest of Ashenthorne blazed. Varia stared in horror at the destruction as small frightened animals raced from the forest; she covered her ears at the tortured screaming of burning trees.

"Loben!" she said, her heart racing as she flitted back and forth, uncertain what to do when a mountain of fire rose up over the treeline. She covered her mouth and nose with her hand.

"We must fly as fast as we can get to Erendome!" Loben said with a cough.

"I cannot fly fast if I must pull you along," Varia lamented. As if sensing her deep need of his service, Krahbane the raven appeared, looking like he was borne of the ash of the burning wood, a dark figure approaching against a blackening sky.

"Mount his back and let us go, oh thank you, blessed Krahbane for assisting us!" Varia said, and Loben pulled his weapon from his belt as he jumped onto the back of the bird. Fast they flew, but Varia was becoming aware that she had not properly fueled herself, and knew that Loben had not done so either, but on fierce determination alone, Varia knew she would make it to Erendome, or die trying.

When the two arrived to the outer wood of Erendome palace, a frightening scene greeted their eyes: The dragon Evara y Bliw was being held at bay by hundreds of Vorku and Wilhvyre warriors, and though she wobbled as if dazed, she gazed at the soldiers to cast her spell and breathed out her putrid smoke. Many fae fell from their ranks, dropping lifeless to the ground. Varia hovered near Loben and Krahbane and put her face against Loben's shoulder to hide her eyes from the sight. When she could bear to look again, she saw why the beast had not already destroyed her family's castle home; Rumendah, with all of his might, was holding her at bay with one of his ancient fae tricks.

"We must stop her!" Varia said.

"But how?" asked Loben. "Even Rumendah cannot hold out much longer. If you look closely, you can see the purple energy rays he emits with his hands are wavering and turning white. He is losing his power. He is very old."

"Old and powerful," Varia said to show her encouragement, but she saw Loben was right: Rumendah was fading.

Playing behind Evara, oblivious to her wrath, was Smote. He leapt across the meadow chasing yellow butterflies and diving down onto the ground as he tried to catch them. Varia looked at Loben and Krahbane.

"Do not follow me, do not risk yourselves! Nor try to stop me." She opened her pouch and found her nectar, and downed as much as she could take in three sips before handing the vial to Loben. "Drink this, stay strong." Her heart begged her to linger, but she flew toward Smote, keeping behind Evara, freeing her mind of any intent lest the monstrous dragon hear her thoughts. *She cannot hear just my thoughts though,* Varia realized, and knew now why the dragon was disoriented. *She is hearing the thoughts of all the fae trying to stop her and cannot focus enough to unleash her wrath.* Varia flew beyond the treeline to the meadow where Smote pounced about. She approached the dragon, hoping his mother had not somehow turned him against her, and she held out her hand. He stopped what he was doing, and stared at her. Then he bounded toward her, and the force was as great as if a tree were falling on her. She braced herself, but a leathery nose brushed up against her entire body in a careful greeting. She hugged Smote's snout.

"Come my love," Varia said, and she flew as fast as she could toward the northern forest of Llangdwig, even though the path before her was murky and dark with smoke. Much to her amazement and relief, Smote followed her, and eventually she was able to mount him and fly faster. She did not notice that Barghest the Grey was also flying fast behind her, managing to keep her and the young dragon in his sight.

Evara the Blue shook her head, crazed and unable to take in the thoughts of a swarm of fae. She roared and the noise caused a ripple in the waves of time, so deafening it was. Far afield, the humans stood still, and they could smell the burning woods and feel disaster looming. They mobilized and headed in the automobile toward the fires of the Hammershins. Meanwhile, the dragon Evara blew more flame, lighting the trees around Erendome. Another fire, and this time there would be no escape. The castle would burn. Evara the Blue looked at the blaze she had caused and readied for another attack; Loben saw his moment and motioned for Krahbane to fly.

"Go as the wind, my friend, for we must stop this beast from flaming once more. If we do not, Erendome shall perish!" Krahbane called one last angry caw before entering the fray, much to his detriment.

The black feathered bird clawed angrily at the serpent's face, and Loben propelled himself over Evara's back, barely missing being struck by her spiky, ravaging huge head. Loben climbed onto her hard scales and inched his way to the top of the large head, up her spine while Krahbane continued with his constant pecking. In the distance, Rumendah collapsed, his wings shuddering as he fell to the ground from where he hovered. Krahbane the raven, feeling his comrade's fall, attacked with renewed force. Loben grabbed the dragon's head. He held on with all of his strength, unable to maintain his balance as Evara's feverish pitching dizzied him. Loben's body was thrown against the dragon's head, scraping and bruising him. Finally finding footing, Loben regained his composure and, using his good wing for balance, made his way to the dragon's ears. There he shouted, "Evara y Bliw! Stop! Your dragonling has gone with Varia of Ashenthorne back to Drakotanith! Find your child! For if the hatchling enters the portal without you, your opportunity to return to your own realm may be lost forever!"

As if ruminating on this possibility, Evara's head thrashing ceased and she lowered her huge body to the ground, lizard-like. Loben released his hold on her scaly head and floated to the ground, and upon feeling his feet touch earth, he tucked his wings behind him, ignoring the pain in his injured wing, and ran for cover. Krahbane, however, seemed to take the last opportunity to thrust. The bird flew headlong into the dragon's snout, and she lifted her face to the sky and the bird was raked by razor teeth. In a puff of black feathers, Krahbane fell and lay still on the cold ground. Loben mourned his dear friend but was relieved to see the dragon began turning and with a sudden winglift, off she went into the sky, after her baby, and after his wife too, Loben realized. As soon as the dragon threat passed, Loben rushed to Krahbane's aid, expecting to find the bird dead. Movement stirred within the bird as Rumendah approached.

"Get these warriors to stop those flames from spreading to the castle!" Rumendah barked as he crouched by his fallen raven friend. Doon was near and gave his own commands, and soon in multiple flights the Wilhvyre and the Vorku worked as a team to douse the fire Evara had ignited, which was moving through three trees. Rumendah held his hand over Krahbane's body. "Bring him to the castle's infirmary," the elder demanded, and four sentries lifted the bloodied corvid and carried him as they flew toward the palace walls.

"Varia flies unaided north with Smote to the portal of Drakotanith to lure the mother dragon away!" Loben shouted over the din of a thousand fae shouting to put out the fires. Dark smoky wind and red flame filled the air around them.

"I am depleted," Rumendah said in a weak voice, "But gather a force to retrieve her! For Evara y bliw shows no mercy. She will slay Varia, if she gets a chance."

Loben waved his cousin Doon over.

"I am too injured to fly, and my steed the raven has fallen. The young dragon also has left, and I have no means to get to the northern woods! But there my wife Varia is alone with both dragons, and while she is brave, I fear her rash decision to try and save Erendome castle will cost her life!"

Doon looked toward the north, which was ablaze. He shook his head.

"We cannot fly the speed of dragons, Cousin, you know this! How are we to get ourselves there in time to help her? By dragon speed and using their wit, they have undoubtedly avoided the fires and arrived at their destination. We are small; it will take us all day and half the night to reach even the outer Hammershins. I am sorry, but unless we can find a willing steed, there is naught we can do for her." Doon laid his hand on his cousin's shoulder in sympathy but turned back to helping Alawe and Durndeng troops vanquish the fire.

Loben despaired, but knew his cousin was right. His mind raced; it was unusual to have a bird friend to assist in the fae world; in fact, Rumendah's Krahbane and his own Zedah were the only two companion birds that he knew of. Loben's mind raced; could Zedah somehow help him? He was about to call her forth, when a chortling sound near his head made him turn. Zedah hovered there. Loben laid his hand on her breast, sending his message of need. Zedah flew fast away, and Loben wondered how on earth the tiny bird, less than a stem in length, could help him.

Varia sent her thoughts for the unruly dragon to rush toward the portal, but the smoke and ash were too much for her, so she had to pin her wings and lower her head against his leathery scales and just hold on in the hopes that he was going the right way. The energy of the forest changed abruptly and Varia knew that Evara was following. She was closer than Varia would have expected; she also sensed the grey faery Barghest was with the mother dragon. A dark foreboding swept over Varia and she realized that she might not see the end of this day, but she held tight to her steed and tried not to let the ride exhaust her.

Soon the heat lessened and Varia risked opening her eyes; they had passed the Hammershins' blaze and were now traversing the thick ancient trees of the Llandwig Forest, the mystical wood protecting the Drakotanith portal. Smote slowed as if cautious, but here Varia looked around. Compared to the ruin and smoke of the forest to the south, this place was calm and untouched, but still it was dark even in midday as the towering branches spread green and lush overhead, creating a vast shaded canopy. Varia breathed in the fresher air and could see ahead the trees turning from golden-barked to silver, and soon the eely black portal loomed ahead. Varia motioned Smote to the ground. She flew before him and cupped his nose in her hand to keep him from entering the portal. He was so large now, yet so much smaller than Evara that she could not imagine that he would be as great a dragon as her one day. Tears welled up in her eyes as she sent a ray of love to the young dragon. She hated to leave him, but knew that the only way to bring peace back to her kingdom was to send Smote home, lest Evara y bliw destroy all her kin. *Both Alawe and Durndeng*, she realized. For Varia was now a member of both tribes, and all the fae were her concern. A tear sneaked away from her and rolled down her face when huge thunder shook the very forest floor. Evara had landed on the outskirts of the wood. It was too narrow for her to fly in; she had to walk the rest of the way to avoid striking the close trees with her huge wings. Varia could hear her coming; fast. She hugged Smote's neck.

"You go with your mother," Varia admonished. "Go with Evara, back to your birthplace." Varia wanted to add, *we will meet again*, but her heart would not let her lie.

Smote dragged toward the sound of the larger dragon crashing through the forest, dejected with his tail on the ground as he looked back once more. Varia's lower lip began to tremble as she hovered above the ferny wooded glen. When Smote went out of sight, Varia was caught off guard when she was smashed from above, and all went black.

Chapter Twenty-Two

In the temporary palace in Rhysgollen forest, Irea hovered over the fae soldiers who were wounded but recovering.

"Everyone here is well tended to," Irea said, checking the last of her injured patients, a Durndeng named Mengwade who had been knocked to the ground in the skirmish over the falling of the Thundendell oak. Two other nurses continued to dress the lacerations of the Vorku.

"Yes," agreed Hoondeen, flitting into an adjoining empty chamber where she found a chair and rested after also attending to the Vorku warriors. Irea followed her, and as dim light filtered in from a window created in the ceiling above, Irea could see herself in the dark-haired faewoman. Irea had never seen another fae with black locks, and could not pull her eyes from them.

Hoondeen's daughter Kurnoon flew into the room, followed closely by her sister Dunheen, the two striking female faeries resembling men in their pants and tunics until Kurnoon let her hair down and swished her dark tresses over the tops of her wings.

"Mother," Kurnoon said in a low voice. She looked over at Irea, and stared at the Alawe. Irea sat down on a nearby bench to rest her weary wings. Kurnoon spoke in a quiet voice to her mother, as Dunheen, the younger sister, approached and listened in.

Soon Hoondeen turned toward Irea. "Irea of Erendome, Princess of Ashenthorne, these are my daughters with King Struben, Kurnoon and Dunheen, princesses of Thundendell, land of Birkendore."

Irea rose up in the air and nodded in greeting, staring now at the two younger fae. Their hair was shaded brown, lighter than hers, but she could see the squared jawlines, the high foreheads and chiseled cheekbones favored the queen's and her own face.

"Greetings," said Irea while crossing her hand to her shoulder in the royal-to-royal Alawe method of salutation, something Irea had never done before in her lifetime.

"Mother, who is she?" Dunheen asked, as if not believing Irea could talk of her own will.

"I will let her tell you," Hoondeen replied, motioning with her gaze toward Irea. Irea alighted softly to the floor of the makeshift infirmary where the wounded fae were being treated.

"I am . . ." Irea began, but her words stuck there. Here she was, a faery of distant royal lines who had lived a peaceful life, only to discover that she was in reality a potential future queen of two tribes! She took a breath and lowered her wings humbly behind her, and gathered her thoughts.

"I was raised an Alawe, in the court of the royal prince and princesses, as their cousin," Irea said. "My uncle, King Dreya of Ashenthorne, was an excellent mentor to me, and his sister, the princess Liope, the one who raised me as her own, was a lovely, fair faewoman whom I miss very much, as she was killed nearly a cyton ago."

Hoondeen nodded encouragement as Dunheen and Kurnoon settled themselves onto two flat stones in the corner of the makeshift hospital room. Irea paced with light feet as she continued her story.

"This is what I was told, that my mother was princess Liope, and my father was the brave warrior Ria, who was killed in the human uprising of Vellinta four cytons ago." Irea looked at the two sisters, who were sitting rapt listening to her tale. "But as it turns out," Irea said, "none of these stories is the truth, for I am, in fact, your half-sister, daughter of your mother Queen Hoondeen of Birkendore, and daughter of the man I was told is my uncle, King Dreya of Ashenthorne."

Kurnoon flew straight up in the air, she was so surprised, and Dunheen stood.

"You, our sister?" Dunheen said, her skepticism evident by her raised eyebrows. "Impossible! You are an AirWalker."

"Why were we never told you had another daughter?" Kurnoon wondered aloud as she lowered herself to the ground.

"It was a secret we had to keep for the safety of many," Hoondeen said simply. "But that is no longer the case, as the truth has come to us, and we are to embrace Irea as one of our own."

The sisters looked at each other, uncertain until Kurnoon walked over to Irea and rested her hand on her shoulder, and Dunheen followed suit. Irea returned the universal fae greeting of acceptance. They all smiled shyly at one another.

"The woods are ablaze!" shouted Prince Moont, Loben's father, as he entered the chamber. He stared a moment at Irea before continuing. "We must go to Erendome, there is trouble there and they need reinforcements to help with extinguishing the fires!"

"Where is Loben?" asked Hoondeen.

"He is there, with his new AirWalker wife, though do not ask me how he managed to fly on an injured wing. Leave a few attendees for the wounded, and nourish yourselves well, the flight to Erendome is long and now dangerous, with humans in between and the Hammershins and Ashenthorne on fire!"

Moont seemed to hesitate before he added, "And I do not know if the rumour is true, but it is said that dragons are the cause of the blaze!"

"Dragons!" said Hoondeen. "Hurry all, we must fly!"

The Durndeng caverns came alive as all who were able bodied readied themselves for the flight to Erendome.

When Zedah returned to Loben's side, she was not alone, but had with her four hummingbirds who resembled her. Loben held up a hand in greeting.

"Zedah, I wonder what your plan is?" he asked the bird, but he found out as the four birds hovered above him, their wing beats furious. Understanding, Loben lifted his arms. Two clutched with their agile feet at his elbows and lifted him up. Once he was in the air, two others grabbed him about the ankles. Zedah led the way, and Loben was able to use his own wings to help lift himself in the air. With the hummingbirds, lucene potion, and by his own accord, they could all fly fast toward the Drakotanith portal. To their left ahead, the Hammershins burned, but the Llandwig forest, a dark mass beneath a burgeoning sky, remained their destination.

Varia came to and found herself dangling from a tree branch, her arms bound above her by a fae rope, her wings wrapped in a makeshift binding cloth fashioned from leaf and vine. Panic seized her as she realized she was alone, abandoned to the elements. Any bird of prey or large insect could feast on her if she were discovered. Her heart raced as she tried to make sense of what had happened to her. She twisted her wrists to see if she could escape, but was unable to free herself.

"I see you are awake now, Sister," Ezia said, his voice menacing as he sat on a nearby limb, his deep voice startling her.

"Ezia! Unhand me! What is it you think you are doing?' Varia asked, angry that Ezia would detain her.

"I am taking you hostage so father will have to agree to allow Alshea to go free! For we cannot continue to skulk around in the woods, forever in fear of capture," Ezia answered. "No part of the woods are safe for fae on the run. Or have you not heard the rumours?"

"What rumours?" Varia asked, a laugh punctuating her question. "There is madness and pandemonium going on all around us! Rumours of humans moving into the meadows? Rumours of dragons escaping from Drakotanith? Rumours of the Hammershins fire creeping toward Ashenthorne?"

"How about rumours of our cousin Irea being the heir of Erendome and Thundendell?" Ezia said.

"Irea?" Varia asked, her thoughts spinning as she wondered if she could cause Ezia to doubt his knowledge. "What nonsense are you speaking of?"

"Irea is the child of our father King Dreya and the Queen Hoondeen of Birkendore!" Ezia spat. "She is a cross-breed, a freak, and she will be the ruin of our two tribes!'

Varia shook her head, pretending not to know it already. "How did this information come to you?"

"I spent time near the castle Thundendell and overheard the EarthSeeker warriors discussing it! If the two tribes' forces combine, there will be no safe place for us remaining

Alawe to hide from the wrath of two thrones. She cannot become queen!"

"You are right about one thing, it is but a rumour. Release me now, Ezia, for there are bigger worries than our cousin's potential queenhood. I promise you our very lives are at stake as we speak, and from dragons, not warriors!"

Ezia flew up and hovered in front of Varia, so close that his furious wingbeat felt like an ill wind. Varia could see the crazed look in his eyes, the set mouth and determined frown. *He is not himself,* she thought, and fear charged through her body as she sensed he may cause her harm. When he pulled his weapon from its sheath at his tunic's belt, her heart jumped and she pushed her head sideways, rough bark from the tree scraping her cheek.

"Do not try to bargain with me!" Ezia said, pushing the Alawe blade against Varia's neck. He poked the tip into her flesh just enough so a small amount of aubergine blood spilled. Varia gasped at the sharp pain.

"Obey me, Sister. I cannot free Alshea from persecution if I do not have you as hostage! We must go and make father bind an agreement to set us all free. Even now Alshea hides in the woods, awaiting my return. You have no choice; you must come with me and cooperate, or I shall leave you here, exposed to the elements where you shall perish!"

Varia felt weakened from the loss of blood and realized that she had not eaten or consumed any nectar for too long. Evening light filled the forest and soon the sun would fall. Hope waned; she would never be able to return Evara and Smote to Drakotanith in time, as Varia remembered Loben's warning, *the portal doesn't stay in one place long.* Angst filled her as she realized defeat.

"I have not eaten," Varia said. "I know not how long I was unconscious, but I am weak and unable to fly, and my wings pain me from these bindings. Unshackle me and feed me so I can be of some help to you, but do not harm me again, Brother, for I am of no use to you dead!"

Ezia leered at Varia and he shoved her tied hands backward into the tree, pinning her wings painfully under her as she squirmed, to no avail. His breath was hot in her face.

"I am in charge," he said in an even voice. Varia quivered under his anger. "I will give you sustenance soon enough, but I will not release you, for you are my hostage. I will trade you to Father in return for a binding arrangement for Alshea's freedom." Ezia whistled into the air and reached up with his knife, the blade still covered in Varia's blood. He cut the rope that bound her hands from the tree but held the ends. Varia dropped like a falling stone and hung in mid-air, Ezia holding the other end of the rope, suspending Varia beneath him. A huge pale grey harrier careened toward them, and Varia tensed. Ezia leapt onto the creature's back, leaving Varia hanging beneath the sharp talons as the bird soared into an elder tree. Ezia pulled on the rope, and Varia used her feet to climb the branch and mount the raptor behind Ezia. The slim bird of prey with an owl-like face stared, unblinking. Once Varia was seated, Ezia pulled her wrist bindings taut, so Varia's hands settled in front of her. She used her fingertips to hold on to Ezia's belt. The harrier lifted into the orange-lit sky, heading in the opposite direction of the dragons she was supposed to be returning to Drakotanith.

Flying with bound wings was terrifying; at every lift, Varia was nearly unseated from the back of the soaring hawk. Because she wasn't using any of her own energy to fly, she grew chilled and leaned into her brother's back for warmth. She could tell the harrier was being used against its will and she sent the message, *I too am captive of the Alawe faery Ezia, and I apologize for my faepeople his rash use of your service.* But the "grey ghost" hawk flew on, and if he received Varia's message, he did not send one back.

The woods grew smoky as they glided out the south end of the Llandwig into the east Hammershins. Varia could not see flames but heard shouts and strange rumbling noises as the inferno raged, and realized the humans were fighting the fire. She listened to the stories the trees told; the humans were using water to douse the blaze. The trees were cheering the humans on, something Varia did not expect. A small smile edged along her cracked lips. *Something good at last,* she thought.

As the hawk careened through the forest's edge, Varia sensed a familiar presence and peeked behind her. There she saw Loben, carried by four hummingbirds, one of them Zedah. The hummingbirds flew toward her and Varia braced herself, frightened that whatever they did to try and save her might unseat her and she would tumble to the ground, her useless wings still bound. Ezia looked up and saw Loben. Before Loben could grasp Varia, on Ezia's command the harrier swooped down. Varia felt herself lurch forward and she free-fell like a twig from a tree toward hard dirt.

Varia felt four strong but gentle feet grab her and stop her from hitting the ground. Amidst a fast-paced flutter of wings, she was lowered to the earth. She pulled on the fae rope that bound her hands and watched as the two hummingbirds who had saved her worked their long beaks on the binding cloth vines that held her wings. One wing was freed, then the other. She stretched and flapped each one to loosen the strained appendages. Loben landed beside her, brought down by Zedah's cohorts. The two faeries embraced.

"I have been so worried about you," Loben said as he stroked Varia's hair, smoothing her long white braid. Varia leaned into him and breathed deeply.

"I am so grateful you saved me!" she said, kissing him. Their mouths met and a spark of remembrance and desire filled them; the same magick spark that had united them in their marriage bound their strength together now. Varia pulled away and looked into Loben's face and saw that the lucene ointment was wearing off, and though he still looked pale, his familiar features shone in the last vestiges of sunlight. Her eyes scanned the shady canopy.

"Where is Ezia?" she asked, the urgency of her dragon mission weighing on her. "We must find a way back to Rhysgollen forest quickly, for Ezia will try and stop us if we linger!" A shadow caught the corner of her eye as Ezia returned on the grey harrier. Commotion filled the air; the grey bird swooped toward the hummingbird pack, Ezia leading the raid. The high-pitched call of the tiny birds filled the quiet forest thicket as they scattered.

"No!" cried Loben. With his injured wing he tried to fly up to protect the hummingbirds, but Ezia returned once more to the fray. The hawk zeroed in on Loben in a straight dive from the treetops like a streak of lightning. Zedah flew between Loben and the talons of the oncoming prey bird. Zedah's small feathered body careened from the blow and struck the ground hard. The hawk rose into the sky as Varia rushed to Zedah's side.

"No, my beloved Zedah, no..." Loben said as he gathered up Zedah into his arms. He looked at Varia, his eyes wet. "She is dead," he said. "She died protecting me!" Loben leaned his forehead against the still bird's chest crooned to her broken body in the old tongue:

Nu blétsian ælfen onuppan ou . . .

Varia held back a sob as she stared at Zedah, her insides twisting that her own brother had caused Loben this pain, and taken the life of their best ally. Loben stood and carried his best friend to a clump of the flower called Old Man's Beard, its white dazzling blooms illuminated in the falling night. He carefully laid her body at the base of the plant, and covered it with nearby twigs and leaves and bark until she was one with the earth. "Fare thee well, my beloved friend," Loben whispered, his voice tight with emotion. He held Varia's hand. "It is my fault that she died," he said.

"The harrier hen, the one called Cromán na gCearc, flew off after the attack with Ezia riding his back," Varia said. "I daresay that bird is a captive of Ezia, and not a willing participant in being his steed. It is only Ezia's fault, not yours, my love." She rested her hand on Loben's face, smoothing the sorrow from his brow.

"Come, we must rest," she said. "Allow me to bring you into a safer place, for your sorrow cannot cause us to be careless in the night." Varia and Loben climbed to the safety of a small crevice in the base of a nearby tree, on the ground but well hidden by plants and fungi. They sat together just outside the cranny under a pendulous leaf.

"We are just on the outer reaches of the Llandwig, and we must rest before we can find Smote and Evara and return them to their realm," Varia said.

Loben handed her his vial. "I have but a little nectar left, but tomorrow, we will find more." He sipped the gooey liquid and Varia drained the flask after him.

While the waning crickets chirped by rubbing their wings together all around them, the forest seemed dark from other than the night. The trees grew thick, making it difficult to see the stars and moon. It was Loben who noted the change. "The blackness here matches the blackness I feel in my heart, after losing my friend Zedah," he said.

Varia found a flat pebble and pulled out a small pinch of the hestus powder. She lit the essence of light by rubbing it on the stone and blowing on the hard surface. A soft glow illuminated their area, and Varia liked the soft mossy bank and fern-lined creekside bed that awaited them.

"I will check for insects," Loben said, and he inspected the den. Finding nothing, he motioned for Varia to join him. "There is water just below for drinking, and I feel the need to move my wings. I will find us a scant meal to settle our stomachs for the night."

"I will fashion some leaf blankets so the chill won't bother us," Varia said. She set down the pebble and upon surveying the area she found several large oak leaves that had fallen nearby. They were dry but not brittle, and softened by recent rains. Varia looked up through the dense trees and saw the sky was clouding up for a sprinkle. She gathered a few extra leaves and draped them over the curling ferns to create a tent-like structure, and she rested on the moss and dragged one of the leaves over her. In the distance she could hear Loben near the flower-laden grave saying his final farewell to Zedah. Sadness filled her as he had his last private moment of grief. Soon he returned, bearing mushrooms, dewberries, and he had filled his empty nectar flask with fine strips of bark and spring water for a simple tea.

"It is light fare, but will get us through to the morning," Loben said. Varia's stomach growled, and she picked up a berry.

"It has been long since I have tasted a dewberry," she said, tasting the sweet but mushy fruit as she popped a whole drupelet in her mouth. She wiped her mouth with her hand, and Loben kissed her.

"You taste good," he said, and he kissed her again, their exchanges berry-flavored.

They continued to eat, slowing the pace, and Varia, remembering how much the Durndeng love mushrooms, fed one to Loben. He took a bite and she could tell that it was delicious to him; she enjoyed the moment as he followed suit with another dewberry, and they ate until they were sated, and his eyes held less sorrow, and then they sipped the bark-tinged water.

Loben flapped his wings after the food was finished, and Varia stood up.

"May I look at your wing?" she asked, and Loben nodded. She gently handled the short stalk where the wing muscles connected to his back and felt the imbalance of energy there. She felt his good wing, and found by tapping into her healing powers that if she rubbed her hands over the delicate wing membrane, she could use her mind to release the tension, the wing so strained from overuse. Loben moaned in pleasure at the relief. Reaching over and taking his second wing in her hands, she noted the opposite   problem. . . underuse. The patch was a scarred, thick spot in Loben's otherwise iridescent member, but it showed no signs of distress. She was careful as she moved Loben's stiff wing back and forth; it was rigid and did not move easily. She tried it several more times until the appendage moved loosely of its own accord. Loben rolled over to face her and pulled Varia close.

"That is so much better," he said, kissing her on the top of her head. "Thank you."

"The patch Rumendah put there is almost healed. I think you should try using it freely now, for tomorrow we must find Evara and Smote, as it is our last opportunity to return them to Drakotanith."

"I too have been thinking of that, for they must be waiting out the night to the north of us, but Evara could decide to fly off and leave this place forever and unleash herself on the rest of the world."

"Let us rest then, as our night has already held much sorrow, and we must begin again before daybreak."

Varia dampened the hestus with a fallen leaf and the dark surrounded them as they curled up together, face to face, in their cozy bed for the night.

"Let us not rest yet," Loben said, and he reached out for Varia, and she nestled closer into his arms, and together they melded in the dimly lit alcove as the thunderous skies above opened, sprinkling down rain, like tears.

Chapter Twenty-Three

 ℱar to the south by Craggyrock Lake, Alshea, Talow, Ulla and Baylo sat around a meager hestus fire in the rainy pre-dawn gloom. The rock outcropping above them did little to protect them from the howling wet wind, and their moods matched the dark sky. Alshea wore the uniform of a Wilhvyre warrior, and picked at the selection of nuts and grains laid before her in the dim light.

"Ezia has a plan to secure the dragon and my sister Varia, who as you all know is the cause of this strife," Alshea said. "He will use her as leverage to have our prisoners' labels released on us, so we can move forward in our plans to begin a new colony, and to start a new tribe of pure Alawe faeries."

"It had better work," Talow said irritably. "For living in the wilderness is not the way I would like to spend the rest of my days! Our forces are as of yet small, my queen. I am considering life in Erendome prison a step up from this nightmare! At least I shall be warm and dry and fed at regular intervals."

Alshea glared at Talow but said nothing. Baylo and Ulla looked at one another and grumbled. Talow winged into the air, his senses alert.

"What is it?" asked Alshea, standing and looking out across the turbulent water of the lake. "What do you see?"

"I see nothing," said Talow, "but I sense trouble. Come, douse the hestus flame and gather your belongings. I feel this is no longer a safe place to be."

"Always moving us around in the middle of the night," Baylo muttered under his breath. "And for what? Nothing ever happens."

A swoop of dark forces claimed them and before any could react, the black and silver-clad Vorku scouts secured them. Alshea tried to wrest her way free but found herself lodged tight between two strong warriors.

"Unhand me!" she shouted, but the soldiers grabbed her and pinned her wings in a binding cloth.

"Send word to the kings that the fugitives were captured," said Wurdu the Vorku warrior. As the four were pinioned, Ezia returned from his attempted capture of Varia just in time to see his entire new clan being spirited away by dozens of enemy fighters.

The morning dawn broke the cloudy sky with rosy rays as Varia shivered and nestled in closer to Loben, who wrapped his arms around her. She listened to the gurgling stream, and the occasional caw of a jay gathering acorns for winter. Varia wished she could stay there in the warmth of Loben's embrace forever, but she knew they must leave to find the dragons. The expected rains had been light and left the forest floor with a dewy sheen, and everything glistened in the few places where sunlight filtered through the abundant trees. Varia stood and Loben joined her.

"My wing is much improved," he said, kissing her on the nose. "I think I can fly! I will try my wings and go and find us nectar and return here; you drink from the stream." He walked a few steps away from their sleeping area and lifted himself into the sky and hovered. He grinned down at Varia.

"Just a bit stiff," he called to her. "But I can do it!" He zoomed up into the canopy and soon she couldn't see him any longer. She put on her tunic and belted her supply pouch. Soon Loben returned with a leaf wrapped full of food.

"We still have mushrooms and berries too," Varia said, motioning toward the leftovers just outside their fortress, now damp with raindrops, but still edible. Soon they ate and drank from Loben's collected full vial of nectar. Varia closed her eyes and focused on Smote; she sensed his presence to the north.

"I know where Smote is, let's hurry before Evara wreaks more devastation in this realm," Varia said. Holding hands, Varia and Loben flew toward the wayward dragons.

Rain splashed during part of the journey but they dried quickly when sun peeked through the clouds as they approached the northern-most end of the Llandwig forest.

"Hopefully the rain will help with the fires," Loben said.

Varia used all of her senses and tried to tap into the universe, as she had seen Rumendah do before. She received many messages, and could not easily focus on her question about the fire, but finally was able to sense it: animals fleeing for their lives, the fae all fighting the blaze as one, the trees dying but the fire lessening, even the humans working to save the land.

"There is little we can do from here to help, Loben. They are making progress putting out the blaze, if I have guessed it right. We are on our own quest."

"No truer words have been spoken," Loben said in a low voice.

"We must fly in to Llandwig silently," Varia said in a whisper. "Evara slumbers now, I can sense her breathing in a rhythmic way, but if I know Smote, he is rambling about, and he may get too excited if he sees me."

"Do not forget about the grey faery Barghest, for he is undoubtedly guarding the pair."

"I had forgotten to reckon him in. Do we have a plan?" Varia asked.

"Can one reason with a dragon?" Loben answered. "Because that is the only plan I have." Varia considered a moment as they flew on hushed wings toward a meadow glen where the huge beast Evara lay curled up asleep, her tail wrapped around Smote, also asleep. Barghest was not in sight.

Varia felt motherly emotion at seeing her young dragonling snoring peacefully in Evara the Blue's embrace, and wished that he could somehow still be hers forever. Logic told her that they were of two worlds, fae and dragon, and their paths were not meant to cross. She motioned for Loben to wait in a gnarled alder edging the lea. Loben called Varia with his hand and pointed to a catkin hanging in the tree; Varia swooped over to it with him. They shared the bitter fruit of the alder and she grimaced at the sharp flavor, but the alder catkin had more energy- producing fuel than even nectar. Fortified, she indicated with her hands that she would go and try to lure Smote away from Evara, daring not even a whisper within the keen ears of the she-dragon.

Loben kissed her before she flew low and quiet toward the sleepers. Smote was opening and closing his eyes; Varia smiled, knowing that he had been scolded by Evara and had to "wait" for his large mother to finish her rest before he could play. He snapped at the grass blowing nearby until he saw Varia; he leapt up from his spot and flew out of the giant's tail embrace. Varia watched Evara's eye, but it did not open. Varia flew toward the woods, Smote galloping behind, himself now the length of a sapling tree. In the open meadow, Varia flew backward a few times so she could witness the majesty of her young charge: he gleamed teal in the morning sun, his scales shiny and sleek, and he looked proud as terrified rabbits and partridges fled for cover in his path. When he reached the alder grove, he looked up, writhing happily as he saw Loben. Loben flew down to him and put his hand on the dragon's snout in an affectionate way. The two fae sat astride his neck and flew toward the Drakotanith portal, to send Smote back to his own realm.

"You have grown!" Loben told Smote as he patted his neck, now out of earshot of Evara the Blue. Smote soared through the trees, making a game of it as the two faeries held on; he would seem as if he would crash into a tree and then veer dangerously, and do the same on the next one, using one big wingbeat so they were gliding through the air. Varia giggled; it was fun riding Smote this way, but a tugging at her heart made her know that there were many things she and Smote had yet to experience, that she would miss when he went "home".

A roar filled the air far behind them, and Varia sighed. "Mum's awake," she said. Loben nodded.

"It would appear so. Send her a message."

Varia concentrated, and sent Evara a message that she and Loben were in the woods with Smote, and they wanted to make an agreement. Another reverberation shook a few leaves from the trees, but they could hear the heavy wingbeat of Evara's flight. She arrived fiercely fast, an impressive figure as she landed and trees fell in her wake. Varia felt sympathy for the dying trees and knew the sooner she could get the dragons to Drakotanith, the better off her world would be.

We ask that you leave our realm, as this place is not fit for dragons, Varia sent the thought to Evara as she neared. Evara lowered her behemoth eye toward Varia, but Varia knew not to look directly into it.

Why should I leave? Evara sent the thought to Varia and Loben, and trees quaked (and so did Varia).

You do not belong here, and should not wreak your wrath on innocent trees, faeries, and humans! Varia said in her mind.

Humans! Since when do the fae care for the lowly humans? Evara thought back.

Varia did not like where the conversation was heading, and she changed the subject as she watched Smote playing nearby in a sunlit meadow, his body a gleaming teal jewel.

Your offspring, Sm . . . Fletheroth the Green, deserves a life of freedom from persecution, Varia tried reasoning with the dragon, *and that is something he will get only in Drakotanith.*

Evara seemed to consider this advice, and Varia took the quiet moment to inhale. The trees lost leaves as the thunderous thoughts of Evara ripped through the stillness of the woodlands.

I will set you a task, to ask me a riddle," Evara sent. *If you ask me a riddle I cannot answer, then I shall willingly return to Drakotanith with my baby, never to return to this land.*

Varia was relieved, but saw Loben shaking his head 'no' even as the word 'yes' sprang from Varia's lips.

"Yes, we will take the offer," Varia said aloud, and a ring of smoke appeared from nowhere and encircled them all, then disintegrated, leaving a golden chain of light which crumbled and dropped to the forest floor and disappeared.

"What was that?" Varia asked, and just then Barghest hovered above her, lowering himself to her level.

"That was a dragon agreement," Barghest said. "The only way out of a dragon agreement is for the dragon to slay you."

Varia felt the blood drain from her face but she whispered to Barghest, "How does it work?"

"You usually have until nightfall on the same day the bargain was made to comply," Barghest said with a shrug.

Varia was glad she had a little time to think of something and that she didn't have to be clever on the spot.

"We shall return shortly, but you must have Evara and Smote . . . er, Fletheroff, stay here. That is the only way the agreement can still remain in effect."

Varia was fairly sure that she couldn't demand anything of Evara but Barghest looked up at the tree-height dragon, who closed her eye lazily and settled down for a nap. Varia grabbed Loben by the hand and they sped to the south to regain their wits, but not too far before they stopped in a linden tree to catch their breath.

"A dragon riddle?" Loben said as they sat on a branch and sipped some of the nectar in his flask, as they had vowed to keep nourished this time.

"I am no good at riddles!" Varia said. "Perhaps we can get help."

"I don't know," Loben answered, and he shook his head. "Perhaps Rumendah can help us?"

"We do not have time to seek him!" Varia said. "For we must hurry and get the dragons back to their land. Do you have knowledge of any riddles?"

"A few," Loben said, "but none that a tricky dragon couldn't guess!"

"Try one," Varia said. "We are desperate."

"Okay." Loben sat on the rough bark of the limb and absently beat his wings in place as he thought a moment.

"Here's one:
> I am always hungry,
> I must always be fed,
> The finger I touch,
> Will soon turn red.

What am I?"

Varia thought a moment and then looked to the west, where the remaining smoke from the Hammershins fire filled the air.

"Fire?" she asked. Loben nodded, and Varia laughed. "Fire riddles for a fire-breathing dragon!" she said, and Loben smiled sheepishly.

"You try it, then. It's not so easy, under pressure."

"Very well." Varia sat beside Loben and stretched her legs out in front of her as their wings brushed against one another.

"How about this one: *The more you have of it, the less you see.* What is it?"

Loben looked perplexed as he tried to work it out in his mind, but then his eyes lit up. "Is it darkness?" he asked. Varia nodded but frowned.

"We can't use the ones she would already know, Loben. We have to invent one."

"We have to make her think the answer is obvious when it isn't, so she'll guess wrong," Loben agreed. The two of them sat together, sipping the nectar and chewing on more of the catkins that Loben had stored in his pouch as they worked out a riddle they thought would trick Evara.

As the day grew warmer they came up with a riddle they thought would work. Standing, they held one another close as they readied themselves for flight.

"I love you Loben. I was unable to say it before, but I am sorry for Zedah's passing. Your life would be simpler if you hadn't met me," Varia said, leaning her head on Loben's strong chest.

"That is true," Loben said, kissing her on top of her head. "But I would not trade it, complications and all, for anything, Varia. Yours is the love I have waited for all along. And if today is the day we end our immortal lives, I am glad we have had this time together."

Varia smiled and held Loben tighter. "I feel the same. We must go, and stay strong for each other. I will do the talking, since the deal was made with me," Varia said. "And if it goes badly, please Loben, escape. I don't want us both to die."

"The same goes for you, my sweet, for if one of us should perish, the other should go on, so our love will be remembered."

They kissed one more time and flew to the place where they had left the slumbering dragon.

Smote bounded up to Varia and Loben like a deranged fox whelp when they entered the forest break, flying low. The woods were still; all wildlife had fled upon Evara's initial arrival and the trees seemed to barely dare to breathe.

Barghest woke the sleeping giant with a gentle whisper: "My queen, the fae return."

Evara went from slumbering to upright, rising her whole height above the treeline before lowering her head to the level of the fae, who alighted in the crotch of a whitebeam.

"Have you come up for a riddle for me, faeries? For if you have and you succeed, I will go directly into the portal to return to Drakotanith and fulfill the end of my obligation."

"We have," Varia said aloud, noting that when she chose to, Evara could quiet her thoughts so that they would not level the local flora.

"Proceed," Evara said with her thoughts.

"Very well," Varia began, remembering that she had to be very careful. She could not add any extra words, or say anything that could be construed as part of the riddle if it was not part of it, according to Loben. Varia took a deep breath.

> *"Until I am measured*
> *I cannot be known,*
> *Yet how you will miss me*
> *When I have flown.*
> What am I?"

Varia waited for the dragon to absorb the words, not daring to speak another sentence. She cleared her mind, as did Loben, so that the answer would not pop out in her thoughts unexpectedly. Evara seemed to be waiting for the solution to come to her from them and she moved her giant head closer, as if seeing if she could intimidate it from their minds. Instead, as Varia had suggested, both faeries focused all of their attention on Smote. *Watch him play*, Varia had told Loben as they came up with the right words for the conundrum. *Think of our experience with him, but do not let your thoughts slip toward the riddle's answer!* Varia remembered the first moment she saw Smote, how he had hatched from his egg, and how when he ate, he grew. She recalled calming him when he was stuck in the cave walls, and how much she enjoyed riding on his back, frighteningly fast though it was. She remembered all of her sweet memories with him, and felt a heavy sadness in her heart at having to say goodbye. Evara glared at her.

"I can tell you took good care of my hatchling," Evara said, her thoughts gentle. "Yet your love for him has addled your mind, for I find the answer to be obvious. The answer to your riddle is Fletheroth y Gras, known as Fletheroth the Green, or to you, Smote. My baby dragon is the answer."

Varia's heart thrilled and Evara realized her mistake, too late. Her roar caused Varia and Loben to drop to their knees with their hands over their ears, and the deciduous trees in the forest all around them lost every leaf, naked limbs now exposed to the elements.

"I am wrong?" Evara's thoughts thundered through the woods.

"The answer is 'time,'" Varia said evenly. Evara raged again, and her dragon screech could be felt all the way to the seashore. Smote flattened himself to the leafy forest floor until his mother was done 'yelling.'

"Very well," Evara said, her head low in disappointment. "A bargain is a bargain. Let us go then, to the portal. I will leave this place." With her nose she nudged Smote up from the ground.

Barghest flew to the top of Evara's spiked head and rode there as she ambled through the tight forest, and Loben flew ahead and led the way, sensing the magical doorway. Soon they entered a part of the woods where the leaves were still intact on the trees, and there, between two Scots pines, was the wavering blue circle that outlined the dragon realm's entryway.

"Go and good tidings," Loben said, giving the fae hail sign of goodwill to Evara. He patted Smote on the nose, and the dragon breathed out a happy curl of smoke.

"Farewell my sweet Smote," Varia said, and she held him, careful to avoid his sharp scales, not allowing her tears to fall. She choked in a sob, her heart wrenching as she said her final goodbye. Smote nudged her gently and the tears did finally fall. Varia grabbed him and held him tight, wondering how she could ever let go. She could hear Loben explain the process of entering into the portal to Evara and she was grateful for the extra moments with her beloved child-dragon.

"You must all be touching one another, and hold on tight, it is a bit uncomfortable," he reminded her. "Do not let go of Smote— your baby—until you enter Drakotanith!"

Loben grasped Varia's arm and pulled her away, and they stayed back as first Barghest, holding Evara's horns, entered. He disappeared in a fizzle of purple electricity. Evara went next, and worked her huge body halfway through, her tail wrapped tightly around Smote's middle. Loben grabbed Varia's arm tighter, as Varia herself hadn't noticed until then that she was leaning in as Smote moved closer to the vortex, awaiting his turn. He cast a sad look to Varia and Loben as he neared the portal behind his mother. The faeries waved, and Loben wrapped his arm around Varia's shoulders, holding her closer, for her soul was being pulled toward the disappearing young dragon. Smote was about to enter the portal, his mother's tail the only thing left of Evara y Bliw in this world, when a pale blue shot of light buzzed around the baby dragon's nose. It was Ezia.

Ezia tried to wrest Smote from his mother's clutches and a terrible muffled roar came from the other side of the portal opening.

"Go!" Loben shouted as he flew toward the vortex. "Varia, we must stop him, he will interrupt the flow and Smote will remain stuck here forever!"

Varia hesitated; could Smote somehow stay? But logic won and she flew to the drama unfolding; Ezia had a rope around Smote's snout, but Evara's tail still was firmly gripping her baby. In the meantime, the circle of light was beginning to wobble, and looked unsteady as if it may snap shut at any moment, leaving Smote and his mother's tail on this side of the abyss. Loben grabbed Ezia, and in mid-air they grappled for control of Smote. Varia whooshed down to release the nose bindings. The baby was free but confused and tried to squirm from his mother's grasp.

"Go with Evara, your mother, dear Smote," Varia said in a quiet voice to calm him. The beast was baffled, and Varia stroked him. Soon his snout entered the portal, and Ezia and Loben lost control of their fight and thunked up against the hide of the young hatchling. Ezia tried pulling on the dragon to stop him from entering.

"The dragon cannot go through! He is my only hope at freeing Alshea, who has been recaptured!" Ezia yelled like a mad faeman.

"He is already in the portal, it is too late, one cannot come back out!" Loben tried reasoning with Ezia, and they grappled further, but Ezia never released his hold on Smote. A shiny teal scale popped off in his hand, and Varia could sense the pain it caused her young charge. She slapped Ezia across the face.

"You dare harm him?" she asked, tears welling in her eyes. "He is my child!" She grasped for the scale and it landed on the forest floor, but Ezia had her by the wrist.

"Do not touch me thus, Sister!" Ezia said as Evara the Blue's tail with Smote wrapped inside slowly disappeared into the brink. Loben flew down and grabbed Ezia.

"Unhand my wife," he said, twisting his grip until Ezia flew backward in pain. He clutched at the nearest thing to him to stop his fall, the tail of Smote, as it went into the magical doorway, and his shocked expression was the last thing Varia saw as the purple light of the portal blinked out, Ezia on the other side, trapped in Drakotanith with two angry dragons and one unruly grey faery.

Chapter Twenty-Four

Varia screamed as she watched her brother and Smote disappear. "Smote! Ezia!" she called, reaching out for the portal, but Loben pulled on her and stopped her.

"They are both gone, Varia. I am sorry."

Varia hovered into Loben's arms and sobbed against his tunic. "I know that Ezia was against the throne of his own father King Dreya, but, I loved him when we were children, irascible as he had become. I hate to think of him trapped in that wretched Drakotanith!" Varia sniffed. "And what will I do without my beloved Smote? I miss him already!"

"There is time for tears later," Loben said, kissing her cheek. "For now, we must find the kings and tell them the dragons are gone from Feyllan, and see what progress the fae have made in fighting the fire of the Hammershins."

Loben flew ahead, and Varia followed, glancing back a final time to see the spot where her brother and Smote had been pulled into the dark realm of the dragon lands. What greeted her eyes was an idyllic woodland setting of trees and sunlight, of evergreens and broadleaved saplings, all breathing a sigh of relief.

Loben and Varia flew south-west toward Hammershins, and soon they saw the black smoking corpses of the trees that had perished in the fire. Varia's insides twisted as she assessed the destruction, the filmy air difficult to breathe.

"I see no flame," Loben said. "I think that the fire is out!"

"I am surprised, but this does seem to be the end of it," Varia agreed as they moved through the still graveyard of smoking tree bones. "Perhaps last night's rain helped." Soon they emerged onto the open plains where the human house loomed in the distance. The char marks inched in the fields toward the home but stopped abruptly. Varia dropped down to the ground to examine strange ruts and valleys there. "This is strange," she noted.

"That is the mark of one of the human's automobiles," Loben said. "The humans used it to transport themselves to this spot, since they cannot fly."

"It is very wet here, too," Varia said. "Wetter than the small rain would have left on the earth."

"They must have carried water here from their wells, using the automobile to bring the liquid to douse the fire. I have heard of it before," Loben explained. "It was the humans who helped put the fire out, Varia."

"That is the story the trees told, but I did not understand how they managed it," Varia said as she studied the human house where she and Loben had first met, the green fenced pastures behind the home now dotted with fat white sheep.

"Maybe they are not the enemy I thought they were," Varia murmured. "I would like a closer look, I have not seen a human up close before."

"We need to use caution, though because most cannot see us anyway, we can risk it," Loben said with a shrug. "It is not far out of our way if we wish to return to the castle."

Varia looked at Loben. "Which castle?" she asked.

Loben hesitated. "Let us see what is happening at Erendome, after we inspect the humans," he said. He took Varia's hand and they flew through the sheep pastures toward the home of men, now with smoke rising from the chimney, the mown green fields enclosed by the now-repaired ancient rock walls, and a new road for the automobile reaching out into the distance.

As they sailed in for a better view, Varia saw several male human beings unloading strange items from the clunky devices called automobiles. The men were soot-covered, which gave them a rough, even frightening appearance, and their odor was strong, of smoke and the meat that they ate, like the scent of carnivorous wolves she remembered seeing as a child, the wild canines that once roamed the countryside. The wolves had long since been killed off by humans, which Varia found to be blasphemous, and it was one of the reasons she had never wanted to meet a human, so barbaric were they. She hovered near to get a better look, and was surprised to find that the humans were shaped much like her faepeople, only large and stocky, with coarse

224

hair and loud voices. They were removing tools that they had used to douse the fires, she guessed: unusual weapons with large flat metal ends. There were rolled up unfamiliar tubes, like a hollow flower stem, and she wondered what they were used for. Water dripped from them. She saw stacked up carrying devices that could hold water, buckets much like the ones that her tribe used to collect honey, only less decorative.

"Thought we might lose the farm there, Eddie," one of the men said to another.

"You were brave, thought we may lose you, Harry," said the other, and Varia could sense the emotion the human felt as he said those words, and she sensed the fear, and triumph, and relief flooding into him. She closed her eyes and allowed the sensation of his emotion to fill her, and felt those things with him as she came back to herself.

She took Loben's hand and flew toward the sunflower fields, mostly to get away from the smell.

"They are brave men," she said as they alighted on a browning seed head, the late summer heat having crisped up the plants. "It is not what I expected."

"They do not understand nature, though they live in it," Loben said. "They have somehow separated themselves from their earthly roots. It is a mystery, but they are different yet alike to us. I find humans to be one of life's greatest conundrums."

Two human children raced around the fence that led to the sunflower garden and tore through the aging stalks. Varia felt like she did when she first saw Smote: curious, and even a bit smitten. She flittered down to their level and watched them frolic. She was startled when the girl human, just old enough to run and play, pointed at Varia.

"Faery," she said, and Varia felt a rush at being recognized. While her instinct was to fly away, she hovered in front of the tow-headed child's face, the girl's blue eyes sparkling with excitement at seeing Varia. In spite of herself, Varia smiled and waved.

"Pretty," the girl said. The boy child stopped running and grabbed his sibling's hand.

225

"Come on, Lizzie, I hear a frog!" he said, and laughing he ran with her toward the pond at the far end of the patch.

"Not so fast, Peter, wait!" she heard the girl call as Varia returned to Loben, who was grinning.

"I was seen by a human!" Varia said, a sense of wonder still with her.

"That human child won't forget that she saw you, but her family will tell her that she is imagining it," Loben said. "Humans can't tolerate believing in faeries, it stands in the way of their ordered world."

"Let us fly to Erendome, Loben," Varia said. "I would like to tell the kings that we have no enemy between us, and that the humans should be welcome to stay, even if they have reclaimed their home in our realm. We must also inform them of what happened to Ezia at the door of Drakotanith, and I dread having to say those words to my father, so much has he lost already."

Though the fields near the Erendome trees were charred and the forest of the Hammershins in the distance shadowed the realm with eerie black tree skeletons, the palace of Erendome itself was spared. As Varia and Loben flew up to the front gate, a crowd of faeries cheered.

"Here come the dragon conquerors!" they shouted, and Varia felt that tricking Evara and losing her beloved Smote and the unfortunate Ezia hardly seemed to be anything to celebrate, but both she and Loben allowed the fanfare.

"I wish to speak with King Dreya and King Struben," Varia announced, her voice formal as they awaited the opening of the ornate gate.

"Enter, Princess Varia of Ashenthorne, Defender of Erendome, who has returned!" the unknown guard at the entry called. Another cheer went up, and Varia was pleased that she had regained her original title of "defender"—the title she'd lost when she was put into the Erendome prison cell just moons before. She and Loben were cheered all the way through the main doors of the castle, and fallen meadow flower petals were gathered and tossed overhead as the fanfare continued.

Once Varia and Loben entered the palace, the crowd was left behind and the usual castle affairs seemed to be commencing, with one major difference; the Vorku army, in their stark black and silver uniforms, made for a heavy presence in the airy hall. Varia's reaction was gut-felt, having been chased by the soldiers before. Her nerves overcame her and she grasped at Loben's hand. He understood.

"I too have been a Vorku prisoner, on more than one occasion," he murmured. "But now, they are welcome here, as are we." At the doors that led to the private quarters of the king, the pair was stopped.

"We are here to see my father King Dreya, and my husband's uncle, King Struben," Varia announced. The Wilhvyre guard, a young one at that, flitted about, uncertain as he seemed to try to collect himself. He bowed awkwardly and opened the ornate wooden doors to the chamber. Varia and Loben entered, and upon seeing her father, Varia soared to him and hugged him.

"Father!" she said, her eyes filling with tears. "Oh, to see you back in Erendome! It fills me with great joy."

"My daughter, I am so relieved to see you!" King Dreya said. Behind him stood King Struben, who greeted Loben with a hearty arm shake. Queen Hoondeen embraced her nephew as well. Behind Dreya, Irea came from beyond the curtains that separated different rooms of the chambers. Varia flew to her and the two fell into each other's arms.

"Ah, too long has it been that we have shared a moment together!" Varia said, leaning her head against Irea's raven hair.

"I have missed you so much, Varia," Irea whispered. The two stared into each other's eyes and their Devic spirits mingled, and they were one again, as they had been since they were faechildren.

"So I presume that the dragons have been returned to the realm of Drakotanith?" Dreya asked, a hopeful tone in his voice.

"Yes," Varia said, keeping her voice even. She meant to mention Ezia, but said instead, "It is done. And not an easy task, I may add!"

"This we already knew," King Dreya said as he sat in his throne, and to Varia's surprise, King Struben sat in the one

227

once reserved for her mother beside him. She liked seeing the two kings of the fae side by side.

"You, dear Varia, and Loben, are the first to accomplish it. To trick a dragon into their own realm once it is released has never before been done since the very portals were shut down from outside worlds. While it is true that dragons and humans once co-mingled, that is precisely because the beasts were unleashed from Drakotanith and never put back in their proper place." The king nodded in an approving way. "And as we know from the old stories, many humans and faeries perished, and all of the dragons that ventured into our realm were eventually killed by human beings. Your beloved Smote and his mother would have surely suffered the same fate had they stayed here."

Varia put her hands to her mouth at the thought of harm coming to Smote. "I am glad we succeeded then, though I do have sad news to report, Father. Your only son Ezia was swept into the Drakotanith portal with Smote and his mother Evara the Blue, and the grey faery Barghest. He is stuck in another realm, and I know not how to bring him back."

An anguished look crossed Dreya's face, and Irea gasped. "There is no way to come back from that dark place without the proper magick and spells, Varia," Dreya said in a gloomy tone, shaking his head.

"The king is right," came a voice, and Varia saw Rumendah, still bent and weakened but very much alive, come into the room. Beside him hopped the raven Krahbane, though the bird was injured; his face was deeply scarred and one eye was missing, and in its place, was a strange bright glassy-looking stone. Varia got the sense that the bird could somehow see through the sparkling dead orb, and she wondered about it as she hugged the elder fae. "I am glad you are safe!" she said. "And Krahbane too."

"These are difficult times, and we are all lucky to have survived," said Rumendah. "Ezia's venture into the land of Drakotanith is a loss, certainly."

"It is a shame that your brother turned against his throne, but I fear it is not the last thing that will bring sadness to this court, for we must decide what punishment the once-princess Alshea will face now that she is known to be a traitor against my throne. For we sent the Vorku and Wilhvyre armies after them, and they have been captured where they were flying free in the woods like common sparrows."

Varia's eyes widened at the news. "You mean, she will stand trial?"

"No, it is known by all what she did, and even why she did it, but her final fate is still to be decided. Her most trusted appointees, Talow and Baylo and Ulla and others, were all part of her scheme to overthrow the crown. They have asked for release into the wilds, but they must pay, Varia. Surely you understand that."

Varia nodded as Loben clasped her hand.

"All the royal heads are here now, shall we discuss their crime and get this grievous act over with?" King Struben asked. Dreya looked around.

"Yes, with the exception of your Prince Doon, who now ministers to the Thundendell oak, we are all here," Dreya said. "A council we still make. Let us proceed."

Within moments the hall was assembled with a circle of seats for the leaders of the two fae tribes, and in all the history of Feyllan none had ever witnessed such a gathering: King Dreya of the Alawe, King Struben of the Durndeng with his Queen Hoondeen by his side; Princesses Varia of Erendome and the newly anointed Princess Irea of Erendome and Thundendell were present, along with Elder Rumendah and Prince Loben of Thundendell. They sat with their wings tucked behind them in a circle and discussed the matter of what to do with Alshea and the others as the raven stood in the corner and preened.

Wing-plucking was dismissed immediately, but banishment was mentioned over and over again.

"I say take them to the Mysty Island," Rumendah said. "It is the penal colony used by many fae and pixie kingdoms. I have heard it told that the fae there have come to a peaceful understanding. They have learned tolerance out of necessity. Instead of warring, they work cooperatively, all skin colors, all tribes, united. Rather like here." Rumendah motioned around the room.

"I tell you I fear escape! For this grey faery that went with the dragons, I believe he was once banished by my tribe to the Mysty Island, and that he must have found a portal there to Drakotanith! My feeling is that the Mysty Island is not secure." King Struben shook his head as he spoke.

King Dreya chortled. "And that is less of a punishment, to be banished to the dragon realm?" he asked.

"There is no joy in that place," Varia agreed. "Going from an island to a hateful world such as Drakotanith? There is no comparison. I agree, the Mysty Island is the sanest solution."

"It is certainly better than pulling off their wings," Loben said, his voice somber. "This is difficult for all of us, but especially, for King Dreya and Varia, who must send family members afar. I suggest that we allow Rumendah to decide; he has a clear head, and is connected to the families but not swayed."

"Very well," Struben said, putting his hands in the air in an exasperated way, indicating he was done with the conversation.

"I too agree," said Dreya. "Rumendah, is that your choice then, that my daughter Alshea and her cohorts be banned to the Mysty Island?"

"It is," said Rumendah, his voice clear. "For while it saddens my heart to say so, it is for the ongoing safety of the kingdoms of Ashenthorne and Birkendore that I decree it must be so. I shall arrange the prisoners' passage to the Mysty Island on the next noon sun, and we shall have to say goodbye to one who would have undoubtedly been a fine queen, had she allowed the rule to come to her in time."

Varia put her face in her hands. "Ah, first I have lost a brother, now a sister! And yet gained another! This is a strange time indeed," she said. Loben put his arm around her shoulders.

"Do not despair," he said. "You have all of the cytons of fond memories of your siblings, and perhaps this is not the last you will see of them, for I have heard of reformed fae returning from the Mysty Island to their tribes."

"We shall see," said King Dreya. He stood, and the rest of the fae joined him. "The circle is open, always unbroken. May the magick of the fae be ever in your hearts."

The others repeated the sacred words to the king and stepped backward, widening the circle, and then turned outward away from where they had been seated. Varia fell heavily against Loben as they walked out together; with so many extra fae in the castle, flying through even large throne room was hazardous.

"I am exhausted!" she said. "This ordeal has nearly broken me inside. I must rest. Will you come to the solarium with me?"

"I will come to your rooms now," Loben said, kissing her forehead. "Will we sleep in a real bed?"

Varia smiled. "I can't imagine it, but yes!" They walked to the portal to the upper chambers, checked that it was clear, and flew up the top floor of the palace together.

Varia took a moment to duck out to the bathing well beneath the top floor balcony window and she let the chilled water revive her. She brought along one of her favorite dresses, made of blue vinca petals and woven sea grasses imported from the southern islands. After bathing she dried and clothed herself, taking time to dip a comb into the water that flowed in a steady trickle there and smooth her white hair that fell to her waist. Refreshed, she returned to her childhood room. There Loben, now also having bathed in another part of the castle, joined her. He looked handsome in his fresh tunic and leggings, and he tied his long brown hair back with a grass hair tie, pulling it behind his shoulders. Varia reached for him, shaky and exhausted.

"I ordered food to be delivered here," he said, holding her against his chest. "Everyone in the castle is most accommodating, Varia. I had expected anger and hatred, and instead find respect and appreciation. I am much relieved."

"We so-called 'banished' the dragons," Varia said with a sigh. "I suppose it is true that we did save everyone by tricking Evara, though I must admit my heart still yearns for Smote, dragon-spell or no."

"I miss the little . . . er, big . . . lad too," Loben said. He sat on the edge of the bed and patted it; Varia went to him, arms outstretched, and took his hands in hers.

"Do you remember when you gave me that special necklace for our wedding?" she asked.

"I do," Loben replied.

"I still have it, let me show you. I knew not when I would see it again, but hopefully it is still safe in its hiding place." Varia fiddled with the tight box that was carved into the frame of the bed, and it opened. She pulled the necklace from its stashing spot and held it up, the bright airy rooms lit by the silver dollar pods, causing it to gleam.

"Allow me," Loben said, reaching for it. He stared at it, and unclasped it and put it around Varia's neck and spun her around. "Exquisite," he told her. He kissed her on the lips as a kitchen helper brought a tray of food to the prince and princess; it was more food than Varia had seen in a very long time. She breathed in, looking at all of the choices.

"Oh! There are my favorite greens, a salad of meadowsweed and burdock, and red berries from the guelder rose, and look!" Varia pointed to a special dish on the side. "Mushrooms for you, Loben! Several kinds! And a hearty seed bread as well. We shall feast!"

Loben's kinfolk, perhaps because they did not fly as often or as high as the Alawe, did not seem to have the same desperate need for constant nourishment that Varia's tribe had, but his eyes lit up at the sight of so many mushrooms.

Varia sniffed the tall carafe. "Mead!" she said. "Better than nectar, for a relaxing meal." She took the tray to a small table and chair by the window in the bower and the two sat and began eating, taking their time, chatting and sharing food. The meal was leisurely and Varia wished she could eat more, but soon she was full. She popped a final berry in her mouth for good measure. Loben leaned over and kissed her.

"This reminds me of the night we shared in the forest," he said.

"That was last night," Varia said with a laugh. Loben shook his head.

"It does not seem possible that so much has happened in our lives in such a short space of time. Spring had just ended, and we had just celebrated the Summer Solstice when I met you, and now fall is upon us, looming into the dark time of the sun in just a few days' time."

"We usually feast for the equinox, and have a grand event, but I do not think that my father will wish to celebrate after losing two of his children, one to treason and one to the dark realm of Drakotanith, where it is unknown if he can survive."

"If anyone can survive there, it is Ezia," Loben said. He stood and led Varia back to the bedroom. He pulled her down on the bed beside him, and drew her close to him. He fingered the necklace she wore.

"I know that you miss Smote, but now we can be together, and perhaps have a real family someday, with true fae children, not wayward a dragonlet."

"That is what I wish for," Varia said, kissing him. He stopped her and removed the necklace and laid it carefully on the bedside table. Soon they both were resting, ready for a relaxing evening together, uninterrupted, and full of love and promise.

Chapter Twenty-Five

When Varia woke, it was with a start. She looked around for Smote, and felt her heart crash when she realized she was home in her Erendome bedroom, and he was not there. She stood and prepared to go downstairs to the dining hall for breakfast. Loben was still fast asleep, and seeing him that way made her realize how little he had slept since she'd known him. Deciding to let him linger in bed, she dressed and entered the next chamber. She was surprised to find Irea there.

"Greetings!" she said, hugging Irea. "I did not know you were still staying in the upper flats."

"I was staying in the guest rooms with Queen Hoondeen and my sisters Dunheen and Kurnoon, and their entourage, but this is, after all, my home. I decided to sleep here last night." She pointed to the adjoining sleeping chamber.

"Sorry if we took over our childhood common-room," Varia said. "It is strange that I should have a husband now, and that was our first night spent in a real bed! But I do not even know where I shall be living next. Everything is so confused lately."

"You do not need to tell me, Cousin . . . I mean . . ." Irea stopped herself. "Long have I called you Cousin! But we are sisters in actuality. I will have to grow used to using the new word, but in my heart, it has always been so."

"In my heart, too," Varia said. "I have known through our connected Devas that you were always so special to me. I am grateful for you, whatever the name was or will be."

Irea and Varia hugged and held one another. When they separated, Varia had a tear in her eye.

"You are exhausted and just being silly," Irea said, offering her a soft leaf wipe from the nearby dresser to dry her eye.

"It is nothing," Varia said. "I just realized that we are all separated now; I am with my husband, you are part of the Durndeng tribe as well, Alshea is . . . well, she is banned. Our days here in the solitude and beauty of our father's home are behind us, dear sister. We are now facing a new world, a new life, and I had not anticipated it, nor did I have time to properly say goodbye to what once was."

"I was rousted from my sleep and blindfolded and imprisoned by Baylo and Ullo, in the dead of night, and left in that dank place with my uncle King Dreya. All would have been lost if Rumendah hadn't arrived soon afterward. At first I thought, halfwit! Allowing himself to be caught, what sort of sage is he? Until I realized that he had planned his own capture all along, and used it as a ruse to stay hidden while he muttered his ancient incantations and invented a false version of himself, and escaped so freely I wonder still how I could not do it too, though I tried."

"It is best not to ask, for I have heard it tell that it is wise not to meddle in the affairs of wizards," Varia said, "for they are hard to control and difficult to reason with, much like dragons. My moments with Rumendah were some of the most confounding of this whole ordeal!" Varia laughed, and Irea joined in.

"Well, we are safe now. But today will be difficult, as Rumendah has summoned a strange type of bird from across the seas to take the prisoners to the Mysty Island."

"I am saddened that we are at that point," Varia said. "Join me now, I am on my way down to have breakfast in the dining hall?"

"I will, and you had better eat, you look half starved!"

"I have had two meals in a row, and then to continue like this and I shall be fat and contented the rest of my days," Varia said. She clasped onto Irea's hand and they soared down to the main floor, where the palace pantry was bustling with activity. As they entered the hall, most of the fae stood in reverence, their heads bowed. Varia felt her face flush, and once they found their seat at the King's table, Varia leaned over to whisper, "What was that all about?"

"They are grateful to you for returning the dragons to their realm, and they believe me to be the next ruler of Erendome," Irea said with a shrug. "Of course that is just silly, it will be you now."

Varia was about to pop a dandelion flower into her mouth and she stared at Irea. "What nonsense are you talking? I am the youngest, I am not to be queen!"

"Varia, you are true heir to the throne. Think about it, I am a child of two tribes! I cannot be queen. But now you are the sole remaining child of King Dreya. So, it is you." Irea's voice softened and she touched Varia's face. Varia looked around the room and could see some of the fae she'd known her whole life stealing glances at her, and looking away shyly when caught. She shook her head.

"No, it is you," she said. "You are the eldest."

"Time will tell, Sister," Irea said with a shrug. "But I think you are mistaken."

Varia continued to eat her dandelion salad, keenly aware that eyes were on her now. She remembered when she was but third in line to the throne, an anonymous princess in the Erendome castle, and no eyes followed her. She found it difficult to swallow.

Loben stood beside Varia, who wore one of her formal gowns, as did Irea beside her. Loben had been given fine garments and he looked rested and handsome in his soft leaf-made tunic and pants, although his eyes carried a sadness in them, Varia noted. They stood with the two kings and this time, Doon was there, looking regal in his Vorku uniform. Before them the meadows near the Erendome whitebeam sparkled; rain had fallen through the night, but the sun was breaking through stubborn grey puffy clouds and asserting itself across the plains. Two large and rather awkward looking seabirds stood in the field, white albatross with ebony wings and a serious expression marked by a black streak over their dark eyes, shading threatening orange beaks. Rumendah stood beside them, closing his eyes and placing one hand on each bird's breastbone, sending them the information they needed to know before they began their journey to the Mysty Island to the northwest.

"Bring the prisoners!" shouted King Dreya, and the once-great Princess Alshea was led out by a uniformed Wilhvyre soldier. She wore a plain shift, her hands shackled before her, her wings trapped in a binding sack. Her white hair fell lifelessly past her shoulders and her eyes avoided the hissing and booing of the faeries who gathered on the palace greens. Following her in an equally drab tunic was Talow, his wings also bound, his hands tied. Behind him came Baylo, then

Ulla, and by the time the four were walked from the prison to their mounts, the roar of the crowd was deafening. The other discontents, including Harah and a few stragglers, had already been banished to the wilds to fend for themselves.

The albatross hopped from foot to foot, fidgeting at the noise. Rumendah reached up to calm them with soft words and gentle strokes as the prisoners were led to a nature-made dais of a flat-topped gleaming stone.

King Dreya sat on a stone throne that had been placed on the boulder cytons before, and he stood and towered over the treasoners.

"It is with great sadness in my heart that I must ban the once-princess Alshea to the Mysty Island!" he shouted, and murmuring commenced, accompanied by wary nods toward the enormous birds.

"I also banish to the Mysty Island my once-trusted Wilhvyre FlightSoldiers, Talow, Baylo and Ulla, for treasonous acts and rising up against the throne of Erendomc in the land of Ashenthorne, the jewel in the Feyllan realm," the king said matter-of-factly. Another mutter went through the gathered faeries, and a few wails, from family members of the banished three. Irea and Varia clutched hands as Rumendah escorted the unfortunates near the no-nonsense birds. The mollymawks reached back with their vibrant beaks in a menacing way, as if to warn the captives not to make any untoward moves.

Two Wilhvyre and two Vorku lifted each prisoner off the ground and onto the awaiting albatross; Baylo and Ulla on one bird, Talow and Alshea on the other. The bound faeries were each given a sip of nectar from a vial that Rumendah held, and a package of stores was tied onto the back of the prisoner seated in the rear position, in this case Ulla and Talow.

"You are banned for all eternity, or until the Erendome court deems otherwise," King Dreya said, his voice lower now as it was time to say goodbye. Alshea, who had been stoic until this moment, stared at her father.

"It was with a strong heart that I did what I did, Father," she said, her chin raised in defiance. "I usurped your kingdom for the greater good of all, so that the abomination that is the EarthSeeker clan would not force itself into our life! Look around you, Father! They have done exactly that! You have chosen the enemy, complete strangers who differ from us in every way, over your own children!"

King Dreya looked stricken at Alshea's words, but he held up his hand.

"Look around you, my daughter," he said. "What you see are friends, new family. We are all faeries of Feyllan! We are not so different, but all rise as one for the common goal of the future of our clans. I fault myself for pretending the Durndeng were extinct, but it was to protect my own heart and my firstborn Irea, and we have lost much in our secretiveness and inability to cooperate with these new kin. Be gone, until your mind can fathom that all fae are one fae, and that we as faeries must stay together to fight the outside influences that threaten our very existence!"

Alshea burst into tears and had no place to hide them, as the birds were growing impatient with waiting and were moving about, ready to fly. She had to use her hands to hold on to the binding that would keep her in place during the turbulent flight.

"Go then!" shouted the king. Long black wings extended, the birds flapped high into the sky, and all the fae watched in silence until the albatross bearing prisoners were a tiny speck, and finally, they disappeared into the horizon, and they were gone.

At dinner, the meal was nearly finished when King Dreya stood in front of his chair. All stopped eating, and the musicians stopped playing. He cleared his throat.

"There has been too much sadness and strife of late, and too many lives lost," he said. "It has been decided that the Durndeng shall relocate Thundendell to the willing tree where their temporary castle is housed in Rhysgollen, and honor always the recovering but gravely injured Birkendore oak. Those who are not part of the reparations will be staying in Erendome and Ashenthorne. So much loss, including Prince Loben's beloved hummingbird friend, Zedah..." the king allowed a quiet moment upon saying the favored bird's name. He cleared his throat. "No more grief!

King Struben and I are ready for celebration. The Autumnal Equinox is in two days, so we shall have a feast! The wounded recovering in the infirmary at Rhysgollen are being fetched, the workers relocating Thundendell summoned! We shall have a party to end all parties."

A cheer went up in the dining hall, and the place swarmed with activity as many left to go tell loved ones in the outlying fae homes, and others talked about the upcoming event.

"This is much needed," Loben said, caressing Varia's face. "For the king is right, there has been too much strife of late."

"This is terrible!" Varia said. Loben and Irea looked at her, questions in their eyes. Varia shrugged. "I have naught to wear."

Irea and Loben laughed as Varia took another sip of her burdock wine.

Varia spent so much time readying herself for the Autumnal Equinox Feast, as it was dubbed, that she lost track of Loben until the eve of the event. Though they ate meals together and of course slept in the same bed at night, she had barely seen him. Irea, however, had been at her side, doing the same: They had sent for flower essences for their hair, perfumes, new gowns, they had glossed their wings and sparkled their skin. It was nearly time to go to the feast when Loben came in to the bower. He looked around the room; there were petals and stones and powder and materials and concoctions strewn about.

"Devas!" was all he said, and Varia smiled and hovered over to him and kissed his nose.

"It takes much effort and care to become beautiful," she said. She flew to the special table where her crown rested next to Irea's and picked up Alshea's, fingering the ornate metals that twined around the precious gems.

"What a loss for our faepeople," she murmured, picking up her own princess crown and balancing it on her head, making sure her pointed ears were not hidden by its weight. She added in a few bracelets and then her hand went to her neck.

"Loben!" she called, for he waited in the adjoining chamber in a chair now, absently fanning his wings as the sunset light outside filled the room with orange rays. "Have you seen my necklace? I seem to have misplaced it, though I know I left it here." Varia hoped no harm had come to it.

"Ah, I forgot," Loben said. To her surprise he reached into his pouch and pulled it out. Varia looked at him, confused.

"I had it . . . altered. I hope you don't mind," he said. He held it up, and it glittered in the sunshine. In the center, Varia spotted a familiar sight.

"Oh!" she said, reaching for the necklace, for there was a most precious object now attached: Smote's scale. It gleamed teal and green as a tear rolled down Varia's cheek.

"How did you . . . ?"

"I retrieved it after Ezia dropped it, but I had not the heart to give it to you before now. Autumnal blessings, my fair wife. I am blessed to be your husband." He held the necklace up after Varia admired it and she turned around, lowering her wings so he could place it around her neck. He did, and Varia felt the hard scale there.

"I do so miss him," she said, "but he is in a better place, with his mother, in his own world." Varia sighed. "I am blessed to be your wife Loben, and thank you for this exquisite gift. I shall cherish it always."

Loben pulled Varia into his embrace and they stood together, allowing the rays to bathe them in the last light of the evening. Irea walked in and stopped in the doorway as they held one another.

"A touching scene," she said. "But you must stop yourselves. We have a party to attend!"

Irea flew to the Great Hall before Loben and Varia. Doon, looking handsome in his formal clothing of dark woven leaf fibers, held his hand up for Irea.

"May I escort you, Sister?" he asked, and Irea smiled, and accepted his hand.

"You have yet to call me that," she said.

Doon nodded. "I have only now realized that this change in our family can be of great benefit," he said. "Please forgive my coldness to you before."

"Consider it forgotten," Irea said. They floated to the ground and walked through the center of the Great Hall, where a sea of faeries parted to allow them passage. The fae, all dressed in their fanciest attire and wearing ornate hats and glittering finery, bowed as Irea and Doon joined their fathers on the dais where the thrones were occupied by King Dreya and King Struben.

Varia and Loben entered next, and Varia watched as her faepeople, both Alawe and Durndeng, offered the same recognition to her and to Loben. They walked hand in hand and Varia rose up and stood by her father's throne, Irea beside her. Rumendah, looking weary yet stately in an ornate white robe, sat in a chair further back next to Queen Hoondeen and the lavishly decorated princesses Dunheen and Kurnoon. Rumendah smiled at Varia, and she sent her Deva over to give him a spirit hug. Understanding, he nodded.

King Struben and King Dreya stood, and the crowd cheered yet again. Dreya reached his hands out, silencing the partygoers.

"Never have the halls of Erendome seen such an act of unity and friendship!" Dreya said. "It is a privilege to have the most illustrious members of our community, and of the Durndeng community known as Birkendore, from the castle called Thundendell . . ." A louder, deeper cheer went up as some of the Durndeng added in their joy. "We shall celebrate Mabon tonight as we move into fall, and together in the next few weeks we shall gather the stores we will need to last another winter, and assist our friends as they move farther into the Rhysgollen forest, further from the Ashenthorne boundaries, but knowing they are always most welcome here. We welcome the dark time of the sun and give thanks for our bounties, but tonight is especially important, because King Struben and I have a mutual announcement to make."

Kings Struben and Dreya were a sight none would forget; the kings were both dressed in their celebration attire. Dreya wore a long blue soft robe of a shimmering imported material, and his gold crown set on his head commanded attention. Struben wore a floor-length tunic the color of the Moonglow Mountains to the east, soft grey and lustrous and bound with a stiff black shimmering belt. His silver crown perched regally over his dark hair. The two, though different, were forces of strength and courage. Several bowed down low to the two kings, and a buzz of whispers filled the hall.

"Rise!" King Struben called forth. "For I, King Struben of Thundendell, realm of Birkendore and Rhysgollen, proclaim the Princess Irea of Erendome, as my wife Queen Hoondeen's firstborn child, to be my next heir to the Durndeng throne!"

A gasp went up in the crowd. Varia's heart thrilled to hear that Irea would be Queen of Rhysgollen someday! Irea herself was obviously not informed that this would be the case; Varia could see her gripping onto their father's throne, to keep her knees from buckling. Varia laid her hand on her sister's wrist and sent strength from her Deva to Irea's. Irea recovered some and managed a wave to the crowd, all of whom were murmuring approval.

"And I," said King Dreya, looking at Varia, "hereby proclaim Princess Irea of Erendome, as my firstborn child, to be my next heir to the Alawe throne!" King Dreya said. Shock registered in Irea's eyes, and Varia grasped her arm to keep her from stumbling as she waved again. The room erupted.

"Father! What is happening? How can I be the queen of two realms?" Irea whispered to Dreya.

"So it shall be, my daughter. Too long have you been hidden behind the banner of the throne, when your rightful place all along was beside my dear Varia and yes, Alshea and Ezia too. For while I mourn the loss of my children, I rejoice in the fact that I have reclaimed you. You are a symbol of the future, Princess Irea. Your blood, a mixture of two fae tribe's, is sacred, and so you shall be queen of all of our combined fae."

The audience had stopped talking to eavesdrop on the conversation between Irea and the king, but he looked up and smiled warmly to his clan.

"Food and drink!" he called. "And merriment all around, for we have much to celebrate. We celebrate the fall season, a time of harvest and bounty, and now, the future queen to two thrones!" King Dreya clapped his hands, and lovely music filled the Great Hall as court musicians began to play. Loben gathered Varia into his arms, and she leaned her head on his shoulder as they moved away from where Irea was being swarmed by well-wishers.

"Do you fret that you will not be queen?" Loben asked, running his fingers along the intricate patterns braided into her hair. Varia looked into his golden eyes.

"I do not!" she said, and it was the truth. "I have never expected to be queen of this realm, and never once did I entertain the idea over the cytons, for I was content to be a princess of this castle where I was raised, to run in the fields with my siblings, to play with birds and the animals, to learn the secret names of trees. This has been my home, and I want it to be yours too, Loben. For I wish to stay here, and live in this palace, if you will be so willing."

"I am comfortable here," he said, "and would be happy to call Erendome my home, though there is no reason why we cannot live in both places, and travel between them. For now it is like we have two homes, the new Thundendell castle at Rhysgollen, and Erendome. We are free to come and go as we wish."

Irea joined them and Varia hugged her. "Queen Irea! Of Rhysgollen! Or perhaps Ashenthorne?"

"Whichever king retires first," Irea said with a shrug. "I have much to learn! Will you help me!"

"I shall!" said Varia, "as I can."

"And Loben," said Irea. "Will you help me learn the ways of the Durndeng fae? For though they are half my blood too, I do not know all of your customs."

"I would be honored," Loben said. He reached out and took Irea's hand. "You will make a fine queen."

The music continued, and Doon pulled Irea away to the middle of the Great Hall to meet his friends, where the fae swayed to the uplifting music, and some even flew up in the air and performed acrobatics at their excitement about the events in the castle. Loben and Varia stepped down off the dais to join them, but King Dreya pulled on Varia's hand.

"I know you wish to remain a free spirit, Varia, for you are more like a warrior than a queen," he said.

"I am not disappointed," Varia said. "I am instead grateful."

She kissed her father's forehead and followed Loben to the hall, where she looked around at the fae around her, their faces full of light, and energy, and goodness. The music swept over her as Varia closed her eyes and danced with joy in her soul.

Cat Spydell

Cat Spydell is a mom, animal rescuer, environmental activist, and author of *The Time Traveler's Apprentice at Hollywood High*. When she isn't writing or working on her publishing endeavors, Cat enjoys spending time horseback riding, bodyboarding in the nearby Pacific, and attending live music events.

Please visit
www.WorldNouveauBooks.com
for more titles from Mischievous Muse Press

www.ingramcontent.com/pod-product-compliance
Lightning Source LLC
Chambersburg PA
CBHW070511030726
47503CB00004B/1235